EVERY FATHER'S FEAR

BOOK 2: EVERY PARENT'S FEAR

JOANNA WARRINGTON

2020 Joanna Warrington

All rights reserved

Disclaimer and Background to the story

Every Father's Fear is the standalone sequel to *Every Mother's Fear*. It is a fictional story based on the thalidomide disaster; one of the blackest episodes in medical history, which had devastating consequences for thousands of families across the world. Thalidomide was used to treat a range of medical conditions and was used in particular as a mild sleeping pill. It was thought to be safe for pregnant women, who took it to alleviate morning sickness. Thalidomide caused thousands of children worldwide to be born with malformed limbs and the drug was taken off the market late in 1961.

I would like to thank the following people for their help with this project: Lorraine Mercer MBE, Lisa Rodrigues CBE, Margaret French, Karen Braysher and my wonderful writers' critique group in Eastbourne, whose comments and advice were invaluable.

The characters in this story are fictitious. Any resemblance to actual persons, living or dead, is coincidental. The story reflects the situations and experiences that families and thalidomide survivors might have faced and draws on real events and the actions of some of the key figures of the time: Enoch Powell, Jack Ashley and Dr Kelsey, for instance.

St Bede's School is very loosely based on Chailey Heritage School in East Sussex, the first purpose-built school for disabled children in the UK It was founded in 1903 and where many of the British thalidomide sufferers were cared for and educated. There are various schools around the UK called St Bede's. The name is coincidental. The school in this story bears no relation to any of these schools.

I have used the word 'handicap' and 'handicapped' in this book because this was the terminology used at the time, rather than the more modern term, 'disabled' or 'disability.'

The events in the book regarding the press campaign are loosely based on what happened in the 1970s.

PROLOGUE

1969

It was gone midnight. Shadow stood in the garden watching, as Rona went from room to room checking the locks on every downstairs window and pulling the bolts across the front and back doors. Bill was already asleep; the sound of his snoring escaped into the garden and reverberated like a pneumatic drill.

Despite the enormous rust-tinged moon bathing the garden in a swathe of light, Rona didn't appear to see the shadow dart between the apple trees. It stopped at the end of the garden. Tonight, it had a plan. Power was an intoxicating feeling that was lacking in other areas of the Shadow's life. Shadow knew everything about Rona and her daily routine. Shadow had watched Toby grow into a young boy. Born with phocomelia as a side effect of his mother taking the drug thalidomide during pregnancy, Shadow watched Toby learn to cope without arms. It took years for Shadow to plan a campaign of fear, driven by angst and pain and it was time to deliver. Life wasn't fair, but this was about revenge.

A light came on in the bathroom directly above where

Shadow crouched. The window swung open a few inches and there was a squeak as the taps were turned on. Rona was getting ready for bed.

Heart hammering, Shadow worked fast on the window below the bathroom - the dining-room window. Pulling out a screwdriver, Shadow eased it into the gap where the window met the sill and with a hard push, the worn lock broke. With a small amount of pressure and little effort, the lock popped open and the window inched up smoothly. Shadow slid in through the gap, tiptoed across the room and hesitated in the hallway before going into the kitchen to put an envelope on the table.

1
CHRISTMAS 1960

Rona 'Is all this festive glitter getting you in the mood for love?' Rona asked Marion, glancing round the room decked out in streamers and tinsel for the hospital's Christmas party.

'Maybe.' Rona wondered whether Marion was still having an affair with Simon. She hoped not. The idea that they might be still carrying on disgusted her. Both women worked at the mother-and-baby home. Rona was a midwife and Marion was a medical secretary with a nursing background and they worked under Doctor Simon Gerard. Rona had discovered their affair when she had caught them together and threatened to expose them to the hospital's board of directors unless they ended it.

Rona gave her a nudge and a cheeky smile. 'I've seen the way Doctor Alistair looks at you,' she said encouragingly. Alistair was single and as far as she was aware didn't have a girlfriend. A much better prospect, Rona thought.

Carrying their drinks, Rona and Marion walked over to the window, taking in the panoramic views over London. The city twinkled under an expanse of sky, heavy with the threat of snow.

'No Bill tonight?' Marion asked.

'He's got a bit of a cold.'

Marion frowned. 'Is everything all right at home? I get the feeling that something's bothering you. You haven't seemed your usual self lately.'

Rona sighed. 'I may as well tell you. We've been trying for a baby and it's just not happening. Bill doesn't want to adopt. He's made that quite clear and I do, because what alternative is there?' She brushed away a tear. She loved her job and marriage, but being a mother was all she'd ever wanted. 'It's hard to watch my sisters play happy families when inside I'm hurting.'

'I'm sorry, I can't imagine what that must be like. When I meet someone...' Marion glanced round blushing, her words trailing off. Simon was watching them.

Rona took a deep breath. 'Anyway, it's Christmas, we should be enjoying ourselves.' She clapped her hands excitedly. 'I'm going to fix you up with Alistair. There's no way you're going home on your own tonight.' Rona's eyes twinkled with mischief.

Marion rolled her eyes. 'Don't you dare.'

'You look fabulous in your new dress. He'll want to dance with you for sure.'

Marion was wearing a navy, knee-length puffy swing dress with a white spotted collar. 'It's not new. It's an old faithful dress I pulled out of the cupboard and pressed into service. I had my hair done though,' she added, patting her lacquered bouffant.

The dancing was energetic and frenzied. Everybody - apart from a few male stragglers around the perimeter of the room, jived and twisted. Rona and Marion put their drinks down and went to dance. After a few songs the lights dimmed and the music slowed and Alistair appeared at Marion's side, taking her hand and pulling her close as other couples joined them. Rona watched them. They looked good together, but then she noticed Simon leaning against the wall, with his face set like stone, his eyes cold, burning into Marion. And in that moment, she knew the affair hadn't ended. Rona caught the worried look on Marion's face. At the end of the dance Marion hurried off in the direction of the toilets. Worried, Rona followed her. Along the corridor she could smell cigarette smoke and the voices of two men chatting. Hanging back, she waited at the corner of the corridor out of view, straining to listen. Inching closer, she caught sight of Alistair and Simon. She held back and pressing herself against the wall listened to their conversation.

'I know you like Marion, but she's bad news, believe me.'

'Why? She seems very sweet.'

'Just between us, please don't breathe a word, especially not to her, but...' and then Simon's voice fell to a whisper.

On Monday Rona was walking past Simon's office and heard raised voices. She stopped to eavesdrop.

'What's going on between you and Alistair?' Simon asked.

'Nothing. He asked me to dance that's all. It's not a crime,' Marion said.

'He's no good for you.'

'I'm not with him, I'm with you.'

'Are you sure about that?'

'Of course.'

'It didn't look like it.'

'It was only a dance.'

'I don't like you dancing with other men, especially not him.'

'What's wrong with him?'

'He said you'd be easy because you've been single a while.'

Rona gasped.

'He wouldn't say that,' Marion challenged.

'It's what most men are like. They think with their cocks. You're lucky that I'm different.'

Marion shook her head. 'Are you though? You want your cake and eat it. Otherwise you'd do the decent thing and either leave your wife or end it with me.'

'You know I love you, but I can't leave just yet. We agreed a plan. Are you backing off?'

'No... but when are you going to leave her? I do understand how difficult it is for you, but I want to be with you.'

'I've poured so much into this relationship, then you shut me down by dancing with that idiot. How do you think that makes me feel?'

'I'm sorry.'

Rona felt angry that despite her warnings Simon and Marion were still carrying on together. Her hand hovered on the door handle as she considered barging into his office.

'I can't leave her until I've saved some money for somewhere for us to live.'

'Haven't you saved anything? You can move in with me.'

He scoffed. 'Your place isn't big enough. You know that.'

'How long will it take you to save?'

'I don't know, Marion,' he snapped. 'I've got debts I need to clear first.'

'You didn't tell me you had debts.'

'I didn't want to burden you.'

They fell silent. Rona waited, checking both ends of the corridor but there was nobody else around.

'Maybe...' Marion began.

'What? Have you got a bright idea? A way to make my debts magically disappear so that we can be together?' His tone was stroppy.

'I could lend you some of my inheritance.' There was a cautious tone to her voice.

'No, that's your money.'

'One day it will be our money.'

'You might need it. I need to sort out my own mess, it'll just mean it will take longer for us to be together. Maybe a year or two.'

'That long? Surely not?'

'Sadly, yes.'

'Take some of my money, I'd rather you do that, than wait two years to be together.'

'I'm not sure. It's not right.'

'Please... take it.'

'Are you sure? They're my debts not yours.'

'The money's sitting in the bank gathering dust.'

'Well if you're sure and don't immediately need it. I will pay you back.'

'I know you will.'

Rona hurried back to the ward, her heart racing, incensed by her discovery.

2

FEBRUARY 1961

Marion
'Please tell me you're not serious, Simon?'

Seeing the light leave Doctor Gerard's eyes as he slumped back into his chair, everything about him defeated, Marion knew the answer to her question.

'Keep your bloody voice down.'

'The door's closed.'

'Walls have ears.'

'Let's get the facts straight.' Marion's voice was shaky. 'You let a nurse kidnap a baby and falsified the papers?'

Facing each other across the doctor's desk, they teetered on the cliff of an argument, but in the face of her harsh words, he fell silent as they processed the enormity of what had happened the night before.

The doctor explained. 'My head was all over the place. Rona threatened to tell the board of directors about us.'

Marion snarled, 'Don't you dare use me as an excuse.'

'She was desperate for a baby. If you were desperate, you'd do whatever it took.'

'I can't believe I'm hearing this. What you did was wrong. It's a crime.'

'He was one of those thalidomide babies. He's probably going to die anyway,' Simon said dismissively. 'He might have all sorts of things wrong with him. He'll have twisted organs and who knows what else. I told her to put the baby in the cold room to let nature take him, but she refused. Thought she knew better.'

'It's not for you to play God.'

'I play God every day, I'm a fucking doctor and I'm telling you that baby will die.'

'You won't be a doctor for much longer.'

'What does that mean?' Simon got up and lurched towards her, grabbing her arm, his face full of fear. 'You've got to stay quiet, please Marion, I could lose everything,' he pleaded.

'Your job, your precious wife and family.'

She shook his hand from her arm.

'I've worked hard, I'm not about to throw it all away because of a little affair.'

Marion's heart slammed in her chest. 'I've given you the best years of my life and you call it a little affair?' She let out a sob.

'Why don't you take the day off? You're in no fit state to work. I'll come round and see you later.'

'You're the one who's in no fit state to work,' she gulped.

'Calm down. I really think you should go home.'

'Why should I? Because you're afraid your secret's going to get out and you'll be struck off the register? Well I hope that happens. You're never going to leave your wife, are you?'

'Yes, of course I am. I've promised you, haven't I?'

'I've waited long enough.'

'I just need to see the kids through school.'

A soft knock at the door closed their angry exchange.

'Come in,' the doctor barked, switching into work mode.

'Everything okay?' Nurse Hilda asked.

'What is it Nurse?' Simon asked and turning to Marion he said, 'Wait a moment.'

'One of the mothers, Sandy, in bed five is asking how her baby is. I've just come on my shift. She said she had a boy last night but hasn't seen him yet.'

'Close the door.' The doctor waved for Nurse Hilda to sit.

'Can you go and explain to the mother that she's lost her baby? He died during the night.'

Nurse Hilda stared at Doctor Gerard in disbelief. 'I'm sorry, Doctor, but you need to do that. It's your responsibility.'

'You're a woman though.' He flinched. 'I'm not good with all that emotional stuff.' He had a poor bedside manner; it was no wonder he was getting her to do the dirty deed. 'Nurse Hilda I have great faith in you. You'll offer tea and sympathy and a gentle hand in this woman's hour of need.'

'But you delivered the baby. With all due respect Doctor, it would be more professional coming from you. That's just my opinion and I'm sorry if I've spoken out of turn. She needs to know what happened and why her baby died. Only you can do that,' Nurse Hilda insisted.

'I'm sorry Doctor, but yes, I agree with Nurse. It won't be easy. These things never are. How on earth can you explain to his mother that her baby was born without arms and died soon after birth? The poor woman. But it's got to be done.' Marion shook her head and stared at the floor.

'Marion's not feeling well,' the doctor said in a sharp tone. 'I was just persuading her to take the day off.' Turning to Marion he said, 'Take a couple of days off.' Leaving her with no option but to go, Marion hated the way he was slamming dismissing her from the room so that she didn't cause him trouble.

'Right, I better get on,' Nurse Hilda said, turning to leave.

Marion went to change out of her uniform and afterwards saw that Doctor Gerard's door was open but he wasn't there.

Passing the ward she saw him at Sandy's bedside delivering the news in his brusque manner, unable to look at her as he spoke, knowing that what he was telling her was a pack of lies and that her child was out there somewhere, being fed and clothed by another woman. Her heart went out to the woman.

3

1961

Marion Entering the gloomy corridor to her flat in a converted Victorian house which she had inherited from her late uncle - it was so dark after the bright lights of the hospital - Marion thought about the silence awaiting her. Working at the mother-and-baby home gave meaning to her life, it filled her days with noise and purpose, laughter and womanly banter. What else did she have on in her life? Her cat was an admission that she'd never have a family. She had given in and taken in an old moggy. It hadn't stopped her succumbing to the needs of an unhappily married man who paid more attention to what was missing in his marriage than to any meaningful future he could have with her.

What would it take for Simon to leave Carol, his wife? All she heard were endless excuses. His eldest child needed support getting through his O levels. And Jackie, at ten would soon be starting secondary school and Francesca, who was closest to him, would miss her dad too much. 'It's too disruptive, I can't do it, the timing's not right,' she heard over and over but the longer the affair went on, the harder it was for both of them to break free.

Meeting became routine. But when the stolen hours were over, she never felt satisfied, and craved more. The sense of disappointment that settled inside her, knowing that the affair would never come to anything was crippling. It was like being offered the hard toffee penny in the Quality Street tin after the best were gone. She suspected it was different for Simon. She added a sparkle to his life. She could see it in his face, spent as he lay on her bed after sex, drowning in his own glory, ready to face the ongoing shambles that was his marriage.

Raging inside, Marion made herself a cup of tea. Simon had a way of turning his mistakes into hers and blaming her for his actions. How dare he blame her for him planning a crime with Nurse Rona, lady high and mighty and send Marion home to stop her talking? How convenient for him. She deserved to be treated with dignity. He'd given her the clearest signal yet that his marriage and his job came first. But who could blame him? Of course, that's what he's going to do, but it didn't help her situation, it made her raw and bitter, as she considered the question, were they over?

Shortly before seven that evening, she heard the familiar sound of his car engine outside. She listened for the slam of the car door, and his key in the lock as he came in the house. Fury bubbled inside her when she thought about the gall of the man.

Her feelings of anger though melted away when she opened the door, a floral assault of roses, lilies and freesia hiding his face, the sweet smell easing the tension between them, a peace offering perhaps, but with a cautionary note that challenge and strife lay ahead.

Tilting the bouquet to one side as she looked at his face,

something unsettling happened. Perhaps she looked at him for a second too long through the heady scent of floral notes, but something passed between them as she felt the pull of attraction and he held her gaze.

'Sorry I sent you home.'

His hand brushed hers as he passed the bouquet into her arms and an electric charge surged through her making her tingle and all thoughts about it being the end of the road for their relationship, evaporated. At the sink, arranging the sprigs in a glass vase with Simon next to her, she was torn between an urge to hug him and going back to the hard shell of an hour ago that had formed around her aching heart. He was watching her intently as she moved around the kitchen. She noted the smell of day-old after-shave mixed with the stale odour of cigarettes and surgery.

'What you did was wrong, unethical, underhand. I always admired you for your professionalism.'

Her words were cut off by the twist of his fingers in her hair, wrapping the length of it around his fist. Her head snapped back and when she turned to face him, his lips were parted and his eyes were full of lust and longing. A thrill shivered through her as their lips met. He was like a potion; from the first time they'd kissed she had to taste him. The fact that he belonged to another woman only made her desire more intense.

He gave a small nod as if an agreement had been made, something decided between them as he led her through to her bedroom, pulling her onto the bed, lifting her skirt and tugging at her knickers. One hand clamped to her breast, his tongue in her mouth, he was too desperate to bother with foreplay. He plunged into her, feeling his way, thrusting forward, his face red and beaded with sweat. Afterwards he collapsed on top of her, his weight crushing her tiny frame.

An awkwardness settled between them. 'We need to talk,' he said.

Moments ago, she felt hopeful. With his sexual appetite spent and cold semen trickling down her legs, she could sense that things were different; it was like the approach of autumn after summer. There was silence while he shifted up the bed, pulling the sheet over his lower body as if to cover the shame of their act.

'What are you going to do?' she asked.

'How do you mean?'

'Are you going to tell the police or the hospital directors or tell Rona to bring the baby back? Surely, you're going to do something, or you could end up in prison.'

'Don't be ridiculous.'

Annoyed with her, he swung his legs over the side of the bed reaching for his trousers heaped on the floor.

'Don't go yet, we need to talk.'

Ignoring her, he pulled his pants on and hitched up his trousers.

'I'm just going to forget that it happened. Rona's got what she wanted and if she feels she can give the poor mite a chance, well good on her. But I think she will be very disappointed.'

'But he wasn't her baby. It wasn't for either of you to make decisions about his life and if he gets ill he will need to come back to hospital and then there will be questions asked.'

'She's got a plan if that happens.'

Marion shook her head.

'The mother didn't want him. And nobody wants to adopt a handicapped child.'

'I think you should discuss it with someone.'

'And risk everything,' he snapped, shooting her a warning look, with sarcasm dripping from his voice. 'Are you that fucking dense?'

She flinched, his words cutting through her, but she wasn't going to be defeated. 'Don't talk to me like that. You've committed a crime. If this gets out...'

'How will it get out? Only Rona and I know what happened.'

'And I know, too.'

Leaning down, he took her chin in his hand and gripped her tightly, with his eyes smouldering. 'And you'll keep it a secret, do you hear me?'

His words spiked her with fear. 'Are you threatening me?' Blood pounding in her head, she chanced, 'If I'm interviewed by the police I'm not going to lie.'

The punch came from nowhere, she wasn't expecting it, he'd never hit her before. Reeling with the shock, her face stinging with pain, she inched away from him, her insides squeezing as she tried to make sense of what was happening. She opened her mouth to speak but the words wouldn't come, swallowed by the thought that she might upset him further.

'You won't be speaking to anybody. Do you understand?'

'All right.' She sniffed, tasting blood in her mouth.

'Because I want you gone.'

There was no remorse, all she heard was hatred.

'I'm not going anywhere. I love my job.'

'If you don't go, I'll sack you.'

'You can't do that - I've done nothing wrong.'

'I'm sure I can think of a few things; you're not indispensable.'

She feared he meant business. 'You can't knock women around and get your own way,' she said wiping her nose.

'I'm going to give you two month's pay. That will tide you over.'

He'd never been like this with her before, he was a different person and she didn't know how to handle him. 'You think you can just chuck money at me, hoping I'll disappear. And what about my mother's inheritance. You can pay that back.'

'I will, when I can, but either way, Marion, you can't stay.'

Putting his shirt on, he looked as if he couldn't wait to escape. How she longed for a man to treasure her in his arms.

'You'll regret this,' she said. She felt like a prostitute, used, dirty and despised. He'd pay for this, there was no way she was going to let him get away with it. She hadn't worked out how, but she'd see to it. She had all the time in the world to plot her revenge.

He pulled out a wad of cash, throwing it on the bed, amid the debris of their hasty lovemaking. She stared at the money feeling like a piece of meat, a toy for him to play with, now discarded. He'd planned to do this.

'Take it, but we're over.'

'Do you think I'd want you after what you just did to me?' she shouted. She was numb and shocked with disbelief that he could turn like this from a loving man into a monster.

4
1973

Jasper and Sandy

Jasper drove deeper and deeper, Sandy's arms and legs imprisoning his body, her heels pummeling his buttocks. He let out a sharp but melodious cry, her orgasm preceding his by seconds. Their bodies parted as he rolled off her, out of breath and sweaty, splaying his arms and legs across her and the bed.

'I wonder if any of my little swimmers will reach their target.' He turned to her, smiling and kissed her moist lips.

He'd always longed for a son, to kick a ball around a field and lately, seeing their married friends raise families, it was getting to him. Sandy never talked about having a family unless he raised the subject. She'd channeled all her energy into raising funds for the thalidomide families and giving talks on thalidomide at various events. He admired her energy and efforts but each month when her period arrived, his heart sank.

She frowned. 'We've talked about this before; we said we'd wait.'

'I know we have, but we've waited long enough. It would be nice to have children.'

'I'm not sure.' Her eyes were misty and instead of looking at him she stared at the wall, a finger in her mouth.

'What's wrong? You look frightened. You know I love you, very much don't you?'

'It's nothing.'

She sat up abruptly, tucking her long blonde hair behind her ears. With matted bed hair and no make-up on, she was still very beautiful. He counted his lucky stars every day he was with her. After their parting when he took the job up north, he thought he'd never see her again. And now here they were, twelve years later and practically an old married couple. At least that's how it felt sometimes. He'd never forget how his luck changed in that heart-stopping moment when the lift doors in the New York hotel opened and there she was in a stunning yellow dress.

She swung her feet onto the floor, with her back to him.

'Talk to me, Sandy.' He put both hands on her back, kneading the knots from her neck, trying to coax her gently back to bed.

She pushed his hands off and stood up. 'I need the loo.'

Puzzled, he lay there waiting for her to finish in the bathroom. He heard the flush of the toilet, a whoosh of water as the taps turned on and a moment later the boiler cranked to life as the shower started running. Disappointment hit him. It was Sunday. They usually stayed in the rumpled bed, talking for a while and reading the papers. They liked making a morning of it before getting up. Something was wrong. He sat up and saw her open handbag on the bedside table, bulging with items that couldn't be zipped away. It was daring him to look inside. He inched closer. A niggling thought wormed in his head. She was on the pill and was keeping it a secret - she had to be. Otherwise she'd be pregnant by now because although they weren't officially trying for a baby, they weren't using contraception either. He knew they could conceive because it happened by accident, the first time they'd made love. He was ashamed of himself every time he remembered their clumsy lovemaking in a seedy hotel in Brighton. They'd only ended up in bed together because the trains to London were cancelled.

Feeling uncomfortable, he couldn't resist looking inside her handbag to see if he could find any pills. With guilt flooding through him, he reached into her bag and fumbled around. The shower stopped. He didn't have long. He searched her bedside drawer and found nothing there either. The bathroom door opened, he slammed the drawer shut and sat back, his hand sweeping through his hair as his heart thudded.

'Sit down love.' He patted the bed as she came in, wearing a towelling robe and rubbing her damp hair.

She slumped onto the bed and faced him.

'Are you on the pill?'

'No.'

She turned away and rubbed her hair vigorously, making him wonder if she was lying.

'I know we're not technically trying, but I thought nature would take its course. Maybe we should see a doctor.'

'Children are a tie.'

'Are you saying you don't want children or just not yet?'

She put the towel down and faced him, a sad expression on her face. 'It was hard losing our baby. I know that it was twelve years ago, but I still feel the pain. And to think he would have been at secondary school now. Everything that could have went wrong.'

'And I wish I'd been there for you, but I didn't know you were pregnant, you didn't tell me. And if we hadn't bumped into each other in New York, I would never have known. We wouldn't be here now.'

'It was easier not to tell you. We'd split up, you were miles away in Manchester. I went along with what Mum wanted me to do and was going to have him adopted. It would have been easier if he'd lived and gone to a new family. I feel such a failure giving birth to a handicapped baby and being told that he'd died.'

Jasper cupped her face as tears watered her eyes. He pushed a damp strand of hair from her cheek and kissed her lips. 'Now you listen to me,' he said kissing her again. 'It wasn't your fault. Ten thousand babies were born worldwide to mothers who took thalidomide. You couldn't help having morning sickness, none of those mothers could, or insomnia or whatever else they took the tablet for.'

'I know all that, we've talked about it so many times, but it doesn't get any easier. It's hard to move on and just forget it happened. I'm terrified of having another baby.'

'You mustn't be scared. I'm here this time. I won't let anything bad happen to you.'

'I might never want a child. I'm sorry Jasper that's just the way it is.'

'Can I ask you something?'

'What?'

'The baby was definitely mine?'

She looked flabbergasted. 'Of course, he was. Why would you ask that?'

'For the same reason I asked if you were on the pill. It's just that we haven't been using contraception in a while. I assumed you were thinking, if it happened it happened.'

NOW THAT SHE'D opened up, maybe it was time he knew the truth. She'd always been a very private person and really struggled to talk about her feelings, even to close friends. Her parents, and especially her mother, were stiff and starchy people. They were cold and matter-of-fact and kept their feelings and emotions bottled up. The thought of laying her feelings bare in all their rawness made her feel sick inside. He was her husband; she knew she shouldn't keep secrets from him. She'd been brave enough to tell him about the baby they'd lost, or perhaps it was the wine talking that evening in New York, mixed with the glamour of being away in the Big Apple where life was an ocean away. She had to find a path through her closed mind and be honest. She hadn't lied to him - but had been horribly dishonest through her omission. It would stir a hornet's nest if she kept it to herself any longer and she was running out of excuses. She felt sick with fear as she braced herself for his reaction. He was going to be devastated.

'There's something I need to tell you. Something that happened early in our marriage.'

She should have been open from the start - it wasn't an issue then. All she had to do was open her mouth and let the words out and he'd have cuddled her and said how awful it was for her - and that would have been that. She should have told him. But at the time, it was impossible.

'What?'

'I had an abortion.'

She watched his face drain of colour and immediately wished she'd kept it to herself. Did he really need to know? But the cat was out of the bag. It was as if she'd slapped him. 'I didn't tell you I was pregnant.'

'You killed our baby. I can't believe you'd do that.'

'I'm sorry, I was struggling.'

Jasper got up and paced the room. 'Why the fuck would you do that,' he screamed.

'At the time it seemed to be the only way out. You would have persuaded me to keep it.'

'Your worries are my worries, otherwise what's the point in marriage?'

'I wasn't myself Jasper. My mind was all over the place.'

He put his head in his hands and grunted. 'This beggars belief.'

'I'm sorry. I know I've let you down.'

'We've lost two babies. How could you let me believe that we only have one dead baby between us when there are two?'

His matter of fact statement punched her in the gut. There were times, usually in the middle of the night when a hollow pit at the bottom of her stomach ached for the babies she'd lost, guilt swallowed her whole.

Jasper let out a sigh. 'You've done everything behind my back.' Silence filled the bedroom and it felt as if it would consume her.

'I'm sorry. I didn't mean to hurt you. And that's why,' she said softly, 'I'm on the pill for now.'

He uncovered his face and stared at her. 'What? You just told me you weren't on the pill.'

She had to tell him. She couldn't keep insisting she wasn't on the pill, he'd have found out in time, because she'd probably be careless and leave the packet lying around. She wasn't ready for a baby. But would she ever be? In his eyes she was a disappointment.

'I am, for now - until I'm ready.'

'You mean only until I discovered you were on it.'

She put underwear on and pulled trousers from the wardrobe, dressing in a hurry through a flood of tears. 'What if Distaval is still inside me? What if it's seeped into every cell and vein? It just felt that I would be jinxed again. That's why I had the abortion, that's why I went on the pill,' she cried. 'I didn't intend to be on the pill for long.'

'That nasty drug has long left your body.'

'What if we did have another baby and I suffered from morning sickness again? You have no idea how bad it is. With the first one it felt as if my body had been taken over by aliens; the sickness was that bad.'

Tossing clothing on the floor, she caught the loving expression on his face.

'I'd make you hot ginger tea and help you through it.'

He wasn't helping. She wished he hadn't raised the one subject she'd tried to avoid discussing. Blinking, she buttoned her blouse, with a crushing feeling of helplessness washing over her.

5

1973

Bill Rona tilted her head towards Bill, mustering all the strength she could and whispered, 'Find Toby's real mother.'

Her words sliced through him. In the twelve years of Toby's life she'd never suggested this. They'd got on with things, as couples do, hiding the ugly secret of his birth and the crime Rona had committed, to the point that they had listened to their own lies for so long, they struggled to distinguish them from the truth––it felt like the truth. But now she lay dying and probably knew it, dipping in and out of consciousness, high on morphine. Bill knew that death did strange things to people.

'What Rona?' he asked, his ear at her face.

'If you don't find her...' she wheezed as her words drained her strength. 'she will find you.' She mumbled something else but it was muffled.

Bill kissed her chapped lips and stroked her papery skin. Should he consider her wish? On top of losing her, he now had this burden. If he found Toby's real mother, the police would be involved; it was inevitable.

He kissed her again. It would be the last kiss, their twenty-year marriage soon committed to memory. The room smelled of death, sweet, cloying and oozing from every pore, as her body shut down, ravished by cancer. He knew Rona wouldn't want the vicar to say she'd fought and lost a battle, or she'd tried hard and failed, or that she'd given up. Rona was a practical woman and being put on the courage pedestal wasn't her. She'd want to be remembered for welcoming new life into the world as a midwife and making so many parents happy. That's why he'd fallen in love with her, the practical and strong side of her nature and it was what he would miss most. Without her he had no idea how he'd cope. When he tried to face the reality of what life would be like his mind was like a hamster's wheel, turning but going nowhere, he had no vision for the future, it was a black well.

He'd always imagined that he'd go first. It was the natural order of things. Men went first. She was the healthy one, until this. She didn't drink or smoke and was careful about what she ate. If anybody deserved to die, it was him. He'd let her down, with his unwillingness to adopt. And if he'd encouraged her to move into a different area of nursing, then maybe she wouldn't have been tempted to snatch Toby.

Rona opened her eyes and stared straight up - at what Bill didn't know. And then she closed her eyes and he knew she was gone.

In an instant time slowed. Sounds distorted; the clatter of the tea trolley and bedroom alarms. The hospice routine continued as if nothing had happened. He felt as if he was drowning, he couldn't breathe. A nurse put her hand on his shoulder.

He wanted to cry; it was hard to hold back. Every pent-up emotion crashed into his mind. He stifled the tears, because now was not the time or place. He'd wait until later, behind his own closed door when Toby was asleep in bed. The reality of being a single dad hit him. He was the dad of a boy who wasn't even his, a boy he hadn't wanted. It was a strange thought. Until now Toby was more Rona's than his. But he couldn't think like that and chastised himself for it. Toby was just an innocent kid; he didn't know any different. He'd loved his mum and life would never be the same for either of them. In the hierarchy of grief, Toby's grief came first.

Bill stood up in a fluster. 'I've got to go. Toby will need picking up from his grandmother later on and I need to go home first.'

The nurse rubbed his shoulder. 'She's at peace now, free from pain. You go; we'll look after her. You can come back any time. We won't be moving her today. A doctor needs to certify the death.'

6

1973

Bill

Shutting the door on the outside world, Bill slid to the floor, crouching against the wall with his head in his hands, allowing his sorrow to well up to the surface. Leaflets were scattered around the mat—a scout jumble sale and a family fun day in the village hall this coming Saturday. A cheery day out, surrounded by happy faces was the last thing he needed. He scrunched up the leaflets and threw the ball at the wall, as if it were a grenade. He reached out to pick up Rona's Betterware and Littlewoods catalogues and hurled them towards the stairs. He'd give anything now for Rona to be here disturbing his favourite programmes with her silly questions about which dress to buy.

With no more tears inside him, he staggered to his feet and went into the sitting room. The coffee table was strewn with half-drunk cups of tea: pages from the *Daily Mail* littered the floor, a headline declaring, 'Europe Here We Come', with a picture of Ted Heath signing the Treaty of Rome the previous year but Britain's membership of the EEC had just come into effect. It was the start of a new era, one that Rona had looked forward to. Life went on.

Rona's yucca plant, occupying a bright spot in the room, felt like a judge waiting to condemn him for leaving the place in a state. Going into the kitchen he realised that he hadn't washed the dishes in days. The sink was piled with dirty pots and pans. Meat pie stuck to plates and needed soaking. The bin overflowed, the floor was sticky and the hob was greasy. Clearing up was the last thing on his mind and he didn't feel like doing them now. All he wanted to do was curl up and sleep for days.

The phone rang, making him jump. They'd just had it installed and he was still getting used to the sound as it rang through the house, but having a phone was so much easier than running to the phone box down the road.

It was the hospice on the phone wanting to know which funeral director he'd be using. He wasn't ready to arrange Rona's funeral and he had no idea of her wishes. Celia would know. And then a thought hit him. My God. I have to tell Celia that her daughter is dead.

Bill went to his mother-in-law's house, a twenty-minute walk away from their home in Blackpool. Celia was picking Toby up from school every evening so that Bill could spend time with Rona at the hospice.

It was an early January day and Bill braced himself against the chill. Light snowflakes swirled around him. The settling snow glinted under the orange street lights. His mind was fixed on how he was going to break the news to Toby, who would be sitting at his grandma's kitchen table building his Airfix kit. Bill rehearsed the conversation he was minutes away from having. 'Is she going to die?' Toby had asked many times over the past weeks and Bill had immediately replied, 'No, son, she's not going to die.' He'd met denial and made friends with it. He harboured hopes that the doctors were wrong, or maybe it was just easier to lie to Toby.

For weeks life had been about arranging the mundane, like making last minute arrangements for people to collect Toby from school. Bill had taken too much time off work to visit the hospital and attend appointments with Rona. His customers were understanding but he knew their patience would soon wear thin. They wanted their house extensions and their roof repairs finished. He didn't want to let them down, but the number of unfinished contracts was mounting. He was overwhelmed. As he approached Celia's house, he wanted to collapse, right there on the doorstep. There was no denying it; he was swamped. Steadying himself and pushing all thoughts of work to the back of his mind, he pressed the doorbell. Toby needed him to be strong.

7

1973

Jasper

Jasper was at his office window in Fleet Street adjusting his tie. People were spilling from the passageway which connected Hand and Ball Court with Fleet Street. Some of them he knew. Sam, the editor was crossing the Court. Jasper loved the view over the close-packed district, synonymous with the newspaper industry. It wasn't just a street; it was a way of life with its own style and philosophy. Some journalists referred to it as the Street of Shame on account of the long boozy lunches. The street had its own characteristic smell. The alleys and courts were haunted by the smell of newsprint. He caught the delicious ghost of it now, in his nostrils as he stood watching the rain make dusty tracks down the glass.

The traffic in the street below seemed to go silent, as if he'd put it on mute. It was over. He was never going to have a child. He suddenly saw his life through a tunnel, narrowing down with him stuck inside.

It was hard for him to focus on the day ahead and the stories he was writing about. There were notes and memoranda scribbled on coarse office copy paper on his desk. He turned to the files on the shelf, his eyes scanning for the file on the thalidomide story. He pulled it out and losing his grip, the file thumped to the ground, the contents cascading across the floor. Jasper stared at the mess. The toxic face of Enoch Powell stared back. When Powell was Minister for Health in the sixties, he had a lot to answer for. He refused help to the thalidomide families or to meet any of them, stubbornly refusing a public enquiry and denying the public the information to understand the tragedy. His government had said that Distillers - the company that had manufactured thalidomide in the UK - had met all the legal requirements of the time, in terms of the testing and marketing of the drug, and what had happened was not Distiller's responsibility. Lawyers, acting for the British families, had sued Distillers, reaching a settlement with the company in 1968 and 1969, but it was woefully inadequate.

'You evil reckless, insensitive bastard.' He kicked the photo as he remembered Powell saying that every medicine carried a risk.

Falling to the ground, Jasper knelt over the mess, the spotlights above reflecting in the slippery wallets containing the newspaper cuttings. There were photographs of thalidomide children wearing prosthetic limbs and photos of the pill that had caused the tragedy. Last night's argument with Sandy still haunted him; it was bound up with the cuttings scattered at his feet. He moved away, couldn't think as he paced the office trying to clear his head.

'Morning.' Sam, the editor breezed into the office. Pointing to the floor, Sam said, 'Christ mate. What's all this mess?'

'Cuttings about the thalidomide story.'

'You're not dragging that old chestnut up again are you? The last time we published a story about that, we had people writing in complaining that they didn't want to look at pictures of handicapped children over their cornflakes and toast.'

'I think it's time the public saw these children as real people. It would be good to find out what's happened to them.'

'Let me call Adam. We need to see where we stand legally.'

Adam was one of the newspaper's lawyers, a young guy in his thirties. He came into the office and stood at Sam's desk. 'Some of the families are in the middle of civil action,' he told Sam and Jasper.

'The whole situation is a disgrace,' Jasper said with passion. 'Road deaths, air crashes and major fires are all followed by searching public enquiries, but the biggest drug disaster of its kind gets ignored.'

'Writs have been issued. It's illegal to bring out facts or comment on a pending trial. Nothing can be published that might influence a judge until every case has been settled by the courts.'

'I hear what you're saying.' Jasper stroked his moustache. 'But I think we need to get to the bottom of this story and dare our readers to look away.'

'I'm all for a story that will sell the paper,' Sam said.

'I wouldn't advise digging into anything to do with culpability. We could have the Attorney General on our backs, taking us to court. The families have been told by their lawyers not to talk to the media.'

'Thank you, Adam. And I get your passion Jasper,' Sam said, frowning as he slumped into his chair. 'Why are you so interested in this story? There's lots of copy to get your teeth into. We've got Idi Admin terrorising Uganda, Vietnam, The Troubles in Northern Ireland and Ted Heath leading us into Europe. It's more than enough to fill the paper and isn't going to have people reaching for a puke bucket. Give the controversial stuff a wide berth, mate.'

'My wife and I lost a baby because of thalidomide.'

The room fell silent as both men stared at Jasper, and Sam turned a deep shade of red.

'Bloody hell mate, I'm really sorry.'

'Me too,' Adam said.

'My wife took Distaval for morning sickness. Our son was born in early 1961 and had no arms. Unfortunately, he died soon after birth. I don't want these children to be invisible. We published early stories about some of the kids, and I want to find out what's happened to them.'

Sam sniffed and taking a deep breath said, 'It's never a good idea to mix investigative journalism with your own personal situation.'

'Writers should write about things they are passionate about.'

'Your work's great and I admire your drive. You want justice for these families. I get all that. But we have to be careful. I'm not prepared to go to prison for this,' Sam said.

'It's my job to keep us out of jail,' Adam said. 'British law on contempt of court means that their writs seal the whole affair in a legal cocoon.'

'It's a denial of free speech,' Sam barked. 'But we have to accept that's the way things are.'

'I'm not writing a pack of lies,' Jasper said. 'Try telling that to the mother of the boy who's had forty-two operations or the ones awarded woefully low damages back in 1968 and 1969.'

'We need to be legally watertight if we publish anything. Common law has long held that the right to free speech must be balanced by the right to a fair trial uncontaminated by outside pressure that might sway a judge or jury. I know the cases have been going on for a long time but actually they are only in the early stages of litigation.' Adam said.

'It's tough,' Sam said. 'In my first months as sub-editor I had a narrow squeak when, thanks to a slip by a writer which was compounded by a duty lawyer's misjudgment; we'd accidentally published the previous convictions of a man about to stand trial. I was personally exonerated, but the newspaper was fined.' Sam, pacing the office in silence took a sharp intake of breath and said, 'We could prepare a piece about the background of the drug and how the disaster came about. Adam, did you know that thalidomide was developed by a Nazi, chemical-weapons engineer towards the end of the war? I think we should start with that story.'

'I'd rather interview a few of the families,' Jasper said.

'It's fraught with problems,' Adam warned.

'I'm going to make a decision,' Sam clicked his fingers. 'You're a good journalist and you've made me think. Without any challenge to our oppressive press laws how will these families get justice?' Sam slapped the palm of his hand on the table. 'I'm willing to give you a couple of weeks to go out and gather your articles, as long as you carry on with the other stories you're working on.' And addressing Adam he asked, 'What do you think? From a legal point of view Adam?'

'Far be it for me to tell you guys what stories to go after, but it is my job to protect the paper and its shareholders from injunctions and damages. So, we need to proceed carefully, and I need to see everything before we go to press.'

'We could put it into page proof and send it to Distillers and ask for their comment,' Sam suggested. 'If they comment without seeking a court injunction we can publish and if they seek an injunction against publication, we could test the law by fighting it.'

'Run everything by me first,' Adam said, slapping Sam on the back and heading for the door.

Having convinced the editor, Jasper had to convince Sandy. She hated him working away on business, complaining that she didn't like being left alone in the house.

8

1973

Toby stifled his tears as his mother's coffin was lowered on ropes into the hole in the ground. He'd sucked a Murray Mint throughout the service and bit his lips, the only way to stem the tears and stick to his father's instructions. 'Don't cry. It's not dignified. You can cry when you get into bed later, out of view of everybody.'

A raven - vicar-like and full of its own self-importance - paraded back and forth around the edge of the hole. He named him Blackie, and he was a welcome distraction. It was hard to believe that his mum had died. He kept thinking it was all a horrible nightmare, that he'd wake to her favourite song, 'You Are My Sunshine,' and her cheery face as she drew his curtains in the morning. His dad always woke in a mood, grumbling if something wasn't right and slamming doors as he went off to work.

Parents were supposed to live to old age. That was what he'd always believed would happen. He had known she was ill, but his dad and grandma had reassured him that she'd be okay. The treatment was working, the doctors knew what they were doing, and she was in the best place, they said. Nobody had told him how serious her illness was. His mum was his whole world, his protector and his best friend. He loved his dad, but it wasn't the same. Their relationship was based on their shared love of football. He didn't see much of his dad; he was always working or down at the pub. His mum had always been there, making his dinner, taking him to school, helping with homework, fighting his cause and making sure he was treated fairly. Her warm hugs had somehow made everything all right when he'd been at his lowest ebb. She made time for him, sitting on the end of his bed, chatting and laughing, making up silly stories using his teddies, taking him to different places in the school holidays; particularly the cinema or the beach. When he was at primary school she had given up her job so she could come into school to help him with some of the things he couldn't do on his own. His relationship with his grandma wasn't the same. She wasn't loving and cuddly. She was cold. She scared him and he didn't like the way she had treated his mum. She was always critical and putting her down.

Toby looked around at the small crowd of mourners. There were nurses from the hospital where his mum had worked and who had kept in touch with her, long after she'd given up midwifery, her bingo friends and lots of people he didn't know or didn't recognise. Toby didn't care who they were. Apart from his dad and grandma they weren't important. He just wanted his mum back. Like the song she sang each morning she was his ray of sunshine and nobody else could ever take her place.

Toby leaned over the grave and dropped two white roses onto the coffin. He couldn't contain himself any longer. With tears pouring down his cheeks, he turned away from the graveside and ran to the gate of the cemetery to wait until it was over. Sadness seeped out of him and in that moment a crushing realisation dawned on him. She wasn't coming back. Ever. She was gone.

9

1973

Bill

Bill wanted it to be over. He'd followed tradition and invited the mourners back for tea and sandwiches and to share their memories of Rona, but all he wanted was to usher them out of the door so that he and Toby could be left in peace. He was in the kitchen alone, while his guests were in the front room. Checking that nobody was coming, he crouched down and opened the cupboard door below the kitchen sink, delving between the bleach and washing powder for his bottle of whisky. He was down to half a bottle. He hadn't meant to drink quite so much the previous evening but he couldn't help himself. It was the only way to dull the pain.

The phone rang and, closing the cupboard door Bill went to answer it. It was another silent caller. There had been several in the past few weeks. Bill wondered if there was a problem with his phone line.

Putting the phone down, Bill could hear the high-pitched laughter of Celia, his mother-in-law. That bloody woman. How inappropriate at her own daughter's funeral to share her appalling jokes. At least when Rona was alive they were able to keep her at bay, only seeing her when they had to and longing for her to get on and sell her house in Blackpool and move up to Yorkshire. She had been planning to move for some time. Rona had breathed a sigh of relief, glad that her overbearing mother was planning to put distance between them. But now that Rona was gone, Bill realised that he needed his mother-in-law to be nearby to help out with Toby. Rona's death changed everything. Celia couldn't move, not now. He unscrewed the lid of the whisky bottle and took a gulp, welcoming the amber liquid and its numbing effects as it warmed through his veins.

No matter what he did for Celia, it was never good enough. He'd come to dread her requests to fix a broken shelf or lug a piece of furniture from one room to another. He'd long given up making an effort to please her, because she was never satisfied. He took another swig of whisky. I must stop he thought. But the liquid slipped down his throat so easily, blocking the pain flooding through his body and pushing his problems to the back of his mind where he didn't have to confront them.

Bill wiped his mouth, tucked the whisky back in its hiding place and returned to the front room. A row of mourners was squeezed along the small settee, elbow to elbow, their plates of food balanced on their laps. Celia turned to him with ill-concealed criticism, smelling the whisky on his breath. He may as well have downed the whole bottle–– the sneer on her face would have been the same. No matter what he did he would always fall short of her expectations. The one thing she wanted for her daughter was to marry a professional man––a lawyer, a doctor or a civil servant, but not a humble builder who came home with grubby hands and mucky overalls. In her eyes Bill was beneath her daughter.

'For goodness sake,' Celia tutted loudly, 'I despair of you, Bill. What have been doing out in the kitchen? You've guests to look after.' Without waiting for his reply she garbled on, raving about how beautiful Yorkshire was, and how she couldn't wait to move.

'I didn't think you'd be moving, not now,' Bill said. He left out the words, 'Now that Rona's gone,' saying them in his head instead, because Toby was in the room.

Celia carried on, without acknowledging Bill. 'Some people think it's all sheep, rain and dour stone cottages, but it's beautiful. It's filled with rolling hills and silence, roses around door frames and tea pots in windows.' She put her empty plate on the table and focused on gathering more food, packing each sandwich onto the plate, as if building an office block. Bill had forgotten this uncouth side to her. It only seemed to come out at his house, as if she'd parked her manners on the doorstep before coming in.

'But Toby needs you *here*.'

She turned to face him, and Bill lowered his gaze to the carpet. She always had that effect on him, just when he had regained his confidence to challenge her she knocked it back, reducing him to a nervous wreck so he was powerless to defend himself. Bill could tell she wanted to know what he was going to do and if he had a plan. He didn't have a plan. He was juggling balls, trying to work, keeping a house and bringing up a handicapped child. It wasn't going to be easy. But one thing life had taught him was you had to rely on family to get you through. She was the only family close by and she still had her health. She didn't have an excuse not to help.

'Bill, it may sound harsh, but you'll have to toughen up if you're going to make a go of being a single dad.' Bill winced at her words and there were a few shocked faces around the room. As if expecting accusations for being insensitive, she added, 'Well of course I'll help dear, we all will, but I'm not going to put my life on hold. It's been a plan of mine to move to Yorkshire for a very long time.'

'But I'm going to need somebody to go into school to help

with Toby's personal care. I can't think who I'll ask.' Bill knew it was wrong to bring this up in front of Toby, but frustration rained down and he couldn't help himself.

'Rona made things very difficult for herself trotting up to the school every five minutes. He's at secondary school now, and there's a nurse to help him.' Turning to Toby, she said, 'You're a big boy now. You can take care of yourself a bit more.'

'Mum liked coming in to school to help me.' Rona had fussed over the lad's needs and going into school had kept her busy.

Toby reddened and Bill wished the floor would swallow them both up.

'Mrs Stevens the school nurse, helps me with my personal care. That's not the problem.'

'You find secondary school a bit overwhelming?' Bill said.

'It's much bigger than primary school. I don't like it when the other children stare at me in the corridors and in the playground. They gawp at me as if I'm a circus freak.'

Now that he had been at the school for several months, Bill had thought things would get easier. After all, Toby was used to being stared at in the street. He'd had twelve years of it. The worst day was when they were at the swimming pool and a mother pulled her child away from him, as though Toby had something contagious.

'Every time I go into a class, I feel thirty pairs of eyes on me, watching and judging,' Toby told him many times. Bill hoped things would improve as the children got to know him.

Toby was perched on the settee next to his Great Aunt Maud who was rubbing his back. 'I don't think you should be discussing all this now,' she said and smiled at Toby. She looked away but not before Bill caught the downturn of her lip as she glanced at his flipper-like arms, the cause of all this bother. He hated pity more than revulsion. 'This is Toby, accept him for God's sake,' Bill wanted to scream.

Celia gave a dramatic sniff and stood up. 'I think I'm going to be off now. It's been lovely seeing everybody,' and as if suddenly realising she needed to be sad, she added, 'although I wish it wasn't at my daughter's funeral, God rest her soul. I'm glad she's not suffering anymore. I suppose we must be grateful for that.' She didn't bother to hug her grandson as she left.

Bill was glad to shut the door on Celia.

One of Bill's aunts was in the hallway. 'What can I do to help, dear?'

The sympathy in his aunt's tone made Bill want to hug her. At least somebody was on his side, but his aunt wasn't getting any younger and would need help herself, at some point. The thought of that overwhelmed Bill. Was anybody going to be there for him? 'Can I wash up?'

'It's okay, you'd better be getting off now.'

'Are you sure dear? It's no trouble.'

The washing-up was the least of Bill's worries. There were so many problems hitting him from every direction. How was he going to go on, without Rona? She was his rock, his world. Everything had come crashing down when she'd taken her last breath.

BILL SWITCHED the kitchen light off and before heading upstairs to bed, he went to stand at the kitchen window, with the sudden feeling that somebody or something was watching him. He stared at the trees and thought he saw a shadow. Squinting as his eyes acclimatised to the darkness, an eerie feeling shot through him. 'Silly bugger. You're imagining things.' He was going to have to get used to being alone. Alone in mind, body and soul. Alone in the darkness with the sound of silence buzzing in his ears.

10

1973

Toby

'Can you mix it in?'

'Do what darling?'

'Mix up my food.'

'Come on Toby,' Celia said in a condescending tone, making Toby's face heat up as she stood over him. He hated feeling powerless. 'You're not a baby. You're twelve years old and practically a teenager. You do *not* need your food mixing in.' She spat the words out with a mixture of amusement and disgust. 'Really, it's time you grew up. Your mother has babied you for long enough.'

'But it tastes better mixed in. It's how I like it.' Toby tried to sound assertive, the way his mum had taught him, but he knew it was pointless arguing with his grandma. She always got her own way and it was deliberate. His mum had taught him to eat with his feet, but his horrified grandmother never allowed it. She said he looked like an animal in a yard. 'As you get older,' she said on many occasions, 'your body will struggle to twist and turn and you won't be able to bring your foot to your mouth, so you may as well get used to being fed.' He'd always eaten with the fork between his toes. It was easy and he could eat fast and be in control. He didn't like it when other people fed him. Why did everyone think he had to conform? He felt cross. He just wanted to be himself and get on with his life without the burden of artificial arms or somebody helping him. Did it matter that he used his toes instead of his fingers?

He stared at his food, his potato was in one corner, peas in the other, with two sausages swimming in a pond of gravy in the middle. He hated peas but when they were mixed in he couldn't taste them.

'Open wide.'

Toby winced, closing his eyes so that he didn't have to watch the peas. They were like a pile of garden waste going into his mouth. He'd seen other children being made to eat food they didn't like but they had a trick that worked for them. They squeezed their nostrils together because that way they couldn't taste the food—but that wasn't an option for Toby.

'Stop being so dramatic and just eat it.'

Toby swallowed the peas without chewing them.

'I'm out for the day tomorrow,' Celia said, cutting up pieces of sausage. 'I'm having lunch with friends. I won't be able to walk you home.'

Toby's stomach twisted into a million knots at the thought of leaving school alone. As much as his grandma irritated him, it was a terrifying prospect to walk home on his own. The bullies were going to get him. It was only a matter of time.

11
1973

Toby saw his tormentors as soon as he turned the corner into the road leading away from the school. It was the second time that Grandma had left him to walk home alone. He knew that he had to get used to it and, when nothing happened the first time, he was lured into a false sense of security, thinking they'd moved on to somebody else and would give up picking on him and calling him names.

The Trio were half-way down the street and waiting for him by the entrance to the park. They knew the short-cut he took and where they wouldn't be seen picking on him. Bob, Jim and Des. Des, the worst of them.

Toby froze with panic rising inside. He tossed a coin in his head. Should he turn around and go back to school pretending that he had stomach-ache and ask one of the teachers to drop him home? No, that was the coward's way out. He had to face up to this. It's what his mum would have told him to do. He carried on walking, but more slowly. He felt a prickle of cold as he approached them, his shoes sticking to the pavement. He was outnumbered. There was no way he could outwit them.

They'd spotted him and were nudging each other. With panic rising, Toby considered knocking on one of the doors of the houses lining the street, but that would be plain nutty. What would he say to the stranger who answered?

'Look at Frog,' Des yelled. 'What an idiot. He's going to go rushing back to school. Baby.'

Des always seemed to know what was on Toby's mind; it was as if he could smell and touch the fear oozing from him. They were casually leaning against a fence. Bob took a pack of chewing gum from his pocket and gave a piece to Jim and Des. He removed the wrapping and put it in his mouth, chewing blissfully. On his own Bob wouldn't scare Toby but the three of them together were a formidable force and Toby knew that they were deliberately chewing gum to look big and intimidating.

'Frog, where's Mummy today? Does she trust you to walk home alone now? That's brave of her,' Des called over. Des laughed. It was an infectious laugh to his cronies hanging out with him, but it scared Toby.

He carried on walking, even though his legs were wobbly.

'Mummy's boy,' Bob jeered, spitting his gum into the road.

They could taunt him about his arms but not his mum. If they knew she was dead, Toby wondered, would they carry on? Perhaps they didn't care one way or the other. He couldn't see them taking pity on him. They were lucky, they all still had parents.

Be strong, Toby told himself, but his heart was hammering in his chest and it was hard to be strong. Part of him wanted to run over and kick them between the legs. But he was crumbling inside and felt the blood draining from his face. If only he had two arms and if only there weren't three of them. He wanted to hit them where it hurt but mostly he just wanted to collapse by the roadside, go to sleep and not wake up.

Quick. Think. His mum had told him to tease them back.

She'd said ignore them and they would get tired of teasing. But they never got tired of it. He was different. He was the odd ball and the only kid in the school without arms. He'd always be the school freak. Sometimes he wondered what it would be like to go to boarding school like his grandma kept suggesting. There were boarding schools for handicapped children, with other people like him, a place where he could shut himself away, surrounded by people of his own kind, people who weren't going to mock and judge and call him names, because there would be something wrong with every child. They would be his equals. He was sick of feeling self-conscious.

Toby carried on walking, on the opposite side. His shirt was sticking to his back and his forehead was wet.

'Oi, flipper hands, I'm talking to you,' Des shouted, his tone deep and menacing as he stepped out into the road. Toby stared ahead and ignored him. Melanie Peckham was standing at the bus stop, reading a book and was oblivious to what was going on. It was a shame that Melanie was a girl. Otherwise they might have been friends. He considered getting on the bus with her and asking if he could go home with her, but that would be plain weird.

The pack of them were in front of him. They'd crossed the road, blocking his path. Toby couldn't ignore them. They were all taller than him, even though they were in the same year. All the girls thought that Des was the bee's knees because he looked like Georgie Best but, unlike Georgie, Des didn't have a clue how to kick a ball. In fact, all three were lousy at footie. None of them had any interests apart from smoking behind the bike shed and picking fights with other boys.

'Mumsie-wumsie tell you to ignore us? But she's not here now, is she?'

Toby's eyes stung and his cheeks burned. He blinked hard and knew that he mustn't cry, no matter what. *Ignore them, ignore them, ignore them.*

'I said, where's Mumsie today? What about the old girl with the bandy legs? Is that your granny? It's not like them to let the little crip walk home on his own,' Des sneered.

Des was bent so close now that Toby could feel his breath on his face. Melanie was looking up from her book with alarm and in that moment the bus pulled up. This was his chance to escape, his only chance. He darted around Des, dodging Bob, just before Bob's foot moved to trip him, but he managed to get on the bus, and Melanie followed. The bus wasn't going in the right direction for home and he had no money. Now he had a sea of faces staring at him. He was used to the whispers, the stares. He wished he had a superpower; invisibility or the ability to fly—or even just the superpower of having arms. A million pair of eyes followed him, they burned into him everywhere he went. He moved towards a row of empty seats at the very back, with Melanie following behind him. He was relieved the conductor was upstairs. Toby hoped to get off before he came downstairs to check their fares. Des, Bob and Jim had their faces pressed to the grimy rear window as if they were pretending to be in a horror movie. In a moment of panic, he wondered if they'd get on too, but to his relief the bus pulled away. Melanie collapsed next to him, her leg touching his as she squeezed in. He flinched and moved away, feeling his cheeks burn. Maybe she fancied him. Now that he came to think of it, she'd smiled at him in maths the other day. It was a warm, inviting smile that told him she liked him. She could have taken another seat, but she'd chosen to sit with him. He wondered what it would be like to have a girlfriend. But then he remembered he wouldn't be able to hold her hand. That was important. To be able to walk along the street holding hands.

'Bubble gum,' Melanie offered.

He stared at the gum longingly, his mouth watering. It was wrapped in coloured paper and looked delicious. 'No thanks.'

He wanted to say yes but he couldn't unwrap the paper.

'Go on.'

'I...'

'It's okay... here.' She unwrapped it and popped it into his mouth before he had the chance to reply. His teeth sank into the gum. Strawberry. His favourite flavour.

'You shouldn't have to put up with those bullies.'

'It's all right. They don't scare me.'

Toby wanted to get off the bus and away from her. He wished she hadn't seen what had happened. It only added to his humiliation.

'That's not how it looked to me.'

A moment ago he'd wanted to confide in her but the shutters came down and all he wanted was the safety of his bedroom.

'I don't want to talk about it.'

'I won't tell anyone, promise.'

Her soft words lifted a suffocating weight from his chest.

'You don't actually live in this direction, do you? You live at the back of the park. I've been past your house. I know where you live.'

He wanted her to shut up. Her chatter was distracting him from working out how to get off the bus without paying. But he needed her help. If he got off the bus too early, he'd have to scoot back along the road and through the park and there was every chance the bullies would still be hanging around.

The bus conductor with his brown leather-battered satchel stood before them waiting for their tickets.

'Two singles to Edgar Road please.' Melanie handed over the coins and passed a ticket to Toby. Blood pulsed in his cheeks.

'Why did you do that? I have money,' he lied.

'No, you don't.'

'I'll pay you back tomorrow?'

'You're coming home with me. My dad will walk you back when he gets home.'

Toby's mouth gaped, a wall of silent tension building between them, unbroken until Melanie got up, indicating it was time to get off.

'You coming, or are you just going to sit there?'

12

1973

Toby

Getting off the bus and walking alone with Melanie back to her house, Toby hadn't the foggiest what to talk about. He felt insanely happy to be with her, but he hoped they wouldn't be seen. He could hear the chants ringing out. 'Flipper's got a girlfriend.'

'When's the maths homework due in?' Homework was a safe subject.

'I'll get my dad to do it for me. I hate maths.' She laughed. She didn't seem the type to cheat.

'My mum used to help me with homework.'

'Used to?'

'She died.'

'Oh, you didn't say, I'm sorry.'

'My dad wasn't good at school. Half the time he doesn't have a clue.'

'It must be hard to lose your mum. Do you think she's gone to heaven?'

'I think she's probably an angel.'

Toby wasn't used to this reaction, not from people his own

age. They usually didn't know what to say to him, or they changed the subject. His voice splintered as he tried to sound calm. 'Yes, it is hard.' There were a hundred and one things he wanted to tell her, about what it was like to lose your mum but if he started, he knew he wouldn't be able to stop the conversation going to a place he didn't want to go. Most of all he wanted to tell her how strange it felt, that his mum wouldn't be here to watch him grow up.

A blanket of silence shrouded the last few yards to her house and then Melanie headed up some steps to a shiny turquoise door and bent to retrieve a key from under a plant pot. She was the same age as him and yet she had her independence. He was envious. In many ways it was as if he was still five years old.

In the kitchen, Melanie poured them a glass of lemonade each, popping a straw into his glass, and for a few moments they stood side-by-side propped against the counter, an unease passing between them.

'Shall we watch telly?' he suggested, feeling uncomfortable.

'Do you want to see my bedroom? It's just that Dad doesn't like me taking drinks into the front room.'

Toby stared at the kitchen bin. He wasn't sure which was worse, the skirmish with the Trio or the confines of Melanie's bedroom, alone with a girl in her private space, stilted conversation, girly smells and pop stars beaming from every wall. Butterflies fluttered around his stomach making him feel queasy.

'Can do.' He felt prickles of heat rise to his cheeks and followed her up the stairs into a small messy room that overlooked the park. Toby's eyes flickered around, searching for a new topic of conversation, averting his gaze from a pile of dirty clothes in the corner. There were two single beds with faded candlewick bedspreads and the walls were filled with posters of Marc Bolan from T Rex.

'If you stand on tiptoes you can just about see your road.'
Toby stood on his tiptoes.
'I've seen you go into your house a few times.'
'Oh.'
Toby wanted to tell her that she was spying on him, but she might not have found it funny.
'You like T Rex?'
'Yeah, you?'
'You Are My Sunshine' filled his head, choking the names of the groups he liked and wanted to share with her; The Beatles, Simon and Garfunkel and more. Now that the song was in his head it wouldn't go away.

Melanie played some records on her new record player. As they sat on the floor in silence, the music evoked thoughts and occasional conversation, but with the music playing there was no need to say very much. The sound was crisp, with a crackle when the needle met a scratch. The radiogram was a beauty on a wooden plinth. Toby longed for a record player and to start buying records of his own. He'd hinted before Christmas, hoping his dad would buy one, but there were no presents, tree or decorations last Christmas. 'I'm sorry son,' his dad had explained. 'I can't get my head round Christmas this year, what with your mum being ill. It doesn't feel right to celebrate, does it?' A recent history lesson about Oliver Cromwell reminded him of that dreadful Christmas. He now knew, first hand, how it must have felt like to live in the 1640s.

'Where's *your* mum?'

'She's gone to look after my auntie for a few days. Says she's left me in charge of Dad.'

The front door slammed and feet pounded on the stairs. 'You up there, Melanie?'

'I should have got the dinner started,' Melanie whispered. 'He's going to be cross.'

The door opened and when her dad saw Toby sitting on the

floor, there was a surprised expression on his face. 'Hello, young man.'

Toby caught the alarm that flickered across her dad's eyes when he noticed his lack of arms, but he was used to it, expected it even, and thankfully it was usually momentary before the person relaxed in his company, but not always.

'Could we walk Toby home, please? He doesn't live far.'

Toby was glad that Melanie didn't explain why. He'd enjoyed chatting to her and listening to music. He didn't want to ruin it by returning to thoughts of the dreaded Trio.

'Okay,' her dad said. 'And we could get fish and chips for supper on the way.'

Toby didn't want to be escorted right to his door. He didn't want to explain to his dad what was going on at school. His dad had never been involved in anything to do with school and he had work to think of.

Toby wished he could stay and eat fish and chips with them. It was better than watching his dad down a few whiskies.

13

1973

Toby

Toby said goodbye to Melanie and her dad and headed up the road towards his house. He lived in a Victorian house at the end of a terrace. Drawing closer, he smelt burning and heard the hiss and crackle of flames. A plume of smoke billowed into the sky at the back of the house. He ran to the fence, peering through a hole and yelling to get his dad's attention. His dad was having a bonfire. Toby wasn't expecting it. They only had bonfires on the 5th of November.

His dad came over to the gate to let Toby in, looking shifty as if he was hiding something. And then he saw why. A box of photos of his mum, their wedding album and her letters sat by the fire. Toby rushed towards the fire, staring at the box in disbelief and confusion.

'Where were you? You're late. I was about to send out a search party.' His dad was prodding the fire with one hand and had a bottle of whisky in his other hand.

Toby wasn't listening. If his dad was that worried, he would have come out looking for him. Toby stared into the red-and-orange ball of rage, plumes of grey buffeting into the sky, ashen debris gliding silently to the ground. Weren't they going through enough pain losing her and now he was erasing her from their lives, with no memories to look back on? He watched the sparks spitting and inside him a spark of anger and hurt burned brightly. He'd save the box, he couldn't let his dad be this reckless, he was out of his mind, he wasn't thinking and would regret it in the morning. But it was hopeless, he couldn't lift the box, he couldn't drag it to safety. All he could do was kick it, but the contents flew in all directions and some of the photos fluttered and rose in the heat and were carried away into the fire. His dad was behind him gathering them in a hurry, as they spread across the garden. He fed them to the flames as if they were food for a hungry dragon. Toby tried to wrestle his dad to the ground with his leg hooked around his dad's leg but he fought him off, pushing him away.

'Get inside, son, just get inside.'

One solitary photo escaped the flames. His dad didn't notice it, he was too busy feeding the fire. It danced up into the air from the heat of the fire before floating through the smoke and coming to rest by the back door. Toby bent down, and picking it up with his mouth, he ran to his bedroom. It was charred and blackened around the edges. But when he nudged the light on, he saw that the image was as bright and clear as ever. It was a younger Toby at the beach with his mum and Blackpool Tower in the background. He was glad that his dad wasn't in the picture, because right at that moment he hated him. His mum was wearing a bright blue dress that merged into the blue sky behind her. She was a picture of radiance; the happy, fun loving mum that he remembered who built enormous sandcastles with forts and towers and always with a flag on the top. Toby stared at the photo for ages trying to relive the day in his head, but there had been many days like it, lazy days on the beach. He'd keep the photo under his bed and look at it every day. It worried him that he'd forget her face and everything about her. This was his only reminder, he mustn't lose it, it was precious. He couldn't understand his dad. It didn't make any sense. Why would he do this?

That night the tears wouldn't stop. He thought the sadness would never go away and every time he tried to think about those happy days on the beach, he felt sadder. The pain ebbed and flowed inside him. He didn't want to upset his dad so he cried as quietly as he could. And then when there were no more tears left inside him, he edged up the bed into a sitting position and said the same prayer that he said every night for as long as he could remember. He couldn't go to sleep without saying this special prayer.

'Dear Heavenly Father, thank you for everything you have given me. I am grateful. If I try to be good, please help my arms to grow.'

When he was younger he thought that if he said the prayer enough times his stunted arms would grow into the normal arms that everybody else had, but as he got older he realised it wasn't going to happen because the damage had been done in the womb and wouldn't ever get better. It was a permanent handicap, but it didn't stop him praying. He understood the story of how he came to be like this. His mother had taken a tablet when she was expecting him, to stop her feeling sick but the tablet had stopped his arms from developing. They were told in school assembly that God could work miracles, you just needed faith. After all, Jesus healed the blind and sick. He cleansed a leper, walked on water and fed thousands with five loaves and two fish. The headmaster believed in these stories, his mum did too, and if all of these things could happen, he reasoned, then anything was possible. A part of him never gave up that sense of hope; maybe one day his prayers would come true.

14

1973

Jasper

Without scoops and exclusives, Jasper reckoned a huge amount of news wouldn't be out there. Scoop journalism got Jasper out of bed in the morning and his intent was to dig away, year after year until the mighty Distillers Company finally recognised its debt to the thousands of thalidomide victims deformed by the drug. It was a ridiculous situation, having to go to court to fight for compensation for damage caused by a drug which had been prescribed on the NHS, and which was passed as safe by the Government. Nobody was at fault. It had been an 'accident.' It was bullshit. He wanted the front page of his Fleet Street paper to demonstrate the outstanding courage of these families. He wanted to batter away until the highest courts in the land decided that a wrong had been done. The only way to do that was to turn the story into a scandal and get into the lives of the families to produce a great human story.

Journalism mattered to Jasper; it ran through his veins. He wanted to change peoples' opinions and influence lives. His work involved copious amounts of time sifting through documents, verifying sources and analysing data. Those were the tools at his disposal. He was adept at tracking down contact information and never made the mistake of rushing into writing his story.

Jasper wanted to be more than a journalist. He wanted to be a campaign journalist, driving change and exposing the truth – lies and errors. At the bottom of this scandal was a government that had betrayed these families.

Jasper's personal crusade was also to campaign for free speech and challenge the way in which the contempt laws were being used. Many papers were backing off from the story because they were getting letters from the Attorney General. Jasper determined that he would keep the story going until the end of time. He owed it to his little boy.

JASPER'S INTERVIEW schedule began in Birmingham. He hadn't been to Birmingham since the construction of the Bull Ring in the early sixties - Britain's first indoor shopping centre. It was symbolic of the new Birmingham as it emerged from the dark days of war and the poverty that riddled large swathes of the city. He found it hard to believe that Birmingham was just a village nine hundred years ago and even since his last visit to the city it had changed out of all recognition. He stared at the boxy grey concrete design. Brutalist architecture, it was supposed to be the height of modernity. Wrapping itself around the town's centre, it was isolated within a web of ring roads, a nasty concrete jungle. If Sandy was with him, she would have made a beeline for the department stores, her beady eye always on the lookout for a new dress or pair of shoes. He had to watch their joint account, she was good at spending above their means and always with the excuse that she needed a new outfit for a charity event. But he was glad of one thing. She was okay about him being away, if it wasn't any longer than a fortnight.

Jasper crossed several roads, darting in front of a Morris Minor, weaving around people as he approached the bus station. Hopping on a bus, Jasper headed for a new housing estate several miles away, to see single mother, Lesley and her four boys. Peter, born with thalidomide damage to all four of his limbs, was her fourth child. Jasper didn't know much about the family or what had happened to Lesley's husband.

Waiting for the kettle to boil in her tiny kitchen, Lesley looped her hair around her ears, banged on the window and wagged a warning finger. Her granddaughters, who she apparently looked after a couple of days a week were squabbling over the doll's pram again. She poured two mugs of tea, handing one to Jasper.

'Biscuit?'

'I'm okay thank you and thanks again for agreeing to be interviewed.'

'No problem. We're used to it.'

'Who else has interviewed you?' Alarmed, Jasper was worried that journalists from other newspapers had beaten him to it.

'None of you lot.' She smiled, offering him a chair at the kitchen table. 'Trainee doctors and surgeons, medical students, those kinds of people. The poor lad, he's had a lifetime of them poking and prodding him and going to hospital for various operations to his feet and shoulders. It's not been easy. He's got a lumber spinal rod for kyphoscoliosis and scoliosis and he's going to need dental work soon because his front teeth have been knocked out because he's fallen over that many times. He's never got on very well with false arms and legs. I think they're realising it's easier to get around in wheelchairs. The doctors try so hard to make them look normal.'

'Where is he?'

'Down south, at a school in Haslemere.'

'Oh, I thought I'd get to meet him.'

'I'm so sorry, I should have made it clear that he wouldn't be here. I protect him from publicity.'

Jasper felt like a prize idiot. He should have checked the lad would be there before coming. But he had also come to find out about the impact of Peter's birth on the family.

'How long have you been divorced?'

'You don't know my circumstances?' Lesley blushed, and making steeples with her hands, she covered her mouth and stared at the table with a frown as if mustering the courage to explain.

'I'm really sorry, no I don't know.'

'It's been hard bringing four boys up on my own. Finding out I was pregnant with Peter was a surprise. I thought I was going through the change. I was forty-four when I had him. The oldest mum in the street. Paul, Ed and John, my older children all have families of their own.

'I can't often get down to see Peter. I miss him so much but what can I do? I don't drive and the train's expensive. It was okay when he was little, but as he got older it was too much for me,' she explained before adding the shocking news that Jasper sensed was coming. 'My husband, Rick, killed himself.' She said it so matter of factly.

With a sharp intake of breath Jasper shook his head, a shocked expression clouding his face. He hadn't seen that one coming. 'Goodness. I'm so sorry to hear that.'

'He jumped from the balcony of our twentieth floor flat in a tower block on the other side of the city. I was at the clinic having Peter weighed and as I walked home pushing the pram, I saw a commotion on the lawn in front of the flats. A circle of onlookers were staring at my husband's body. If I had arrived minutes before, I might have been able to stop him.'

Jasper wanted to say something helpful but couldn't think of anything. 'Life's a shit. I can't imagine what you went through.'

'Every family has a cross to bear. Some have been through worse than me.'

'I know it doesn't compare with what you've been through, but we lost our first child at birth. He was thalidomide.'

'So, you have a personal interest in the thalidomide families?'

'Yes. That's why I'm keen for your stories to be heard.'

'Not a day goes by when I don't think about what happened to Rick. I could have prevented it. There were no indications that he was planning to do it. The anger inside me drives me mad. He took the easy way out and left us all. It was a selfish thing to do.'

'I can imagine you would go over it in your head.'

'It was beyond my control.'

'I hope this doesn't come across as cold-hearted, but could I write about what happened in my article?'

As if suddenly remembering that she was talking to a journalist she looked worried. 'I'm not sure. No. I think I need to respect the privacy of my family.'

'Yes, of course, I understand.'

'Just don't mention our names. You could talk about it in a general way. We're not alone. I know of two other fathers who took their lives, in similar circumstances. I met the mothers at Queen Mary's Hospital, Roehampton. The fathers take it hard - no more than us mothers, but we have to just carry on and deal with it. They have a limb-fitting centre at Roehampton. Peter had his prosthesis fitted there. I've met several thalidomide families there, usually while we are waiting in the queue to see the doctor. I can put you in touch with them. But I'll have to ask them first, of course.'

'Thank you, that would be good. And yes, I've heard of the good work being carried out at Roehampton. It's offered specialised services for amputees since the First World War I believe.'

An awkward atmosphere settled between them, she sliced through it with meaningless chat. 'Those flats were supposed to be high-rise havens, a far cry from the back to back slums our parents grew up in, but they were prisons for young mothers like me, with no garden for the kiddies to play in, and nowhere to hang the washing. That reminds me, I better get the washing in, the sky's getting darker.'

Lesley called the girls in and folded the clothes she brought in. Susan, her youngest granddaughter, hurled herself at Lesley's legs, crying. Anita, her other granddaughter, looking smug, was pushing the pram towards the shed.

'Anita, let your sister share,' Lesley bawled through the back door. 'They can be a right handful,' she told Jasper, before rounding both girls up and plonking them on the sofa to watch *The Magic Roundabout*. 'Mummy will be here to pick you us up soon, you can watch the telly for a bit.'

JASPER STRUGGLED to take in the enormity of Lesley's story as they ate fish and chips on her sofa, watching *Coronation Street* soon after the girls had left.

'I sometimes wish my life could be as dull and predictable as an episode of Corrie, as certain as Hilda wearing curlers or Betty serving hotpot.'

Jasper wondered what to say. He couldn't offer advice and he couldn't soothe away her pain. All he could do was listen and ask the right questions.

'"You're not taking that monster home,"' that's what my husband told me, and he meant it. Lesley was staring at the TV screen as if under hypnosis, her eyes glazed over, and she was a million miles away.

About to put fish into his mouth, Jasper stopped, fork midair, his appetite gone.

Turning to him, her face alight with anguish as if it had

happened only yesterday, Lesley spoke softly. 'They expected it to be routine. He was my fourth child. I could pop babies out like peas from a pod. Giving birth is supposed to be the most wonderful thing but this time it wasn't. My only thought as I looked at his twisted limbs was that he couldn't possibly survive. I kept asking, why me? What had I done to deserve this? Was God playing a cruel joke? And when they whisked him away to examine him, I was filled with shame. Peter's birth taught me that having a child is very much a step into the unknown. We can't choose our children. We just get on with it. Men do the easy bit and women endure the pain and we never give up on our children. How can we? We love them. The doctors thought it was a catastrophic error in foetal development, or a rare genetic deformity called phocomelia and when we found out that it was a drug that had caused it, I felt a huge sense of guilt for taking the drug. It's a guilt that never goes away.'

'Sorry.' It sounded hollow but Jasper couldn't think of anything to say.

'I only took a few pills. I couldn't get on with them, so I binned them.'

'How did your husband cope, in the early days?'

'At first, he threatened to leave if I took Peter home but he had nowhere to go. He'd lost his job shortly before Peter was born and money was tight. He refused to hold him, he wouldn't even look at him. We argued the whole time because I didn't want Peter's brothers to pick up on their dad's hostility. I wanted them to love their brother. It was a horrible time. He wasn't the man I'd married. *He* was the one who turned into a monster. I couldn't get my head around his attitude. Peter was his flesh and blood. He begged me to leave Peter at the hospital, but I think part of it was fear of the unknown and that was egged on by the doctors who thought that Peter would have profound deformities of the internal organs too. He wasn't expected to live. Maybe my husband didn't want to get too attached. That wasn't the issue for me. I was already attached. And Peter chose to live. He was a strong little boy, much stronger than his own six-foot father who took the easy route out. There were plenty of times when I wanted to scream, cry, cut and jump, but I didn't, I'm still here. I don't want people to look at me and see a martyr, an angel or a slave, I'm just me, a mother who gets on with looking after her family. I'm positive, inside me there's always a feeling that life will get better. I don't think my husband had that same outlook. If I'd seen the weak, depressive side to him before I married him, things might have turned out differently.'

'How did Peter's brothers react to his disability?'

'Kids are accepting. He was their baby brother. They took it all in their stride and loved him to bits.'

'It sounds as if you've had a tough time of it.'

'Life is a hard lesson. You play the hand you are dealt. Peter has learned that. But his father didn't.'

The evening ended in light-hearted conversation and Jasper left when the dreary music of Coronation Street began. They had talked all the way through it.

15

1973

Bill and Toby

It was the day after the bonfire and Bill couldn't believe his moment of madness, when he had torn through the house, snatching every photo in sight. But grief was like madness. God never gives you more than you can bear, he had read that somewhere in the Bible. But the theory needed serious testing. He used to behave normally—he was an ordinary man who never did anything to shock anybody. But now it seemed that his every action was irrational and illogical, as if an alien had invaded his body.

How was he ever going to make it up to Toby? He couldn't. Apologising to Toby wouldn't bring them back. The pictures were gone. Bill was overwhelmed with guilt. Burning her photographs was a new layer of guilt to add to the guilt that already sat heavy. He couldn't believe that he'd wished Rona dead in a fit of anger when she had stolen Toby from the hospital after the doctor had put him in a cold room to die. Then there were the endless arguments about what she'd done. And in a fit of anger he'd even, on many occasions wished Toby dead. But the worst guilt of all came from the time he had tried to smother him in his cot. And then Rona's illness came into their lives like an unwelcome visiting aunt. After everything she'd been through-- it should have been him not her. She didn't deserve to die. If he'd paid enough attention when she'd said she hadn't been feeling well, maybe they could have treated the cancer. The boy had lost his mother. Everything was now down to him to get things right, to not screw up. Toby depended on him. But he was failing.

Toby's door was closed. Rona had never allowed Toby to keep his door closed. She was very strict about that. Communication was important to her, she thought children should be downstairs and part of the family, not locked away in their bedrooms doing their own thing. Bill had designed and fitted a special door handle for Toby to use. A growing boy should have his privacy.

Bill hesitated outside the door, uncertain whether to knock or walk in. He sighed, turned and went down for breakfast, picking up the post on the mat. What was he going to say to Toby anyway? He couldn't think of any way to make it up to the lad. Perhaps it was best to give him a wide berth and let him grieve in his own way and get the anger out of his system.

In the kitchen there was a note on the table from Toby in his scrawly writing. 'I'm never going to talk to you ever again.' Bill flinched, the words cutting through him. In a flash he knew what he was going to do. He marched into the hallway and shouted for Toby to come downstairs, his stomach clenched with anger. He would spill it all and tell the boy that actually the woman he thought was his mother--wasn't. His real mother was out there somewhere, unaware that her child was alive and well. He took several steps up the stairs. When he thought of Rona snatching Toby from the hospital, it was such an incredible and unbelievable story that he had a hard time believing it himself.

The door at the top of the stairs was closed; the boy beyond,

Bill guessed was defiant and determined to stick it out. Bill stopped. What was he hoping to achieve? Taking several deep breaths, he felt calmer and more rational. He retraced his steps back into the kitchen and made Toby a bowl of cereal. He flicked through the post and tucked between the phone bill and the gas bill was a postcard of a London bus. He turned it over and read the message. *Dear Rona. I haven't forgotten.*

Bill's heart slammed in his chest and his hand flew to his mouth. He stared at it for several minutes wondering who had sent it and what it meant. He opened the other post, most of which was junk mail. Recently, there had been a lot more junk mail than normal and he was going to ring the companies to ask them to stop sending it.

His thoughts were broken when he remembered Toby's breakfast. He put Toby's special long- handled spoon on a tray, together with a cup of tea with a straw in it and headed upstairs, unnerved.

He knocked. 'I've got your breakfast here.'

'I don't want it.'

'You've got to eat.'

'Leave it there.'

Would this be their life from now on? Depositing food outside his door as if he were a prisoner in a cell?

'Don't you want help dressing? You've got football later.' Bill had taken Toby to the local Saturday football team since he was five years old. It was their special time together and any disagreement or atmosphere between them could be broken by their shared love of footie. It was Saturday, at least the gods had that in his favour, otherwise the impasse between them could take all week to smash.

'I've got my dressing stick. I don't need your help.' Bill had never known Toby to be this stubborn. His dressing stick had been specially made for him at Roehampton Hospital in London, but it was quicker for Rona or Bill to help him, especially on weekdays. Toby wasn't good at getting up in the morning and there was never enough time to leave him to dress himself.

'And I'm not going to football. I'm staying in my room all day.'

'Suit yourself.'

Toby was punishing himself by missing football. He could wage war but soon enough he'd want to go to football, however annoyed he felt towards his dad.

Thinking he should get dressed and wander down to the shops for more food while Toby was stewing, Bill went to his own bedroom and opened his wardrobe, but it was the wrong door. His clothes were on the left side. He stared at Rona's clothes, her scent wrapping around him. He touched each garment, mesmerised and the past reclaimed him.

A glamorous handbag, draped over a gold evening dress she hadn't worn in years caught his attention and he pulled it out, surprised at how heavy it was. In glittery silk it was shaped like a folded napkin, with a scalloped edge, studded with sequins. It tickled his fingers. He snapped open the gold clasp, breathing in the smell of glamour and champagne. He remembered that she'd worn the bag and dress to their engagement party and more recently to one of her sister's parties. He pictured Rona, her sleek hair cascading down her back, the bag slung from her shoulder. He seemed to remember it originally belonging to her grandmother. Of course, it wouldn't have been her mother's. He couldn't imagine her mother giving Rona such an exquisite bag. They had a bad relationship. Bill held the bag as if it was the most precious thing he'd ever held. His mind drifted back to their engagement. In those days, marriage was a passport to freedom, a means of escape from parents and it meant the start of an intimate relationship.

The lining was bright yellow and there was a zip to a pocket for lipsticks and coins. He could feel something inside and, curious, he unzipped it, pulling out a piece of card. It was the business card of a Charles Hanley, a legal firm he'd never heard of. Flipping it over there was a message in spidery handwriting which read, 'Please don't hesitate to call. The first half hour is free.' What had she consulted him about?

Toby popped his head round the door, his face stony. 'Why did you do it? There's nothing left.'

Bill shoved the card into his dressing gown pocket, glad that Toby's sulk hadn't lasted all day. 'I'm sorry.'

'You shouldn't say sorry, not unless you mean it. That's what Mum used to say.'

Bill couldn't disagree with that. He stood up and looked out of the window at the blackened mass in the middle of the lawn.

'And you've ruined the lawn. How's the grass supposed to grow back?'

'All right, all right. Stop being such a know-it-all.'

'What if we forget what she looked like?'

'We won't.'

'You don't know that.'

'No I don't, but photographs are always taken on holiday, or on special occasions. Nobody ever takes photos when people are looking unhappy or at sad occasions like funerals. I don't want to be reminded of the happy times. It only makes things worse.'

Toby flopped onto the bed and Bill sidled up beside him. 'It's not a balanced way of looking back at someone. It makes them out to look a saint. I don't want to canonise your mum. She wasn't perfect, we're all human.'

He'd said too much and wasn't sure what he was saying-- he was rambling and trying to justify what he had done. He knew that he wasn't making much sense. He couldn't get his head around any of it. It hadn't been easy rummaging through the albums, reliving the past and lingering too long on blissful moments that contrasted so sharply with her illness. He didn't want to reflect back on Rona's life through rose-tinted glasses as if everything was perfect, with no cross words and no sad times. Life wasn't like that.

'But what if I have children one day? I'll want to show them what their grandma looked like.'

Bill sighed. Sometimes Toby had an old and wise head on him; he dwelled on the type of thoughts that the average child wouldn't think of.

Bill's eyes anchored on Toby. It suddenly dawned on him that the secret he and Rona had carried for the past twelve years would go on for many years and into the next generation, a big ugly lie. Unless... he broke it. Could he? It was too much responsibility. He hadn't caused the mess in the first place. Telling him the truth was overwhelming. He didn't know what Toby's reaction would be.

Bill fiddled with the bag's zip. The smell of the bag and the scent from the wardrobe floating into the room felt suffocating. As if Rona's spirit had invaded the room.

Toby cut into his thoughts. 'Can I take that bag to school on Monday?'

'Why would you want to take a woman's bag to school?'

'It's Mum's bag. She'd let me if she was here.'

Bill had no doubt in his mind that she would. Rona had always given in to Toby's demands.

'We've got to take something special into school and tell the class about it, then we get to draw it.'

'I think we can find something else for you.'

The bag conjured memories of a time before the big secret, simple times when they looked forward to having a family.

Bill thrust the bag into the wardrobe. He'd decide what he was going to do with Charles Hanley's business card later on.

'You can take your grandad's old pocket watch into school instead. I'll dig it out later.'

. . .

Toby would have preferred the bag. There was something enchanting about it and he wanted to show it to Melanie, but he settled for the watch instead.

'You coming up the shops with me? I need to get some food in.'

'No thanks, I've got homework to do.'

'Do you want some help with it?'

'I can do it,' Toby lied.

It was geography. His least favourite subject. He was struggling but didn't want to admit it and see his dad's embarrassed face when he couldn't do it either and his long rambling explanation about how schoolwork was so different back in his day. Toby doubted it. How could geography change? Earthquakes and volcanoes had happened for thousands of years. His mum would have been able to help, but his dad was a bit thick. He felt bad thinking about his dad in that way, it seemed disrespectful. It wasn't his fault. It was the way he was. But now that his mum was gone, who could he ask for help? He'd have to drop into the library later. The library assistant was a friendly lady who could find books to help. The only other option was to ask his grandma. But he didn't want to do that.

16
1973

Toby and Bill

It was Monday morning and Toby didn't want to get up. It felt as though a hundred knives were piercing his stomach. He dreaded the end of the weekend because it meant seeing the bullies again. He hadn't slept and wondered what they would do next.

'Dad.'

Bill rushed into Toby's room. 'Come on, get up, it's late.'

'I can't, I'm ill.'

'You're not ill.' Bill pulled the blanket off Toby.

'My tummy's really bad,' he whined, pulling an agonised expression.

'If you want me to help you get dressed, you'll have to get up. I haven't got time for games. I can't be late for work.'

'I can't get up. I can't go to school.'

He didn't want to tell his dad about the Trio and risk looking like a weakling. But his strength was cracking, and he couldn't fight the tears.

Bill perched on the end of the bed, forgetting about the client he was seeing that morning. The client was renowned for being a stickler for time, often waiting on his driveway, pointing to his watch, as Bill got out of his truck, even if he was five minutes late.

'You like school.'

'I never said that. Anyway, I've got tummy ache.'

'Maybe you just need the loo.' Bill was getting impatient. He could do without this.

'They hate me.' Toby hadn't intended to open up to his dad, but now that he'd started, he was propelled along.

'Nobody hates you.'

'They do. They call me names.'

'What names?'

'They call me a stupid flid or spastic.'

'Just ignore them, son. They'll soon get bored.'

'You don't know what it's like at school.'

'I'm not so old that I've forgotten what school's like. It takes time to get to know people; you haven't been there long.' He sighed and checked his watch.

Sometimes the fear went to Toby's head in the form of a grinding headache. At other times there was a searing pain across his chest, but today it lay in his stomach, a tight ball of knots that refused to go away. When he stood up the pains were worse, but he couldn't let his dad down. He'd have to go to school because as his dad kept reminding him, 'If I'm late for work I'll lose my job.'

'All right I'll get up,' he said reluctantly, dreading the day ahead.

'Good lad, once you get in that playground you'll be as right as rain.'

That was the last place Toby wanted to be. The playground was like a jungle. He wished he didn't have to go to school.

'There was a boy at my primary school and he is now home-schooled. Why can't I do the same?'

'You do come out with some stupid ideas. What sort of newfangled notion is that? I pay my taxes for you to go to school. The whole point about going to school is to mix with other people. Anyway, who would teach you?'

'We could get a tutor.'

'Don't be daft. Who are you, Prince bloody Charles?'

'Who's going to look after me when Grandma goes to Yorkshire?' Anxiety wrapped around him with the realisation that in future he'd always be walking home alone.

'I've asked Rita next door to make your tea.'

'And when were you going to tell me that? Does she mind? She's got the baby to look after. I don't want her coming round every day.'

'Will you stop asking stupid questions?' Bill snapped. 'You've got fifteen minutes to get dressed and get some breakfast down you.'

Toby's stomach tightened. He got up and when Bill left the room, dressed himself using his dressing stick and went downstairs.

While Bill made breakfast, Toby stared in the hall mirror wishing that he wasn't different from the other kids. At primary school he'd learned to accept that he was unlike anyone else, but now that he was at secondary school, fitting in was the most important thing in the world.

BILL DROPPED Toby at school and sat in his van watching the flow of chattering children as they made their way, en-masse, across the playground and through the school doors. It was the best thing to take his mind off his troubles, but he couldn't summon any enthusiasm. He looked at the business card that he'd found in Rona's handbag and started the engine. To hell with work. He made a snap decision—he'd stop at a phone box, cancel his client and make an appointment to see Charles Hanley. He didn't know what was going on in Rona's life before her death and it was getting to him, he needed answers.

Charles Hanley had a free slot mid-morning and by lunchtime Bill's mind would be settled.

It didn't go down well with his client though. 'You won't be in till after lunch?' the client asked.

'I'm sorry. I've got some business–– to do with my late wife–– to sort.'

'I've been very understanding so far, but you need to put your affairs in order and in your own time, not mine. You gave me a date when the work would be finished. You've put it back twice already. I'm losing patience, Bill. If you don't get back to the job after lunch, I'm finding another builder. Do you understand?'

Bill flinched. The words were hurled like a punch. He didn't need the pressure. The client was an idiot. He never appreciated him when he was on track, sometimes he worked flat out till late into the evening. He could wait; they were idle threats.

17

1973

Toby With a wink, the maths teacher, Mrs Devlin, returned Toby's test paper to his desk. 'Well done.'

Toby wished the test paper would disappear into the inkwell. He didn't want to be the clever kid and the teacher's approval made him more of a freak. Nobody liked brainy kids and he badly wanted to be the class rebel. He contemplated a Bay City Rollers haircut, but it wouldn't make him cool. He was the class flid—with a new hairstyle he'd just be a flid with a quiff. Toby nudged the paper out of the way with his shoulder, but the teacher, now back at the front of the room was addressing the class. 'And top of the class for this test,' she announced, 'is Toby.' Toby lowered his head, his eyes fixed on the 90% scrawled across the front in red. They'd call him a swot or a teacher's pet. He took the paper between his teeth, lifted the desk lid up with his nose and swept the paper from view. He wished he could rip it into thousands of tiny pieces.

'Well done, Toby,' came Melanie's voice from behind. He flinched and hoped the teacher wasn't going to dwell on the test and would press on to the topic they were currently learning; fractions. 'God, I wish I'd put more effort in,' she sighed.

'Swot,' came a whispered remark somewhere close by. One of the Trio, Toby guessed. He kept his eyes pinned to the front, determined not to let the smirks chisel away at his confidence.

As they settled into the lesson one of the pupils leaned forward with a folded piece of paper for Toby. It had been passed along the row from somewhere at the back. Neatly folded into a tiny square, it was impossible for Toby to open. A flush of frustration crept up his neck. Whatever nasty remark was written on the note it didn't matter; they'd see to it that he got the message, delivered with brutal force in a corner of the school grounds where nobody could disturb them. He felt the first chill of fear knowing this was the last period of the day. As the teacher wrote exercises on the board, her voice sounded as if she was talking underwater, over the pounding of blood in Toby's head. His fear was compounded when the bell rang, signifying the end of the day. Anchored to his chair he couldn't move. Desk lids banged as pupils packed away, chairs scraped on the wooden floor and in their haste to get out, as if fleeing a fire, a poster or two was knocked from the walls. Three pupils waited—they were lurking outside the door, beckoning to him to come with them.

'Run along then Toby, your friends are waiting,' the teacher said.

Toby got up slowly in the hope that by taking his time he'd think of an excuse to linger. He hoped the Trio would give up and go home, but the look on their faces told him otherwise. They were enjoying this and weren't giving up. Jostling each other, they were like a pack of hyenas getting warmed up for the hunt. The teacher was packing her books away; she'd want him gone so that she could lock the door.

'Can I ask you something?'

Smiling at him, Mrs Devlin looked up from her bags. 'Yes of course you may.'

'I didn't really understand some of the lesson.'

'Can we go over it next week, Toby? I don't mean to be evasive, it's just that I'm in a hurry.'

'Oh.' Toby lingered for a few seconds. He needed a better excuse to stall for time and couldn't think of one. He wished he could offer to carry her bags to her car, but sadly, with no arms that wasn't an option.

His mind froze and he sauntered towards the door. To his relief they were gone. He stepped out into the echoey corridor; it was empty in both directions. When it was busy, the corridor was like a river. The only child without a paddle, he was pulled by the current, never sure if he'd reach the bank.

He heard the distant hum of chatter from around the bend and as he neared it, he recognised the voices of the Trio. It was too late, they'd seen him. The gaggle of bullies came into view and he turned on his heel and ran as fast as he could in the opposite direction, passing the school library, up a few steps, past the school office and through the swing doors. They were right behind him, his heart raced, and blood whooshed through his ears.

He should have slipped into the library, but it was too late. He couldn't turn back. It was open until four o' clock there was no way they'd wait a whole hour for him to leave.

Out of the building, he ran down the steps two at a time, joining the herd of pupils on the pathway outside the school gate, hoping to disappear into the safety of the crowd. But as the Trio gained ground shouting and flinging their bags around, the crowd parted to let them through and from nowhere the back of a hand belted him hard across his head.

'Teacher's swot,' said Des.

'Think you're so clever,' sneered Jim.

'You flids are rich bastards, getting money from the courts.'

Next to the path was a steep grassy bank that fell down to the road. A foot hooking around his ankle toppled him over and sent him crashing to the ground. He landed on his side and it hurt like hell. In a heap at the top of the bank he was about to hurtle to the bottom. The crowd stood watching and nobody offered to help him. Cries of disgust at the way he was being treated rang out but were drowned by a ripple of cheers. It was always safer to side with the bullies; nobody wanted to be the next victim.

The throbbing inside Toby's head was intense, but he couldn't rub his head to relieve the pain. Every swallow tasted sour and all he wanted to do was curl into a ball and roll into the ivy at the side of the bank. A car stopped by the roadside to find out what was going on. Signifying safety, the smell of warm petrol filling his nostrils comforted him as he heard a door slam and footsteps.

'Clear off the lot of you,' the driver barked at the crowd. The children dispersed and moved along the pavement.

'It's all right lovey. Let me help you.' Terrified, Toby's eyes were still shut as he cowered from the bullies, expecting more blows. Hearing the kind voice, he opened his eyes to see a woman in a pink coat hovering over him.

She didn't hesitate or seem awkward when she saw his hands, surprising him by reaching down to guide him to his feet. 'Where do you live? Let me give you a lift home.'

She opened the passenger door and he got in. Toby had been warned by teachers and his parents about getting into a stranger's car, but this lady seemed so nice and he felt safe. She chatted as she drove and asked him about what had happened outside the school and was there anybody he could speak to at school? Her concern was genuine and kindly.

'You need to tell your dad what happened.'

'I don't want my dad to know. He'll only worry about me.'

18

1973

Bill
By the time Bill parked his van - around the corner from Charles Hanley's office - his head thumped. He got out of the car; he was in two minds whether to show up for the appointment or head home. It was easier to pretend that he'd never found the card. Whatever was troubling Rona had ended with her death.

Walking towards the office a new thought occurred to him. Had Rona consulted the solicitor for a divorce? It was a daft thought; they had been happy, hadn't they? Sickness wormed through his belly. Maybe she hadn't been as happy as he'd imagined.

Pushing away these thoughts he headed in, but moments later, sat in front of Charles Hanley, he struggled to find the right words. 'I found your business card in my late wife's handbag. I'm curious to find out why she consulted you.'

'Her name, address?' Hanley left the room and returned with a file. He read the notes in silence, a frown on his forehead before looking up and his face relaxed into his, dealing-with-clients, face.

'She came to see me a couple of years ago—nice lady. I'm very sorry for your loss.'

Bill acknowledged his kind words but wanted to get to the point of their meeting. 'What can you tell me?'

'I'm bound by client confidentiality. Have you got proof that you're her husband?'

Bill handed him their marriage certificate, Rona's death certificate and her will, showing Bill as executor.

'I can't tell you much, I'm afraid your wife's passing doesn't break my contract to her and during our first meeting she made her wishes clear. I met her at a party.'

'Hang on a minute. What party? My wife didn't go to parties, she had a handicapped son to look after.'

'...and she was worried about something and needed to know her options.'

Bill inched his chair closer to Charles Hanley's desk, his eyes focused on the file. 'Worried? What worries? What are you talking about?'

Hanley raised his eyebrows. 'I'm not at liberty to go into details, but I can divulge the broad nature of her business. This is going to come as a shock but there's no easy way to say it. Your wife was very troubled. She was frightened and didn't know where to turn. My advice to her was to tell you—but she wanted to protect you and the child. You see, she was being followed.'

Bill opened his mouth to speak, but the words were stuck in his throat.

'I'm sorry I can't be of any further help. I've already told you more than I should.'

'What do you mean followed? I don't understand. By who?' Bill asked, ignoring him. 'Was it a man or a woman? What did they want? Did they want to hurt us?'

'I don't know any more than that.'

'I need to know. Could you look through your file again, see if you've written a name down?'

Hanley closed the file.

'Why didn't she tell me?'

'She probably didn't want to worry you. I don't know much more, but I advised her to go to the police and come back to me if she needed further advice.'

The words hung in the space between them as Bill tried to make sense of what Hanley had told him.

'I'm very sorry.'

'Do I need to worry about my son's safety?'

'I'm not at liberty to say any more. I'm sorry but I have another appointment. I'll see you out.'

In no fit state to work, Bill headed home to think. Opening the front door, he missed the predictability of the life they'd once had. He used to sniff the air and know what day of the week it was. Monday, shepherd's pie, Tuesday, corn beef hash, Wednesday, egg and chips, Thursday spam fritters. Now the only smell in his nostrils was fear.

He stood in the garden and lit a cigarette. The garden was chilly—there had been an early morning frost, but he had his duffle coat on and a mug of tea warming his hands. He'd taken to sitting on the bench, listening to the sparrows chirping, his eyes closed against the sun flickering through the apple trees. When he opened his eyes, he was aware of something to his left. A robin was sitting on the arm of the bench. Careful not to move suddenly in case it flew away, Bill turned his head to look at the robin. In that moment their eyes connected, the bird chirping as Bill smiled. With warmth flooding through him, Bill remembered a saying that robins appear when a loved one is near. He closed his eyes, feeling Rona's presence beside him, but when he opened them the robin had flown away, leaving him bereft.

The doorbell startled him. He put down the empty mug

and waited, hoping whoever it was would go away, but it rang again, longer this time. There had been several times lately when he'd opened the door to find nobody there. Bill went into the hallway, looking towards the front door. The fear that it was a stranger––Rona's stalker ––was irrational, crazy even. The doorbell rang for a third time. They weren't going away; he had to open it.

Whatever words were on the tip of his tongue died when he peered out onto an empty street. He looked in both directions but there was nobody within sight. Had he imagined the bell ringing? He was losing a grip on reality. And then, with a sharp intake of breath Bill gasped, his hand flying to cover his mouth as he stared at a woman on the pavement opposite the house, who seemed to have appeared from nowhere, dressed in a dark coat, her arms folded and with a snarl on her face. Was she Rona's stalker? And then, in the blink of an eye, as if to prove that he was losing it, there was suddenly nobody there.

As Bill closed the door, he knew he was being dramatic, the conversation with the solicitor had added fuel to his fears. It was probably a kid truanting from school up to mischief, ringing every doorbell in the street and running off. He glanced towards the telephone. Maybe he should ring the police. But what would he say? Rona was dead. Maybe there was no connection. The woman could have been anybody. He was being paranoid.

Standing next to the phone, made him remember his concern about the growing amount of junk mail they were receiving. He picked up the mail from one of the companies––a firm supplying hearing aids, and dialled their customer complaints manager.

'I'm sorry sir. Mrs Rona Murphy filled in a coupon from *Woman's Weekly* for more information on our hearing aids.'

'It's unlikely my wife would do that. Neither of us have hearing loss.'

'Perhaps she was interested in helping a relative.'

'No. Can you send me the coupon she filled in, please. I want to see the handwriting.'

'Yes, I can do that, sir.'

Ending the call, Bill needed a nip of his finest scotch. Until now he'd forgotten about the bottle he'd cracked open a few days ago. He dumped his empty tea mug on top of the pile of dirty dishes that had sat in the sink for a couple of days, the porridge encrusted onto the bowls and streaks of gravy stuck to plates. He poured himself a measure into the only clean mug in the cupboard, stopping when it was half full, only to swear under his breath and fill it to the brim. Taking the mug upstairs to his bedroom he perched on the end of the bed, staring into the open wardrobe. In his subconscious mind he wondered if he'd find anything in the wardrobe. He took a huge gulp of whisky, welcoming its effects on his screwed-up emotions as it burned its way to his stomach. He needed the crutch of alcoholic oblivion. Finishing the drink and feeling comforted by it, he knelt down to rummage through the undergrowth of her wardrobe, pulling shoe boxes out and scattering them across the floor. An overwhelming emotion was evoked by the smell. Floral tones filled his nostrils, so strong that Rona could have been in the room. It triggered a flicker of memories. Next to the smell, the splash of colour caused a searing pain across his chest as the sun filtering through the window caught a pink shimmery dress and a pair of gold sparkling shoes, a beautiful spectrum of colour bounced across the walls. There was a time when the colours of Rona's wardrobe lifted his mood but now they were just a torment.

As he opened the shoe boxes each pair conjured a memory. Picking up her battered T-strap nurse's shoes, caked with whitener and with worn-down heels, he imagined Rona fleeing from the hospital, clutching baby Toby that fateful night. He could visualise her running, but the colour of the shoes, white, was associated with goodness and innocence and the reality was anything but. She'd taken the baby to safety, or thought she had, but with her death how safe was he? There was a level of detachment between himself and Toby. As much as he tried to convince himself, the fact remained that Toby wasn't his son. Rona wasn't polished perfect white, just like the shoes she had worn, and he wasn't either. She'd broken the law and made a massive life decision in a fragment of time and he was left to pick up the pieces.

With these thoughts brewing, he opened the last box, surprised to find that it contained a collection of envelopes and diaries. His heart jolted. Convinced that he would discover something about Rona, he opened one of the diaries, but it was all about Toby's progress; how he was getting on at school and what he enjoyed doing. Frustrated, he tossed the diary aside. In a box he saw an envelope containing a card. From the date on the postmark he knew it was a wedding anniversary card, but nobody had sent anniversary cards beyond the first few years of marriage. He sat for a long time, not moving and trying not to think.

Fingering the envelope, about to open it, he heard the front door bang and the thud of Toby's bag on the floor.

'Dad?' Toby called from the bottom of the stairs.

Bill tried not to let his words slur. 'Yeah, I finished early. How did you get in?'

'It's okay I got a lift back. They opened the door for me.'

'Who gave you a lift?' Bill was losing track on who was supposed to be collecting Toby. He remained on the floor where it was comfortable, waiting for Toby to come upstairs. When Toby bounded up the stairs and into his own room, slamming the door behind him, Bill wondered what was wrong.

He got up and went to stand on the landing. 'What the

bloody hell's the matter with you? And I just asked you a question. Who gave you a lift?'

'You're always swearing. Mum wouldn't like it.'

Bill wanted to shout back that she wasn't here now, he could swear all he liked, but he swallowed his words. As hard as it was, he had to keep control, even though all he wanted was to curl up in bed with his bottle of whisky and never wake up. When he was asleep, he could forget. He knew that he couldn't hide at the bottom of a bottle forever.

Opening Toby's door, he found him under his blanket, his face hidden. Bill pulled the blanket away, and finding his son's face red with tears, felt a surge of love washed over him.

'Hey, little fella, what's up?'

Toby sniffed and rubbed his nose against the pillow.

'You know you can tell your old dad anything.'

Toby made a grunting noise.

'Let me get you a tissue.'

Bill went into the bathroom, returning with some toilet paper. With no arms, blowing his nose was tricky on his own. It was hard when he had a cold but most of the time Bill caught him wiping his nose on his collar. It drove him mad, but without arms what else was the lad to do? Toby's handicap was most hard-hitting with the little things, it wasn't him being unable to dress, wiping his bottom or eating easily - they were the big things that had to be overcome, they were daily and routine -but it was blowing his runny nose in a hurry, or catching a falling ornament that still caught Bill off guard and wrenched at his heart.

'Has something happened? Has someone upset you?'

'You've been drinking again. I can smell it.'

'I might have had a little tipple.' Bill felt small, as if Toby was a stern adult.

'You shouldn't drink.'

'A man needs something to oil the wheels. What's the matter?' Bill's hands were on his hips.

'Not when you're in that state.'

Toby turned away from him and stared out of the window.

'Be like that then,' Bill snapped and left the room, slamming the door behind him.

He stopped with his hand on the handle, aware that he was behaving like a petulant child. He rubbed his sore head and went back into Toby's room. What the hell was happening to him? He couldn't think straight.

'I'm sorry.'

'Go away.'

Bill sighed and plonked himself on the end of the bed. 'Well look, I'm here for you, if you want to talk about anything. I know it's not easy. But I did go to school, once upon a time. Have the kids been picking on you? You would tell me if they had?'

'Why do you assume that?' Toby asked, pulling himself into a sitting position with a thunderous look on his face. 'As it happens, I got top marks in maths today, but what do you care? You're so wrapped up in yourself.'

Toby's words stung him, but they were true and raw. Bill knew he had to pull himself together.

19

1973

Bill couldn't wait to open the envelope and rummage through Rona's belongings to see what else he could find. He waited until Toby was in bed asleep and went back into his own bedroom.

Inside the envelope was a card with a picture of a champagne bottle with its cork popped and pink ribbons bursting out of it. It mocked him. The writing was large and childish, each letter a different size.

See you in the usual spot.

The usual spot? What the hell did that mean? A thought slammed into him. Was Rona having an affair? Surely not. If she had, he would have guessed, read the signs, been suspicious. He thought they'd been happy. Maybe he was wrong.

When he turned the card over to look for clues, he found more writing.

I'm watching you.

Cold whipped through him. The message was too sinister to be from a lover and yet...

Unable to make sense of the words he returned to the box.

He almost missed the other letter, tucked away at the bottom of a box under a pile of bank statements. It was face down, hiding from him and had a coffee-cup ring in the right-hand corner. It was addressed to Rona in the same handwriting as the other envelope, the same loops and swirls. A hint of mustiness reached his nostrils as he took out a folded sheet of paper, smoothing it with his hands. Perching on the edge of the bed, he read:

Dear Baby Thief,
What goes around comes around.

Bill dropped the letter as if the paper had burned him, a fist of panic squeezing his insides, his breath coming in loud rasps. 'Rona, my love. What was going on? Why didn't you tell me?' He'd let her down and she'd had to cope with this alone. And now she was dead, it was too late to be the supportive husband he should have been.

A new thought took hold inside him. Toby. Somebody knew where they lived. He was terrified of losing Toby, of being arrested for a crime and much worse— Toby finding out the truth.

Bill saw only one viable solution. They had to get away and go into hiding somewhere. He'd do anything to protect them. But even that idea was flawed. It wasn't as though Toby was unobtrusive and wouldn't be easy to find. But why should he up-sticks? He liked the house. His grandfather had built it. Fond memories bled from the bricks. Memory was like an emery board, it smoothed the path to the future and kept him going. He remembered the photographs he'd fed into the fire. Pain seared through him. He'd burned her smile, her pretty face, her beauty, the only hard evidence that she'd walked this earth. And seeing Toby so distraught the day after the fire had pained Bill. He was useless –– as a husband and as a father.

Rona's spirit breathed in the walls and defined his past. Her laughter lived on in the fleeting memories illuminated every time he switched on lights and opened doors or climbed the stairs. How could he step away, or close the door on the love of his life?' His whole world was contained within this space. This house had its own special smell, feel and taste. There had to be another way. He wasn't prepared to live in fear, with terror galloping through his body every time there was a knock at the door or a phone call in case it might be the police or the social services. He just needed to know one thing. Who had sent the letter?

20

1973

Bill Turning into the road leading to the school a few days later, Toby muttered, 'Dad, I don't feel well.'

'Don't try that one again. Have you got a test today that you don't want to do? I've told you before, you need to spend time revising, it's no good thinking ten minutes will do.'

Leaning over to give him a hug, Bill closed his eyes. His brain was a maelstrom of confusion. He opened his eyes and blinked. She was there - the woman - and she was staring at him from across the road. Her arms were folded, and she had the same look on her face.

'What's up?' Toby asked. 'You look as though you've seen a ghost.'

Toby turned to see what Bill was looking at. 'That's the nice lady who gave me a lift yesterday.'

'She gave you a lift?'

Something cold clamped around Bill's heart. What if the woman was Toby's real mother, trying to gain his trust before kidnapping him?

'What have I told you about not getting into stranger's cars?' Bill said sternly.

'I fell down the bank. She was only trying to help.'

Bill found it hard to stay calm. 'Don't ever get into a stranger's car again, do you hear me?'

'What if she offers me a lift, shall I say no?'

'Who is she?'

'I don't know Dad. She didn't say much. Are you annoyed with me?'

'No, I'm not annoyed with you, but you've got to be more careful.'

'Can I wait in here for five minutes, Dad?' Toby asked, with an anxious look on his face. 'There are some boys that I don't like waiting for me.'

'Where?'

'Dad,' Toby said. 'Don't stare.'

'I've got to get on, son.' Bill felt overwhelmed and could feel a headache developing. He found his new role, as a single dad hard; trying to juggle his child's problems with the demands of a full-time job. He turned the key in the ignition and the engine coughed to life.

'Please, just five minutes.'

About to release the handbrake Bill turned to Toby. 'You're shaking. What's wrong? Is someone giving you a hard time?'

'They didn't like me coming top in the maths test.'

'Is that all? They'll get over it. You'll soon be top of everything. That'll show them.'

'Can I move school?'

The question took Bill by surprise. 'You're doing well at this school. Your mother fought hard to get you into this place, and it's got a good reputation.'

'Why can't I go to a school for handicapped children? A boarding school would be nice. They have midnight feasts and lots of fun. Mum told me that some thalidomide children go to residential schools.'

'You don't need special facilities. Your mum spent the last years of her life fighting for you to lead a normal life.'

'I'll never have a normal life.'

'You're a capable lad. If you want to blend in, then wear your artificial arms.'

'You know I don't like wearing them.'

'It's better than using your feet to do things.' Toby was allowed to wear flipflops to school because it was easier for him to use his feet to do things, if he needed to. In the winter he wore boots that were easy to kick off.

'I try not to at school. How can I? The other kids would laugh at me. I put the pen in my mouth when I write.'

'I know things aren't easy with Mum gone. But the dinner ladies are happy to help you eat.' Bill knew that Toby hated being reliant on the school nurse.

'Yes, they do help me, but I don't like being the only child that needs help. I hate being different. And I don't like getting the nurse to help me go to the loo or the teacher to help me wipe my nose. It's embarrassing. I wait till I get home to do a number two. I just want to go to a school where everybody's like me.'

Bill wished he had more time and patience to talk to Toby. There were always too many distractions and problems to deal with. Bill glanced at the throng of children and saw that the woman had disappeared. He wanted to follow her and didn't know when he'd get another opportunity.

'You don't need help to go to the loo. You've got your stick.' Toby had a couple of toileting aids. He kept the devices in the nurse's room.

'I've got to go,' Toby said. 'I'll be late.'

'Wait, just a sec. The lady that gave you a lift, have you seen her before?'

'No, but she told me where she lives.'

'Where?'

'In Halifax Road.'

'What number?'

'How should I know? Why? You're not going to tell her off, are you? She was a nice lady.'

'I just wondered that's all.'

'She said she lives at a house with a hedge shaped like a bird in the front garden.'

With Toby disappearing into the school grounds, Bill got out of the van and looked around. The woman had gone.

As he drove to work, Bill considered his next move. If he saw the woman again, he would approach her and find out who she was. He could worry and wonder, or he could address the matter head on.

Bill turned the van around to head towards Blackpool town centre where he was working on conversions of a block of flats. Preoccupied with his thoughts, Bill didn't see the woman step out into the road in front of him. He braked hard and stopped inches from her. It was the same woman. He was terrified to think that he could have run her over. He froze, his shoulders slumping forward onto the steering wheel in disbelief; a sliver of panic wound up from his chest. Her arms were folded and she was glaring at him. As she moved on, she turned, pinning him with a cold stare. He wiped the perspiration from his face with a towel he kept in the van and rammed the gear stick into neutral, pulling the hand brake on.

He got out of the van and shouted at her as she disappeared into the crowd. Heads turned to stare at him, and the lollypop lady walked towards him.

'Move along please, you're blocking the road,' she said.

21

1973

Bill 'Dad there's a ton of letters on the mat.'

From the top of the stairs, razor in hand and face covered in shaving foam, Bill stared at the snowstorm of mail scattered across the carpet. 'I'll get some more bags from the supermarket later.' The dustbin was already overflowing with rubbish, much of it junk mail and the bin men weren't expected for another three days.

'Why are we getting so many letters Dad? There must be at least a hundred here.' Toby said, kicking the pile as if they were leaves in a wood.

'I could understand it if it was Valentine's Day, what with your dad being such a good-looking bloke,' Bill said, making light of the situation, not wanting Toby to see how alarmed he was. He ruffled Toby's hair and smiled. 'Back in my day, the ladies were queuing for a date.'

'Very funny.' Toby laughed.

It took Bill ten minutes to gather the letters and sort them into different piles on the kitchen table. One letter caught his eye. It was the letter he'd been waiting for and had the name of the hearing aid company emblazoned in the left-hand corner. He tore it open and under the covering letter from the customer complaint's team was the coupon filled in with Rona's details. Staring at the large, childish handwriting, Bill knew that it had been filled in by the same person who had sent the mystery letters he'd found in the wardrobe.

In that moment Bill was clear about one thing. Rona's troubles had not ended with her death.

22

1973

Bill was dreaming of roasting chestnuts on an autumn day. The air smelled pleasant and woody. He stirred, rolling onto his belly. Somebody was banging on his front door and he heard shouting. He squinted at his alarm clock, dim in the faint moonlight shining through thin curtains. Nearly midnight. He sat up in bed sniffing. Was it smoke?

Bill swung his legs to the floor. As soon as he opened the door an acrid, peppery smell slammed into him and made him cough. Peering over the banister, he heard a crackling sound. He had no idea how the fire had started, but they had to get out fast.

Heart thudding, he banged on Toby's door, yelling for him to get up. He turned the handle, rushing to Toby's bedside, surprised that he hadn't woken. Stirring in the gloom, Toby looked startled, but registered the urgency of the situation when Bill screamed for him to get up.

'I need my inhaler,' Toby gasped.

Bill grabbed it from the bedside table. 'You'll feel better when we get outside.'

The fire was downstairs. While Toby struggled out of bed, Bill ran to the bathroom and soaked two towels to put over their mouth and nose. He put one over his lower face and did his best to tie it in a matter of seconds. It would probably slip but it would have to do. He scooped Toby into his arms and held the other wet towel over his face. Toby coughed and spluttered as Bill carried him through the smoke and down the stairs. As they reached the bottom, a loud bang came from the kitchen and the door crashed into the hallway sending billowing clouds of grey smoke into their pathway. The distance between the bottom of the stairs and the front door felt endless. Relieved to be outside, despite the chill night air and dressed only in pyjamas, Bill froze as he stared ahead. He looked past the fire engine, and Mrs Miller, the neighbour in her dressing gown and hair curlers. His eyes were fixed, the circus around him blurring, as if he were hypnotised, by the woman standing on the pavement opposite. The same woman, her face calm and interested, as if she were watching a spectator sport, entertained by the tragedy as it unfolded.

23

1973

Bill

Waking was like rising from the dead. The slow climb out of sleep, his mother-in-law screaming up the stairs for him to get up for work and the realisation that Rona had gone. It hit him hard every morning, like a blow to the head.

He lay there, staring at the ceiling. It had been two weeks since the fire. The same thoughts worried him, intruding his sleep and his ability to get on with daily life. The woman. Had she caused the fire? Who was she? He hadn't seen her since that night but that didn't mean she wasn't around. Somewhere. Anywhere. Waiting and calculating her next move. He felt sick to the core. Groaning, he levered himself upright and pulled back the curtains to reveal grey clouds. They were a mirror to his emotions. Their life was in danger, but he was doing nothing about it. He couldn't continue to do nothing while she worked out her next move.

He was paralysed and unclear. The thoughts tossed and turned in his head but went nowhere. If he went to the police, it would all come out. He'd end up in jail. He couldn't lose Toby and destroy the boy's world.

Was she Toby's real mother? It was a terrible thought which seared through him. His heart jolted. If she was his mother, she had rights. It was time to do something. Too much had happened. The letters, the solicitor, his own sightings. They'd move away. And soon. Only then would this terrible mess go away.

Why was life so brutal? First my wife, now my home and now our lives in danger. How much more could a man take? But in the immediate situation, to be living with his mother-in-law felt like the cruellest blow of all, a trick played by the Devil.

As he dressed, he remonstrated with himself for wishing they could move to a new house and get away from everything to start afresh. The choice was taken out of his hands. His granddad had always told him to be careful what you wished for. Bill had forgotten to renew the house insurance and couldn't claim for the damage it had caused. Although he could do a lot of the work himself, he didn't have the time or the money, and restoring his own house would be too upsetting. They'd lost everything, from the furniture to the curtains and carpet, it was burned to a crisp. All that remained was a charred shell and the only way out of the situation was to live with Celia, or rent somewhere. Despite their plight, Celia insisted that she was still moving to Yorkshire.

'My plans are not going to be disrupted by you, just because you were foolish enough to leave the oven on,' she said over breakfast.

The fire report concluded that the oven had blown up because it had been left on, and was very old which hadn't helped. Bill had gone over the events of that night so many times and was certain that he hadn't left the oven on. He hadn't used the oven that evening, they'd had cold potatoes and ham. Forgetting to turn appliances off wasn't the sort of thing he did.

The oven should have been condemned years ago, Rona had complained for ages about uneven cooking—and he had intended to replace it. But, as his dinner had been served to him each evening when he got home from work, it was one of those good intentions that never saw fruition.

Bill couldn't believe Celia's selfishness, leaving them in their hour of need. 'So you keep saying and I don't want to stop you going.' The last thing Bill wanted was Celia lording it over him with her self-righteous attitude. 'And for your information I did not leave the oven on.'

Celia tutted as she helped Toby to breakfast. 'Just as long as you don't take after your dad with his poor memory,' she remarked to Toby.

Bill went into the hall to put his coat on, thankful that she was taking Toby to school while they were staying there. It saved him time and meant that he could get to work earlier. In some ways living with her was a good thing. With not wanting to spend a second longer in her company than he had to, he'd been putting in extra hours at work. Getting stuck into work had helped take his mind off Rona, but as soon as he stopped, there was a dull ache and morbid thoughts flooded his heart. Grief revealed its ugly side in the quiet moments, and it felt like a crushing ache, without having her in his arms for comfort, and without her laughter buoying him through the choppy waters of life's troubles.

In the hall, Bill hesitated, with one hand on the newel post, as he watched the postman from behind the frosted glass push a letter through the door. He thought his fear had gone. They were safe at Celia's, but his fear was alive and rising inside him. He watched the letter drop onto the mat. It was addressed to him, in large and familiar writing. Thrusting the letter into his pocket he headed out of the house. He'd pull over a few streets away to read it. He didn't want Celia peering over his head, nosey cow that she was.

Leaning into his truck, Bill checked the tools and equipment that he needed for the day. About to close the doors, a red car and a mop of hair caught his eye on the road ahead and in a skip of a heartbeat he knew it was the woman who had given Toby a lift. Banging the doors, he rushed to the front of the truck in time to watch her car disappear down a side road. With his heart thudding he got in and turned the engine on and headed in the same direction. Swerving into the side road, he raced to the next turning. With hands curling into fists, Bill felt the first stirrings of anger, as something uncoiled inside him. He was ready for a confrontation. It was time to put an end to this. He'd have this business sorted out, once and for all.

Bill caught up with her, adjusted his speed to match hers and followed as the woman crossed roundabouts and turned corners. After about ten minutes, just when Bill thought he was going to drive around the town all day, the woman stopped, but it wasn't the same road that Toby had said she lived on. Was Toby mistaken or was this a different woman? Sweating, he wiped his brow and hovered a short distance behind the woman's car as he watched her vanish. Waiting a few minutes, he got out, his eyes scanning the house as he walked past. Crossing the road, he pretended to be more interested in the houses opposite and then walked briskly back to his truck where he grabbed a newspaper to hide behind, pretending to read it. After waiting about fifteen minutes, Bill realised it was a pointless exercise. The woman could be in there for hours and he had work to do.

Before pulling away, he opened the letter.

I know where you are, it read. *You can't run from me.*

24

1973

Toby

The school bus wheezed to the corner near Celia's house, belching thick smoke from its rear. The door opened and Celia stepped on, handing money to the driver for Toby's journey to school. She guided him to a seat, before giving him an awkward peck on the cheek and a small wave. With the bus stop so close and his grandma able to help each morning, it made sense for him to take the bus. At first, he'd been anxious about the idea.

'I don't want to get the bus.'

'You'll be fine,' said Bill. 'You've got to grow up some time. We did a test run the other day and you enjoyed the ride. Anyway, Grandma will help you.'

'Can't you just drop me off on your way to work?'

'It'll do you good.'

That was the problem, he didn't want to be the only kid who needed assistance. He dreaded the stares and the questions from random strangers, usually children. 'How did that happen?' And older people telling him that he was brave to get the bus. Sometimes passengers would talk to him, asking about his disability. It was as if he owed them an explanation, when really it was none of their business. It made him feel uncomfortable. Once he said, 'A magician made me like this.' He often thought of God as a magician, deciding with a wave of his wand who was going to get a perfect body. Looking around the bus there were no perfect bodies. A red-faced overweight woman with mounds of fat coughed and spluttered her way onboard. She bumbled along the aisle and collapsed into a seat, squashing the woman next to her. Toby wouldn't like to be her. The woman probably wasn't happy with the way she was. A couple of spotty, greasy-haired, lanky boys were in front of him. They probably obsessed about their spots and greasy hair, whereas Toby accepted the way he was, because what else could he do? He couldn't wish away his limitations, but he could change the way he coped. Things were looking up for him, he was doing better. The Trio had backed off and hadn't bothered him much in the past few weeks. He wondered if they'd heard about the fire and felt sorry for him with losing his home. Whatever the reason for backing away, it was best not to question things, otherwise he might be jinxed, and it would all kick off again.

Closer to school, the bus trundled past Des's house. It was a flat above the butcher's shop where his dad worked. Strips of sausages and various cuts of meat on hooks hung like Christmas decorations across the length of the window. Des's dad, Mr Clements, stood at the doorway, his arms folded and wearing an apron, watching the world go by as he waited for customers. He looked like the pork sausages he sold. He was short and chubby with a glistening face, so unlike his lanky son.

The driver changed gears to drag the bus up the hill and the engine clanked. Feeling sick because somebody was wearing too much perfume, Toby wished he could open a window to let in fresh air. A boy behind him unwrapped a bacon sandwich, shooting the greasy wrapper at the back of his head. It landed on his lap. Random strangers did such things to intimidate him. Sometimes he was scared, but often not, because he was used to it. Mostly he ignored people. They were the ones with the problem. In his dreams he was much braver and could do all sorts of things. He could plan revenge and get away with it. But in his waking hours he was shy and merged into the background.

As Toby went into the religious studies class for the period before lunchtime, the Trio smiled in unison in his direction. Unnerved by their friendliness he looked away, hurriedly sitting down and burying his head in his desk. Des and Bob were standing either side of his desk. His cheeks flushed as fear took hold.

'Do you fancy coming into the wood at lunchtime for a fag?' Bob asked.

The question hung in the air as a sense of awkwardness settled between them. Was this their way of apologising for the way they'd treated him? Did they want his friendship? Maybe he'd misjudged them. He couldn't decide what their motive was, but this was the last thing Toby was expecting.

With wariness in his voice and a reticence in his gut, he whispered, 'Okay.' It was as if the words had come from somebody else, rather than his mouth. What the hell was he getting himself into? But he knew that there was no going back; he'd agreed. He couldn't lose face. The last thing he wanted was for them to think he was a coward.

'Grab your lunch and meet us over there.' Des said.

He swallowed hard as ripples of bile filled his throat; the sour taste made him retch. As they returned to their seats and the lesson started, Toby mustered all his strength not to throw up.

'Who can tell me what we were learning about last week?' the teacher asked, surveying the sea of faces in front of her. Nobody answered.

'Toby, can you explain what we were learning?'

Miles away in his thoughts, the question jolted him. 'Sorry miss, what was the question?'

A titter of laughter broke out as all eyes turned towards him.

'Wake up will you!' she barked, clapping her hands.

The whole class laughed.

'We were learning about John The Baptist.'

'Good. Elaborate will you.'

Toby stuttered as the class waited and brain fog descended. All he could think about was what was going to happen during lunchtime. He didn't want to go into the woods, but there was no option. Terror galloped through him as he tried to think of an excuse not to go, while at the same time struggling to form a coherent explanation for the teacher. With fear slamming into his chest; an idea came to him, he'd tell Melanie that he was going into the woods at lunchtime. She could keep a watch, from a distance, in case something awful happened. He had a bad feeling about this. He couldn't decide what to do and so when the bell authorised the end of the lesson, he decided not to tell anybody. He'd go and get it over with, share a fag with them and come away, hopeful that they weren't going to pick on him ever again.

25

1973

Toby

'The problem we've got, Flipper, and this is where you come in, is that we don't have an ashtray.' An ominous feeling slammed into Toby - they were still calling him nicknames; it didn't bode well.

Toby and the boys were in the wood that circled the school grounds. It was a secluded place of dense copse and bracken that lunchtime staff didn't bother to monitor, despite knowing the odd pupil smoked there.

Des stepped towards Toby, dry leaves crunching underfoot. His eyes glittered like a bird of prey. He took a cigarette from a packet of Players No 6, while Jim and Bob hovered in the background nudging each other and trampling the flowers carpeting the spongy woodland floor. Toby longed to say something, but the words were stuck to his tongue. He willed himself to step away and run back to the playground, but his feet were rooted to the spot. It was a bad idea to come, he should have known. Why was he such an idiot? But how he longed to be accepted.

Des's eyes trailed over him and all Toby could do was watch

as Des put the cigarette to his lips with greedy fingers, sucking hard, filling his insides with toxins and tar and bringing life to a cruel soul. Toby had never smoked before. He watched the tip of the cigarette glow orange and red and wanted desperately to smoke away the sadness inside him, but doubted now that he was here, in the woods, that he'd be offered a drag. As Des exhaled, smoke curled from his lips, billowing into shapes around Toby's face. The thought of smoking suddenly made Toby want to wretch, even though earlier in the day he'd wanted to try it. He coughed and spluttered and heaved, acid burning his throat, vomit rising like a riptide. He leaned over and spewed his guts. Diced carrot and chewed cabbage splashed onto his shoes. The Trio laughed, lapping up his fear. He put his chin to his chest trying to wipe splats of vomit from around his mouth––but couldn't. He needed help. He couldn't return to the classroom like this. Tears pricked his eyes. He had to get away, but Jim and Bob were gripping his shoulders while Des blew smoke into his face. He needed his inhaler. He was struggling to catch his breath.

'Grip him tight, lads.'

Terror shimmied across Toby's face adding to their evident excitement as Des took the cigarette from his mouth.

'Let me go, please, I'll do anything you like.'

'As I said, we don't have an ashtray,' Des smirked.

'Do you know what temperature a fag burns at?' Jim asked.

'No.'

'Well over four hundred Fahrenheit.'

'A tad warm.' Bob laughed.

A chill snaked through Toby's veins, as he realised what was going to happen. And then he felt hot. Perspiration trickled down his back and unable to disguise the bubble of tears, he sobbed as Jim and Bob tightened their grip, the tip of the burning cigarette an inch from his hand.

'We're doing you a favour,' Bob said as Des pressed the tip

of the cigarette to Toby's skin. It felt as if he'd been bitten by an ant, but a hundred times more painful.

Sobbing in agony, Toby screamed. 'I need water, water,' as he tilted his head, straining to see the angry round red lesion on the back of his left hand.

'Have you brought it, Des?' Bob asked.

Des leaned down to get something out of his bag.

In his confusion, with pain searing through him, Toby thought they had water. He watched Des kneel to undo the straps of his satchel, but it wasn't a water bottle he was getting out. Panic gripped him when he saw the metal. Fearing for his life, his mouth opened in horror and his jaws twitched as the realisation that things were going to get a whole lot worse hit him.

He could hear the distant laughter of pupils on the playground.

Finding strength inside him he screamed, 'Melanie, Melanie, help, help.'

But the only living thing to hear his plea for help were the whispering trees and the distant thrum of a woodpecker.

Des stood up and Toby could see that he was hiding something behind his back, but Toby couldn't see what it was. Jim loosened his grip on Toby's shoulder, Bob tightened his grip and Toby waited–– his heart thumping in his chest, wishing the ground would open up and swallow him. Jim pulled a metal bicycle chain out of the satchel, ordering him to press his legs and feet together while he tied them. Toby's head buzzed. He was going to die. Over the horror of death, his mum appeared, with a warm smile on her face, waiting for him with open arms to take him to safety.

He kicked out, shaking his feet, but it was hopeless, the metal tightened around his ankles and his bones crunched. He lost his balance and collapsed to the ground, hitting his head on a tree stump. Tasting blood, he wasn't sure where it came from and there was mud at the corner of his mouth.

'Melanie,' he screamed, with every fibre of strength inside him.

'Let go of me,' he slurred, before tape flattened across his mouth silencing him. He could only blink wildly when he saw Des wheel round, a meat cleaver in his hand. A buzz cracked through him, a roar in his head and then he blacked out.

When he came round, they were gone. The rustle of leaves in the wind and the screech of magpies in a nearby tree were the only sounds in the wood. He realised that lunch must have ended; everybody would have returned to their classrooms. How long would it be before he was discovered? It could be hours before anybody came. He was afraid of the dark, the idea of sleeping in a wood all night filled him with horror. He wriggled on the damp bed of leaves twisting his body as he tried to sit up, but his head throbbed and remembering the meat cleaver, nausea percolated in his stomach. If they'd used it, he would be dead now. What if they returned to finish him off? Surely Melanie would tell the teacher when she saw he wasn't there, but he couldn't be certain that she would. Wondering if the boys would threaten her if she said something, a deeper fear gripped him. He wouldn't drag Melanie into his mess, but it was a possibility because after all they knew that he was friends with her. Beautiful Melanie, he couldn't bear the thought of them hurting her. If they were capable of doing this to him, what might they do to her? He scrunched his eyes, tears pricking as he prayed for help to come.

Time dragged by. He had no idea how long he was lying there, but the end-of-day bell hadn't rung yet. His mind drifted to his mum, his place of safety and security. He closed his eyes conjuring her image, her soft brown hair and wide smile, recalling the chemical smell of lipstick as he ducked to avoid her kiss on his cheek when she dropped him at school. He'd do anything now to feel those rouged lips on his cheek and her hand patting his head. He'd even drink the horrible Horlicks she'd always brought to his bedside when he wasn't well, or sit with her by the coal fire listening to her tales about life when she was little. His grief sent his mind into all kinds of weird places, like the back of her wardrobe, through bright swirling colours, silky blouses and scratchy jumpers. The sandwiches she used to make, always with a hole in the middle of the bread because the butter was too hard to spread. He couldn't erase her voice from his head, he wanted it to ring through his head and never go away. He found it hard that one day she was here, the next gone, and lying in the silent wood was a reminder that her body was still too. Her energy, her smell and all the things that made her into a human being weren't here anymore. How was that possible?

With all these warm and fuzzy thoughts masking his fear, the crack of wood underfoot took him by surprise. Leaves crunched nearby, he tilted his head, his eyes searching until a familiar figure came into view through a clearing, rushing towards him, shock spreading across her face. It was the school nurse and behind her, Melanie. Seeing him up close with gaffer tape over his mouth and his legs in a bike chain, Melanie gasped, her eyes piercing him as she looked on in horror.

'Melanie, run back to school, find the Head, get him to ring the police,' Mrs Stevens, the school nurse barked.

Melanie was rooted to the spot, her face drained of colour, too stunned to move.

'Come on, we need to get help.'

Blinking several times as if struggling to take in the scene, Melanie turned and ran back through the clearing towards the school.

Relieved to be discovered, but fearing retribution, Toby was alarmed at the thought of what the police would do. Mrs Stevens knelt beside him and taking a small pair of scissors from her first-aid bag, she cut the tape in two places, carefully prising it back. Toby winced, but the moistness of his breath had loosened it around his mouth and after several moments it was off.

'Who did this to you, Toby?'

He didn't want to tell her. He just wanted to disappear, move away and never come back, but he didn't have a choice. Resigned to the fact that they'd come after him and it would be far worse next time, tears filled his eyes and his temple throbbed. His voice cracked. 'I can't say. Please, don't call the police.'

'You can't protect whoever it was. This isn't just bullying Toby. They could have killed you. The worst kind of bullying I think I've seen in all my time at the school. You may not like it, but it's got to be reported to the police.'

'They might kill me. They had a meat cleaver.'

'A meat cleaver?'

'His dad's a butcher.'

He'd said too much.

'Des?'

Toby nodded.

'What's happened to your hands?'

'It's nothing.'

'It doesn't look like nothing. Is that a burn?'

Toby nodded.

'You'll need to see a doctor.'

'I just want to go home. I want my mum,' he sobbed.

26
1973

Bill and Toby

Bill wheeled the van round, swerving recklessly into the road. His palms were sweating, gripping the steering wheel. He jerked his head to look in the mirror. A driver honked his horn in anger.

Arriving on the building site, he was met by his hairy-faced bricky who had a thunder of questions for him. The questions merged into a tangle; he couldn't think straight. He wanted to crawl away to bed and never wake up.

'Come on, Bill, we've work to do. The customer's complaining that we're behind schedule.'

'I know, mate, stop reminding me. It can't be rushed.'

'I'm worried, that's all.'

'Well don't. Get on with your work.'

Bill couldn't settle into the day. It felt like treading water. He was going through the motions as best he could; the contents of the letter burning anger across his chest as he waited for the first opportunity to pack up for the day. He intended to return to the woman's house.

It was nearing five before he could escape. He was on the

point of leaving when a taxi pulled up, parking across the pavement. Celia, her face red and teary got out of the passenger side and ran towards him. Shit, something had happened to Toby.

'What's up?' Bill said, rushing towards her.

'We need to get to the school,' she said reaching out to him, shaking uncontrollably and crying. 'I had a phone call from the Head. He didn't tell me much, just that we need to get to the school quickly because Toby's been hurt.'

'Hurt?' Bill couldn't register what she was saying. He'd never seen her in this state before, not even at her own daughter's funeral.

'Don't they need to call an ambulance?' Bill cried. 'Shouldn't we be heading for the hospital rather than school? How hurt is he?' Bill began to shake. 'I love my boy, please God let him be okay.' It was as if his brain had been shredded from the inside. He couldn't think straight. He staggered towards the taxi, with Celia's arm linked in his. The driver opened the door and he fell onto the passenger seat, glad to be sitting down because he felt like collapsing to the ground.

'I had to call a taxi. I was in no fit state to drive, although how I managed to dial the number, I don't know. I couldn't steady my hands,' Celia said.

Bill focused on the road ahead through teary eyes as they headed for the school.

'They said he's been bullied,' Celia cried and blew her nose loudly.

'Bullied?' Bill gasped in horror. 'Jesus.' Anger swept through him. He wanted to get his hands on whoever had hurt Toby.

'All the times he's had tummy ache and not wanted to go to school, you didn't listen. He was crying out for help. Anyone could see that he was being bullied,' Celia reprimanded from the back seat.

'Why didn't you say something then, if that's what you thought?'

'It wasn't my place.'

'Oh, don't be ridiculous.'

The taxi arrived at the school entrance and two police officers were in the reception area. They looked over as Celia and Bill got out of the car. Dread pushed against Bill like an invisible gale and his stomach knotted as he realised the officers were waiting for them.

'Mr Murphy, thank you for coming so quickly. Sit down a moment, we need to explain what's happened at school today and then you can see Toby. He's in the Head's office and the school nurse is looking after him.'

As the officers explained the events, Bill couldn't process the sheer horror of what had happened. The words were a blur. Toby's hand had been burned by a cigarette. His ankles tied with a chain. Nausea clawed at Bill's throat. He wanted to throw up and struggled not to. This beggared belief. Was he hearing correctly or were they talking about a different child rather than Toby? Bill tried to remember how to breathe. He felt clammy and faint and suddenly the air around him felt too hot. The room was spinning. He needed a drink. Somebody came over with a cup of water and put a reassuring hand on his shoulder. He took a gulp and put his head between his knees. Bill found his strength and looked up at the sergeant. 'What sort of nasty children would do this to my son?'

'We have to take a statement from Toby. We'll need him to come into the station. We have specially trained officers to interview minors and you can stay with him. It's all low-key, nothing to worry about, but as soon as possible if you don't mind,' the officer explained. 'An officer is visiting the boys who did this. They will all be interviewed too.' The officer stood up. 'Mr Murphy, the Head is waiting, please come this way.'

In the Head's office Bill rushed over to Toby, staring at his hand in disbelief. Bill let out a sob as he knelt on the floor beside his son, hugging him tightly. 'You poor, poor boy. This is all my fault. I should have listened to you. I've been so wrapped up in myself. I'm sorry. I'm so sorry.' As Bill stared at the burns, his tears plopping onto Toby's hand, he thought his heartache and anguish would split him in two as it rose like a crescendo. When he'd collected himself, he turned to the Head and Mrs Stevens, the school nurse and said in a sombre voice, 'How could anybody be so cruel?'

There was a mantle of strained silence before Mrs Stevens spoke, her voice barely audible. 'Lots of people will be wondering the same thing.'

'What are you going to do?' Bill asked the Head. I don't want these thugs anywhere near my son. His mother will be turning in her grave. She would be devastated.'

'Don't worry about them, the police will make sure we won't be seeing them for a long time to come,' the Head said in a reassuring tone.

'I hope you're going to expel them?'

'They'll be getting a lot more than expulsion,' the Head reassured him. 'From what the police have told me, they'll be locked away in Borstal for years.'

Gulping in air, as though oxygen had been sucked from the room, Bill said, 'I want my lad to change schools. I don't want him here a moment longer.'

'You don't need to take such drastic action. But it's for us to make sure he's safe.'

'I went along with what my wife wanted. She was determined that he should grow up like other kids and learn to fit in, so that he wasn't treated differently.'

'And she was right. He can cope.'

Bill was rattled. 'But he's being singled out by bullies because he's different. He holds a pen in his mouth, he writes with his feet. To the other kids he's weird.'

Bill could see the Head was trying to uphold the school's

reputation and didn't want this to turn into more of a drama than it already was.

'If you don't mind my saying,' Mrs Jones, interjected with a nervous cough, 'you're talking about Toby as if he isn't in the room. He should be involved in this discussion.'

'Feelings are running high, Toby's been through a dreadful ordeal and needs time to recover. Take him home, have the rest of the term off. There's only a couple of weeks left until the summer holidays begin. I'll organise for homework to be brought to him, so that his learning isn't disrupted. I'll have somebody from the local education authority visit you to discuss your options from September onwards. Please go to see your doctor as well, get the burns looked at again in the morning and it would be good to get the doctor on board regarding your future options. How do you feel about this Toby?' the Head asked.

Toby shrugged his shoulders. What was he supposed to say? Whatever he said he had the feeling they'd make the decision for him. Adults always did and they were talking about him, not to him. He felt like a freak in the classroom and felt the same in this room among adults. And his hands were hurting so much; he didn't want this discussion right now.

'Good.' He felt anything but good, but thought it was what he should say.

A sad accepting smile washed across the faces in the room, as if everybody knew that life wasn't going to work out for him. They felt pity for him. That wasn't what he wanted.

Toby crumpled up his grazed face. His hair felt like bird's nest. All he wanted was to be free to be himself, to tell everybody in the school, in the whole world, look at me, this is me, this is who I am. He didn't want to hide away because they saw his broken parts as a problem. Why should he run back home because they couldn't deal with it, because they couldn't deal with him? All the school cared about was its image in the town and there was a lot of competition with other schools. He could see it in the sports matches and discussion when the exam results came out in the summer.

He had nothing to be ashamed about. He was born this way, and all girls and boys were all God's creation. That's what his mum had told him. *Don't let them break you down.* His mum had drummed those words into him and over time they'd become a part of who he was. There was a place for him–– but was his place in this school or in another one? He wasn't sure. I am who I'm meant to be, his head screamed.

But there was another side to his thoughts. Although he would miss Melanie and a few other friends, he craved a change. A new start somewhere else where he could be free from fear and live each day without worrying about what others were going to say or do. He just had to be brave. He could see from the faces in the room that they didn't believe that it could happen for him. For different reasons they all wanted him to crawl away so that he wasn't their problem. He'd walk away, not crawl away. He had legs to run to reach his goal and wasn't scared of change. The bullies could come at him with a butcher's shop of meat cleavers of varying sizes, he wasn't going to let them destroy him. He was going to rise above it. But the only way to rise from the ashes was to join forces with children of his own kind and to gain in strength, and confidence. It wasn't a sign of weakness to flee to people who knew what he was going through. He didn't believe that for a moment. He wanted to wake up with a warm feeling that he was fighting his battle with those who understood and were fighting the same battles.

'I don't want to be driven away but I've heard there's a boarding school for handicapped children somewhere in the country.'

'It would be up to the local education authority to assess your needs. This school meets your particular needs. I can't see them agreeing to something so drastic given that you cope so well in mainstream education and have found ways to get around your impairment. Many of the children in those schools have complex physical and learning needs, but you'll have to discuss it with the educational officers when they visit you. I won't rule it out as an option,' the Head said.

Rona had firmly believed in Toby integrating into the community. She would not have wanted him to be cut off, removed from society. Celia had resented them coming to live with her, that was plain to see, and listening to Toby, it was obvious that she'd been feeding his mind with ideas. Bill felt like a stranger deposited in the room. Everybody had an opinion, but he was on the outside, pulled in whichever direction they decided was right for Toby. Was he a fraud, an imposter? Who was he anyway? He wasn't Toby's real father; he was just the bloke who'd brought him up and that wasn't through choice. It was different for adoptive parents. They went through a process with rigorous interviews and assessments to check their suitability. They had time to adjust to the idea of parenting. But it had been thrust upon him. There were times when he'd resented Rona for doing what she'd done. He'd accepted that they weren't going to have their own children, but Rona hadn't. He wished she'd told him that she wasn't coping. She must have been out of her mind and in the middle of some kind of breakdown when she snatched Toby from the hospital. He was only a wee day-old baby. Twelve years later and Bill still struggled to comprehend what had happened. But he'd got on with it and kept Toby alive, fed him, clothed him, entertained him and yet every move felt forced and fake; it was all a pretence. One day Toby's real parents could walk into Toby's life and take over.

IT HAD BEEN AN EXHAUSTING DAY; the most traumatic day for Bill since the day that Rona had passed away. Celia and Bill said very little to each other over dinner, but were extra attentive to Toby, asking him how he was and if they could do anything to help him. The police interview, following the meeting with the Head was an ordeal. Bill thought about how he could treat Toby over the coming days. He decided to take the next few days off work to spend time with his son. Work could wait. Toby came first. He tried his best to lighten the atmosphere by suggesting a trip to the cinema and Toby's favourite car museum.

Toby went to bed and despite it being late, Bill and Celia washed up. After a strained silence, Bill dropped his tea towel on the worktop and took a deep breath. 'Thank you, Celia.' Bill found it hard to be humble with Celia. Their relationship had always been strained, but there were times, like today, when he really valued her. 'I know we don't always see eye-to-eye, and I'm sorry for my part in that, but I needed you today and couldn't have gone through all that without you.'

Celia dried her hands and stared at her reflection in the window, unable, Bill thought, to look at him and accept his apology. He'd seen a different side to her today. She was tearful and emotional, the grandma he wanted her to be, but now it seemed the shell was hardening around her once again. But when she sat down, her hands cradling her head, she surprised him.

'The poor, poor little boy. That's what he is, you know?' She looked up at Bill through red teary eyes. 'Just a boy. And he's had that much pain inflicted on him. We're going to have nightmares about this. I know I will. How can we possibly protect him as he goes through life? I wish people could be kinder. Why didn't his classmates stick up for him? Are they all brutes? Surely not. In a bizarre way, it reminds me of how the Nazis treated the Jews. Could those boys have killed Toby? I shudder to think.'

Bill sighed and pulled out a chair. He put his hands on Celia's, and squeezed them. 'I feel angry, but I know that's just a shield for the pain. I want to go round to those boys' homes and confront their parents. But I know it would end up in my thumping them and then I'd end up in trouble with the police. But they are responsible. They raised those brutal monsters.'

'Where would that get you? An eye for an eye never worked. We need to rise above it, but it's hard.'

'Where did Toby got the boarding school idea from? Was it you?'

'I don't like your accusatory tone.' Celia's body stiffened and she pulled her hands away from him, folding her arms defensively.

'You're planting ideas in the lad's head.'

'It's really not a bad idea Bill. You're not coping, you're still drinking too much. I just think it would ease your pressures.'

'Ease my pressures?' Spittle gathered in the corners of his mouth as he spoke. He knew he wasn't coping, but he wasn't letting Celia get the better of him. 'Life is one pressure after another. I get on with it. I deal with it. I'm not plonking my son in an institution and walking away. This is what I signed up to. Parenting doesn't always come in the package we expect.'

'I just think that if he goes to a boarding school, he'll feel better about himself.'

'No, it would give him a very warped, unrealistic view of life and goes against everything that Rona was trying to achieve.'

'I'm sure the staff would be very caring. They've been specially trained.'

'They're paid to do a job,' Bill scoffed, sarcasm filtering into his words. 'They see them as a commodity. Every child needs at least one main adult in their life, but who have those children got? Adults too busy to spend one-to-one time with them and then they're gone when they leave their job. Toby needs continuity. He needs me. His dad.'

'I give up. He's your child, but at least listen to what he wants for a change.' Celia tutted and raised her eyebrows smugly. Bill gritted his teeth. Just when he thought Celia was on his side, she went and ruined it. Bill had nobody to share his pain with and in that moment felt more alone than ever.

27
1973

Toby and Bill

That night, Toby's dreams took a nightmarish turn. The light from the landing formed a triangle on the carpet and in his sleep Toby saw a faceless alien landing on the triangle wielding a blade. He felt the cold knife against his throat. Its sharp edges running around his skin ready to pierce him. And then, just as the knife was about to plunge, he screamed. His dad and grandma appeared in his doorway, their hushed voices soothing him back to sleep.

'We've got to get him some help,' he heard them murmur. 'He can't go back to that dreadful school.'

TOBY WOKE the following morning knowing that it would take time to recover from the attack - that's what his dad and grandma told him. The sun streamed through the curtains. He lay in bed till gone ten, his mind clouded with grey and he had no energy or motivation to get up. He wanted to believe them because he couldn't go on like this. 'You'll get there,' they told him. 'You're made of strong stuff.' His mind and body were struggling to believe their words.

The welts on his hand were angry and purple. Against his ghostly skin they were grotesque, but he knew he was lucky. If Melanie hadn't raised the alarm, he might have died in that wood. He owed Melanie his life; she was the one friend he could trust.

He knew one thing. There was no way he was going back to that school in September. He'd refuse. They couldn't make him. He'd kick, he'd scream, he would do anything, but he wasn't going back, even though the bullies were gone.

BILL WAS LOST. Sadness travelled to every cell. He was angry with himself for being so consumed with his own problems that he hadn't noticed what was going on in Toby's life. He'd let his son down. It was unforgivable. The lad had tried to talk to him, but he'd slammed him down. All those mornings when Toby didn't want to get out of bed because of tummy ache, which should have alerted him to the fact that something wasn't right. He'd hidden inside a bottle of whisky for too long, focusing on his own pain and hoping to dull it. Toby should have gone to a smaller school. Ravenswood was too big and overwhelming for him. There were so many ifs and even more if onlys. If only he hadn't gone to that school, if only Rona hadn't died, if only he hadn't been drunk. There was no way that Toby was going back there in September. 'Over my dead body,' he kept repeating. He was also angry with the school for not noticing what was happening.

Anger burned through Bill when he thought about what the bullies had done. He didn't know their families but often bought meat from Des's father. He wouldn't be buying meat there in future.

Passing the butcher's shop the following morning, his head

still pounding with everything that had happened, on impulse he decided to go in to confront the man.

As he opened the door and walked into the shop he was hit by the smell of blood--the death stench and sawdust. A customer was choosing sausages and Roy Clements, Des's father, was helping her choose which ones to buy. Suddenly Bill felt nervous and waiting for Roy to finish serving, Bill's eyes cast over the pieces of meat on display - the shoulders, the forelegs - that swung on hooks. He thought about the meat cleaver and wondered where Roy kept it. Looking at the fowls dangling in a row, their feet a blueish yellow, he felt suddenly sick and gagged. He imagined Roy taking one down and laying it on the counter, pinching the plump flesh before wielding the cleaver above his shoulder, bringing it down and splitting the bird in two. But as the image danced in front of Bill's eyes, the bird was replaced in his mind by Toby, lying on the counter. He gasped and the customer turned and frowned at Bill.

'I won't be a moment, sorry to take so long,' she said.

'It's fine,' Bill replied.

The customer turned to go after picking up a brown bag containing her sausages from the counter and tutted at Bill as she passed him.

Roy smiled at Bill. He didn't know that he was the father of the boy his son had so brutally bullied. As far as Roy was concerned, Bill was just another customer. 'Good morning. How can I help you, sir? We've got a good selection of meats today, or maybe I can interest you in a pie?'

Bill glanced behind him to check that the shop was empty before speaking. 'You don't know who I am, do you?'

Roy frowned.

'I'm Toby's dad. Toby... the boy your son brutally attacked. So, where do you keep your meat cleavers? Don't you lock them away? You do know they're a lethal weapon, especially in the hands of psychopaths like your son?'

Roy turned a deep shade of crimson, wiped his hands on his apron and walked to the door, bolting it. 'Why have you come here? To cause trouble?'

'You should be ashamed of yourself,' Bill hissed his words and pointed a finger at Roy. 'What sort of monster have you raised?'

'He's my child but he's responsible for his own actions.'

Bill laughed and stepped towards Roy. 'You're his father. You should be teaching him right from wrong.'

'And what do you expect me to do about it?' Roy pulled the blind down to cover the door to stop passers-by from staring.

'Thrash him. The boy needs a bloody good hiding.'

'Meet violence with violence? That your idea? An eye for eye?'

'The boy needs to be disciplined. And you're an utter disgrace. You're not fit to be a parent. Don't you keep those meat cleavers locked away?' Bill spat the words.

'What do you take me for? I'm not a complete idiot.'

Bill knew that the anger building inside him would erupt and result in him thumping Roy if Bill didn't control himself. He took a deep breath, unfurled the fist in his pocket and grabbed the door handle.

'I hope you and your precious son rot in hell,' he shouted as he stormed out of the shop.

THE FOLLOWING day Bill phoned the school to find out what was happening to the bullies. The Head was evasive. 'They've been expelled. Toby is safe to come back in September,' the Head said.

'But they're still in the area. My son isn't safe.'

'Please don't worry Mr Murphy. The police and the social services are taking care of things. Speaking to the professionals involved, those boys will more than likely be sent away.'

'Sent away? To Borstal? That's what they need. A short, sharp shock. Army style discipline to deter them from a life of crime.' Bill had heard that Borstals were sadistic, brutal places. He would be pleased to see them locked away.

'No, they are much too young for Borstal. They'll be sent away to an approved school. Please forget those boys and just concentrate on Toby's schooling. I've arranged a meeting with the local authority to discuss his schooling.'

'Thank you.'

.

SEVERAL DAYS later Bill and Toby met with the education authority. They told Bill they were making enquiries to find the best school for him in the local area but so far, they hadn't found a school to take him. Every headteacher they had spoken to felt they weren't able to provide the appropriate care for a boy with no arms.

'I'm afraid they can see that artificial arms will slow down his ability to write, or in fact do anything, and they do not have sufficient resources to provide him with the extra help he needs.'

'But he doesn't need artificial arms,' Bill protested.

'Artificial arms are the key to his future livelihood; he needs to persist with them. He'll develop all sorts of physical problems if he doesn't. It's not good for the wear and tear of his joints if he continues to use his feet for things that artificial arms could do' the education officer said.

'I'm his father and I know what he's capable of.'

'I'm sorry but the local schools don't have the facilities to cope with a disabled child.'

'What other options are there?'

'Boarding school. There is a school in the north for handicapped children, but unfortunately they don't have a place right now. The only one with spaces for this September is in Surrey. It's called St Bede's.'

'That's a hell of a way. I'd never get to see him.'

'You're a builder, Mr Murphy? Is that right?'

'Yes, but that doesn't mean I have lots of holiday time to swan around the country.'

'Well we actually have some good news on that front, but it will depend on how interested you are.'

'What news?'

'St Bede's is looking for a builder. They've been let down. Some chap has dropped out. They're in the process of building a new unit for the school. It's a big project apparently. If you ring the chief maintenance officer, I reckon the job could be yours and accommodation comes with the job. But they'd be looking for you to start pretty soon.'

This was a lot for Bill to take in, but he couldn't believe his luck.

IT WAS a couple of weeks later, and Bill had discussed the job over the phone in a call that had lasted over an hour. With shoulders slumped, he fell into a chair at the kitchen table like a sack of bricks. He wasn't looking forward to the day ahead and was on edge because he still hadn't heard whether he'd got the job. They were taking their time and had told him he would hear within the week. As each day went by without hearing anything, he resigned himself to the thought of Toby going to the school and Bill staying behind, in Blackpool and rarely getting to see the lad.

Slurping his tea, he saw an envelope propped against a jar of marmalade. The postman must have come early, and Celia had put the letter there. Bill fingered the letter. His brain tingled with excitement as he tore open the envelope and pulled the paper out. The green embossed typeset at the top read St. Bede's School, Haslemere, Surrey.

Dear Mr Murphy,
I would like to offer your son a place at St.Bede's Residential School for the Handicapped this coming September.

Following our discussions on the telephone, I would also like to offer you the position of assistant maintenance officer for the school site which will involve helping to build our new unit.

As Bill read the letter, it was as if a trail of gunpowder shot through his veins bringing his soul to life. All the pent-up sadness, anger and despair melted away, replaced by a sense of adventure. This was the new start he and Toby needed––and it meant Celia could move to Yorkshire.

Bill and Celia had made several phone calls to St Bedes, asking all the questions they needed to know, before Bill had sent in the job application. This was everything he could have wished for. A new school for Toby and a job for him on site. St Bede's took children with various handicaps from spina bifida and hydrocephalus to children suffering from severe limb damage due to thalidomide.

The offer from St Bede's was also about building new memories and starting afresh. He wasn't just thinking of the fire, the bullying and the problems at work, but the fears that had tormented Rona. It was the mystery woman that he feared most if they stayed in the area.

28

1973

Jasper

Jasper hunkered down in his hotel bed in Birmingham city centre, reflecting on the sadness of the family's wretchedness, laid bare, and how the home should be an anchor and a place of refuge. He pulled the sheet up to his chin, tiredness batting against his eyelids as sleep towed him under. He'd write up his notes in the morning.

THE SUN STREAMING through the gaps in the curtains woke him early. His first thoughts were about suicide. Life had pushed Rick to his limits, giving him a tough battle to fight and testing him beyond his endurance. Suicide was a complex issue and a range of things going on for Rick caused him to take his life. He'd wanted to ask Lesley so many questions to get the full picture. What was your marriage like? Was he suffering from depression? How much do you think was down to Peter's birth? Did he have problems at work? He visualised what it was like for Peter's brothers, watching their father go to pieces and then their mother's struggle when he died. It wasn't his business and he couldn't stray from the main theme of his article.

Dressed and sitting at the small desk, Jasper took out his notebook and tried to imagine what it was like for Rick, to be told that his child was severely disabled. It was difficult to understand the mental state that he must have been in, but Jasper tried to conjure up a picture in his head. Maybe he was frightened of failing Peter and couldn't handle the new situation. He was selfish, contemplating the impact on his own life and how it would drastically change. His wife would be focused on Peter. Rick would get forgotten. Jasper played around with ideas as he scribbled random thoughts––crossing some out and ringing others.

As a parent, your natural instinct is to give your child everything, but sometimes you can't, because it's beyond your control, he wrote. *Are we ever equipped for the challenge of parenthood? Faced with a child who was going to be rejected by everybody, father takes his life. With no will to live, his family life is turned upside down...*

Still affected by his chat with Lesley, so many thoughts swirled around his head, he found it hard to write the article. He left the hotel at nine with a few pages of disorganised notes tucked in his briefcase.

29
1973

Jasper

Leaving Birmingham, Jasper thought about the themes he would be writing about. The shocking stories needed feeding back to the public, to demonstrate the gravity of the situation. Distillers should not get away with the crime they'd committed.

Jasper took a train over the moors to the harbour town of Whitby in North Yorkshire, to meet Mick - father of Angela. Angela, like Peter had no limbs and had lived in residential care from infancy. She saw her parents every other weekend and sometimes during school holidays.

'My wife, Pat, made the decision to send Angela away. I didn't have a say. Pat and I aren't together anymore,' Mick explained. His shoulders were hunched and with a quick sniff, he conceded that he'd gone along with it because he didn't want to kick up a fuss. 'The doctors told us to forget her and to go home and have another baby.'

'How did you feel about that?'

Mick frowned. 'I thought they were callous, but I suppose

they thought they were being practical. And nobody expected these children to live. They've defied all expectation.'

The two men chatted in a pub before walking back to Mick's cottage, up an alleyway off Baxtergate. Pushing the gate open, they stepped through a cobbled passageway and up a flight of narrow steps to the cottage. The path between the cottages was barely four feet wide. It was like a row of doll's houses.

'We'd waited so long to have a child and now Pat sent her away, as though she didn't matter, like a parcel delivered to the wrong address. I couldn't understand it, but the wife said it was for the best. So did the doctor. She used the excuse that our cottage wasn't geared to bringing up a handicapped child and at the time we didn't have a bathroom.'

Sipping his tea, Jasper glanced around him and out of the window and into the neighbour's front room. They were so close that he could see what the neighbour was eating.

The cottages weren't family homes and looked more like holiday cottages. It was barely big enough to raise a family. Everything happened in one room. There was a stove and a few cupboards, a log fire and a settee and chair. A set of steep and windy stairs led to two bedrooms.

Mick continued. 'It was as if she was finding excuses, because she didn't love Angela and never would. It had nowt to do with the cottage. We could have moved, although this place has always been ideal for my work at the harbour, and house prices are going up so I'm not sure we could have afforded a bigger place. I don't earn much.' Mick was a fisherman. 'But now I can see things as clear as daylight. She was just a lazy cow. She hardly did any housework. I brought back my wages, I did all the cooking despite working my arse off. I think she imagined life would be a picnic once she had a baby. She gave up her job in a shop without telling me and she spent the whole pregnancy slobbing on the sofa. Pregnancy isn't an illness, for Christ's sake. Me mam had eleven kids and I can remember her carrying the coal scuttle in from the yard and scrubbing the front steps the day before she went into labour.' He got up and flexed his arms. 'Come on, let's go for a walk. I'll show you around as it's nice weather.'

Jasper thought it was a good idea. It was much easier to get things off your chest when you were putting one foot in front of the other. Awkward silences and uncomfortable moments could be filled with pebble throwing or interlaced with comments about the view.

'Everything I do in life is because I have to, there is no alternative. That's just the way things are. You get stuck in and get on with it. Having a handicapped child is no different. It's one of life's challenges and you have to face it. That's what you do. But she couldn't grasp that basic life lesson. She always takes the easy route out of any situation.'

'How long have you been apart?'

'A few years. Bringing Angela up showed me another side to my wife, it was a side I didn't like.'

They were the only ones walking along the planking towards a lighthouse and then back towards a concrete slope to the sandy beach. The temperature was chillier down on the beach and there was a chemical edge to the air. Further along the coast there were dog walkers on the sands. The tide was far out and seemed to merge into the watery sky. The views all around were spectacular. Rising from the harbour, rows of houses built several hundred years ago, criss crossed the bottom of a steep cliff. Perched on the top, Jasper found it easy to see why the haunting remains of Whitby Abbey were the inspiration for Bram Stoker's gothic novel, *Dracula*. The setting sun cast a shadow over the ruins and seemed to echo the disquiet between the two men. Below the abbey stood St Mary's Church, reached by a steep climb of steps. Time and weather had gnawed at the graves, some of them teetering on the eroding cliff edge. Jasper made a note to return with Sandy for a few days, to explore this quaint historic harbour town.

'One day as I was getting ready to collect Angela from the home, my wife said she didn't want to do it anymore.'

'What do you mean?'

'She didn't want Angela coming home. I've always looked forward to weekends, and spending time with my daughter, but when she came home on those weekends I saw things that made my toenails curl. I couldn't put up with it, I didn't like the way the wife treated her, so for several months, while Pat and I fought like cat and dog, eventually breaking up, Angela didn't come home. I felt awful for that, as if I was abandoning her, but it was for her safety. And then Pat was gone and it was just the two of us.'

Jasper studied his face, trying to gauge his thoughts, but Mick's eyes were fixed on a boat in the distance. 'We sat here on the beach one day and Pat spilled out her thoughts. I wanted the child I thought I was going to have, she said. The one that was going to run marathons and was going to go to college or make her a grandma. The one I got was a bad joke.'

'What are Angela's interests? What can she achieve?'

'She loves singing. She's in the school choir. She's got a beautiful voice and a great sense of humour. As far as her future is concerned, I don't know what will happen. She'll need full-time care and that will be costly.'

Mick looked out to sea and for a few moments the two men were silent. Jasper closed his eyes, breathing in the sea air.

'Pat's written her off. My daughter has more drive and determination than my idle ex-wife, I can tell you that for nothing.'

'I'm sure.'

'The thing I want to get across to you is the public's general attitude to handicap. I'll never forget one of the nurses telling us that we'd get our reward in heaven. It's so condescending. What annoys me the most is people coming up to me and saying, God only gives these special children to people who can cope with them. What twaddle.'

Jasper wanted to know more about the things that Mick was alluding to, regarding the way his ex-wife had treated Angela on her home visits. 'How did Pat treat Angela?'

Jasper saw the light leave Mick's eyes and, as he spoke, a wariness crept into his voice, as if he was scared of betraying his wife, knowing it might end up in a national newspaper. 'She said demeaning things.'

'Can you give some examples?'

'You mustn't use our names for your article.'

'No.'

'She was always accusing her of being an attention seeker. It's hard for Angela, I don't begrudge helping her do things, like cleaning her teeth and helping her to eat. But Pat would shout at her, '"You can dress yourself, get on with it."'

With the feeling that more was to come, Jasper waited.

'She used to order her to strip off as soon as she was home.'

Jasper wanted to ask why, but he waited.

''You've got someone else's clothes on, you stupid idiot', she used to scream in Angela's face. "Where are the clothes I made you?" I spend hours making you things.'

'I thought you said she was lazy.' Jasper knew it wasn't the point, but he was curious.

'She is. She lied. She's never picked up a needle or a thread of cotton in her life.'

Mick blew his nose.

'How did Angela take the criticism?'

'It's had a long-term effect on their relationship. She told me she doesn't like her mother and makes excuses so that she doesn't have to see her. They don't see each other much. It's not a loving relationship.'

'You have a close relationship with Angela though?'

'We've got a great relationship. There were lots of small

things that Pat did that weren't nice. When she was telling her off, she would wag her finger in Angela's face. To someone like Angela, who can't defend herself, that's threatening.'

'Anything else?'

'She'd shout, "I'm waiting for you to get dressed, get on with it, you lazy girl." I would also get told off for helping her dress. I think she liked the feeling of power she had over Angela. Pat had a controlling father, she was sexually abused as a child, and I think by controlling Angela in this way, she was dealing with her own demons.'

Jasper listened and looking out to sea they fell into silence for a few moments before Mick took a deep breath and in a bright tone changed the subject.

'I love this town,' Mick said, looking around him and rubbing his stubbly chin. 'I'm a simple man, my world is here. There are towns like Sheffield built on the steelworks and colliery villages around Durham and beyond. I couldn't be a miner, grafting underground and barely seeing the light of day. What sort of life is that? I wouldn't swap the sea for the pit if you paid me. But I can't drive, and neither can the wife, so it was always going to be hard living here; we had to be able to get to hospital appointments.'

'How did you bring her home if you don't drive and how far away is the school?'

'It's in Sheffield. My brother would bring her here and take her back. That was when she was younger, and it was easier to get her in and out of the car and carry her up the alleyway. These days he takes me to see her once a week––sometimes only once a fortnight.'

THE FOLLOWING MORNING, Jasper got up for an early run to clear his head. Shafts of red speared the dawn sky as he emerged from Baxtergate at the water's edge, to see fishermen hauling rope and engines idling ready for a day at sea. He'd started running a few years ago as an antidote to spending hours hunched over a desk. He'd found it tortuous at first, but now it was pleasurable, and he enjoyed pushing his limits. With his feet slapping on the cobbles, he passed window cleaners on ladders soaping shop windows and water dripped from freshly watered hanging baskets. This was a town that cared for its appearance. A gust of wind howled around the winding road that led towards the steps rising onto the cliffs. He stopped to take in the view between the alleyways. His running shoes felt flat and worn as if all of their bounce had gone and he could feel the grooves between each cobble which made his toes sore.

He stopped to browse in the window of an art gallery displaying Frank Meadow Sutcliffe's photographs of Whitby. Sutcliffe's work presented an enduring record of life in the town around the late Victorian era and turn of the twentieth century. Jasper's gaze wandered to a picture of semi-naked children standing in the sea. Transfixed by the photos, he wondered about the plight of handicapped children back then. He remembered reading that freak shows were the terrible fate that awaited backward and handicapped people and that crowds flocked from all around the world to see the freaks exhibited in circuses.

Running on through the tangle of streets, he was out of sorts, as if somebody was missing. Enveloped by a wave of sadness he stopped at a phone box. He was missing Sandy. He pictured her face and eyes and the way they were just before he left, their legs tangled in bed after sex. He felt guilty for leaving her. She didn't always cope well on her own, but this was work. What option did he have?

When they first met, Sandy was a sugar fix, a toy to play with while he waited for his career to take off. She was a stunner and hard to pull away from, but he'd always known that his career came before women back then.

The loss of their baby still affected Sandy. She couldn't move on, and made it clear that she didn't want another baby. The shock of seeing the lack of financial and social support for children struck by thalidomide prompted Sandy to offer help. She channelled her energies into a charity set up to raise money and help the children born with missing limbs and she helped at the local school for the handicapped, St Bede's.

'For years I've struggled to keep my looks and my weight in check so that I can appear in glossy magazines. I'm obsessed by my looks, I've pandered to slimy male bosses who want the perfect look. Well no more. We're living in a world with unrealistic body expectations. I'm done with modelling. I want to do some good in this world.' Jasper was shocked when she made the big announcement. It was so unlike her. She'd always focused on herself. Her world was glamour, fame and vanity but now she was planning to help the less fortunate. But she'd been deadly serious. These days, Sandy talked about the problems of raising money, rather than the problems of smudged mascara. She helped with everything from garden parties to jumble sales, but still enjoyed being the centre of attention, as she trotted round events, using her charm and wit to get wealthy businessmen to part with their money for the cause.

Jasper picked up the phone and dialed their number. Although it was horribly early, it was a good time to phone because he could guarantee she would be in. She hated being woken because she found it difficult to get back to sleep, but he knew she'd be happy to hear his voice. He'd be tied up later and unable to ring. Nervy at night she never slept well alone, her ears pricked at the click of the fridge and the crackle of pipes expanding. She was friends with the neighbours on both sides of their leafy close, in the centre of Haslemere in Surrey, so Jasper knew she was all right.

The phone rang on, but there was no answer. Was she stubbornly refusing to answer because he'd woken her? He hated mind games. Their marriage was too fresh for the rot to set in just yet. Putting the receiver down, he left the booth and ran through the town, climbing the hundred or so steps up to St Mary's Church. Puffed out at the top, his feet still smacking the tarmac, he carried on, wearily, through the graveyard and onto the cliff, where the wind was blustery, and a fine mist speckled his face. He leaned against a fence drawing breath, before following the stone wall that circuited the perimeter of the abbey grounds and down towards an allotment. The red blob of a phone box standing proud and statue-like at the bottom of the hill beckoned him. An hour had passed. She'd be awake by now and getting dressed. Tugging the door, his nose twitching against the smell of old fags and urine, he grabbed the phone and dialed. There was still no answer. Where the hell was she? If she'd spent the night somewhere else, why hadn't she mentioned it? She was meticulous about keeping him updated. This wasn't like her. With mounting concern, he scoured the mental list of people she could be with, and phoned a couple of them, drawing blanks.

And then a thought wormed in his head. She was having an affair. He didn't know where the idea had come from, but now that it had popped into his head, it took root like a stubborn weed. Sandy was beautiful and had admirers. They were devoted to each other. Deep down he knew that, but was this the price he had to pay for marrying a beauty? She must be lonely. It was his fault. He had to get back to London and find out what was going on.

In the tangle of empty streets, he passed gift shops selling Whitby jet, a semi-precious stone created from fossilised wood. He'd return when they opened, to buy Sandy a piece of jewellery. The black would look stunning against her pale skin. He heard a dog barking and a girl calling its name. As he reached an alley the dog jumped out and the girl, not much bigger than the dog, tugged at the lead, trying to restrain the ferocious Alsatian, baring his teeth at Jasper. It looked more like a wolf than a dog. Jasper's heart slammed in his chest with the shock. He flinched, swore and recoiled in fear. Jasper had never been keen on dogs, ever since a bad childhood experience.

Jasper wasn't going to waste any more time. He'd head home, to confront Sandy.

30

1973

Bill gripped the windowsill, his face ashen as he peered into the street. Despite it being early, the woman was across the road, staring from behind a pair of sunglasses. Moving from view, he collapsed onto the bed, and knew in that moment he would have to confront her.

After work, he drove to her house. Soon it would all be over. If she was Toby's real mother, he'd come home and confess the truth to the boy, face the weight of the law, the future and all that it held. He parked the van, icy nerves shooting through him as he stared up at the house With his hands shaking, he locked the van, his earlier bravado gone.

As he strode towards the front door, feet crunching over the gravel, he noticed the woman standing at the kitchen sink. She looked flustered when she saw him.

She opened the door on the second knock.

'Bill.'

'Who are you? And how do you know my name?'

'Mrs Mitchell. Call me Linda. I think you'd better come in.'

The speech Bill had prepared stuck in his throat as he

stared open-mouthed at the thin woman wearing yellow corduroys and a turtleneck jumper. After inviting him in, she turned and led him along the corridor, in a trail of musky perfume, down some steps into the kitchen, where she reached for the kettle to make tea.

'You've been following me.'

'My mother's house sprouts problems daily.' she said, her hand shaking as she poured water from the tap.

Bill frowned.

'Deep cracks run the length of the skirting board.'

'I don't understand. Is there something I can help you with? I'm a builder.'

'Yes, I know you're a builder,' she snapped. 'Don't you remember me? Your shoddy work has caused my mother no end of grief including a heart attack.'

Giving her a watery smile as if he were a pupil unable to express himself properly, Bill stuttered, 'I'm sorry to hear your mother isn't well. Are you saying that she's a customer of mine?'

'That's exactly what I'm saying. Don't you remember your customers? We have met before.'

The woman slammed her mug on the counter, tea sloshing down the sides. Reaching for a cloth she pressed it on the counter, letting out a sigh and a tirade of further complaints about the work carried out to her mother's house. Flummoxed, Bill didn't know what to do or say. He wasn't expecting this to be about work. This was supposed to be about something much more sinister. It was bad enough that a customer had complaints, but he felt sudden relief and almost wanted to cry with joy. Toby was safe, he wasn't going to be taken away. Normally he handled work complaints well, it was all par for the course in his line of work and there were set procedures he followed. But all of the basic questions he usually asked were scrambled in his head and he felt the stirrings of a migraine.

'Can you tell me her address? Why didn't you contact me? I

take great pride in my work and if something isn't up to standard it must be remedied. I'm sorry if I've caused your mother distress. Let me go round there, this evening.'

'Builders are supposed to make our lives easier.'

With stomach twisting, Bill feared she was going to call a solicitor to make a claim against him. This was all he needed.

'You've been following me for a while. Why didn't you just ring me to discuss the problems?'

'How could I complain when your wife had just died and left you with a handicapped son to bring up.' Her face was stony and she was shaking. 'And that dreadful fire. I was walking past when I saw your house ablaze. A friend of mine lives near you.' Stunned, Bill had never encountered an emotional customer like this before. There had to be more to it. She had a screw loose. His heart went out to her. He'd spent weeks making the wrong assumptions.

'Thank you for giving my son a lift home the other week.'

'What a sweet boy he is. Toby isn't it? He told me he's being bullied at school. I'm sorry, look at what you've made me do. He confided in me and now I've broken his trust.'

'He shouldn't have got into a stranger's car. I've had words with him.'

'How is he?'

'Events have moved on.'

Bill struggled to understand why Toby would confide in a complete stranger, let alone take a lift from a stranger. Had he taught him nothing about stranger danger?

'How do you mean?' she asked.

'He suffered the most dreadful abuse at that school. Thankfully the boys who did it will be locked away for years. 'You don't read the local paper then?'

She shook her head. 'Is he okay?'

'Yes, he's moving school.'

'That's good.'

'Do you have your diary?' Bill asked. 'When would be convenient to pop round to your mother's house? Once I've assessed what needs doing, I'll set aside a few days in the next couple of weeks to sort it out. I'm very sorry you weren't happy with the work.'

'Tuesday or Wednesday.'

'Just one thing, remind me when the work was carried out?' Some projects he never forgot, like the extension to Boots The Chemist in the town centre or the renovations to the grand Georgian mansion owned by the mayor, but there were many customers he forgot. He could pass customers in the street and they'd stop to chat, but he couldn't remember them. He usually went along with it, pretending to know who they were.

'Three years ago.'

'Three years?' Bill's mouth fell open. 'You've had this campaign of hatred going all this time and didn't think to just call me?'

'Campaign of hatred? That's a bit dramatic. I wouldn't say that a few stares were a campaign of hatred,' she scoffed.

'So, you didn't send my wife anonymous letters and cards on our anniversary and you didn't send me a letter the other week with one sentence, *I know where you are?*'

Linda stared at him with an expression that said, you're barking mad. 'No, of course not. Why on earth would I do that? I'm sorry I acted weirdly towards you, but I haven't been myself lately. I lost my husband recently. You must think me neurotic and probably I am. I went a step too far, glaring at you whenever I saw you, waiting outside your house and following your van around the town. How hard would it have been to ring you?'

'I'm sorry to hear about your husband. It's not easy is it?'

She ignored his question. 'Have you contacted the police?'

'I'm trying to get to the bottom of it myself. And to be honest I had thought you were behind it.'

'Me? Why on earth would I do something like that?'

'I'd rather you didn't mention it to anybody if you don't mind.'

She nodded.

'You had a year's guarantee on the work and could have contacted me as soon as you noticed problems. You're now well outside the guarantee and I'm afraid I'll have to charge you for the work but if my workmanship is to blame, I will offer a discount.'

'I would have contacted you much earlier, but what with my husband's death and my mother recently diagnosed with dementia, my nerves have been shot to bits. I haven't been myself.'

'I'll take a look and get back to you.'

With head pounding, Bill closed the conversation, said goodbye and walked back to his van. He felt bile rise in his throat and wanted to be sick. She was just an odd customer. But she wasn't the person writing the letters and she wasn't the reason Rona had been to see a solicitor. The sooner they moved away, the better, before anything else happened.

31

1973

Bill

After visiting Linda's mother and assessing what needed to be done to correct his mistakes, Bill returned to her house to explain his plan. She welcomed him in, friendlier and more relaxed this time. A ginger cat meowed around her feet and she went to a cupboard for a tin of cat food. A letter on top of the pile next to Bill's coffee cup grabbed his attention. The header read *Swan's Nest Residential Home for Autistic Children*. His interest was piqued because he was determined to find out more about this woman. He felt that there was something relevant to him, going on in her life.

Linda sat down and quizzed him about the renovations.

'I need to pull up the top floor carpet to secure the planking and joisting. It's uneven to walk on-- and in the front bedroom I need to re-plaster the wall and I noticed there's some mould building up in the bathroom. I advised your mother to always open the window after baths and showers. But I will clean that off and apply a coat of mould-resistant paint. That should have been done but it seems that it wasn't.'

'How much is it going to cost?'

Bill was relieved that she was happy to pay. He needed the money and didn't want to fall out with her. He didn't like it when customers were unhappy and wanted to do his best to sort any issues.

'I'll work it out and get it on paper for you. As I said before, I will give you a discount.'

'Don't worry about it. I've got enough bills piling up, one more won't make much difference.'

'I know the feeling.' Bill wondered if she had children. There didn't seem to be anybody else living in the house.

'It wouldn't be so bad if I had something to show for it, but with my husband dead and like you I'm having to manage on my own with a handicapped child in a residential home.'

'Oh...I'm sorry to hear that.' Bill was surprised and wondered why she hadn't mentioned her handicapped child at their previous meeting. But he also felt uncomfortable when customers stepped over the line of professionalism, pouring out their woes.

'We have something in common, Mr Murphy.'

'Call me Bill.'

'I've got an autistic son who's the same age as Toby. He's been in residential care for years. Some days I don't visit him, and I feel weighed down with guilt but then I think, what's the point? He's so far gone. I have no life. I suppose that's why I get so wrapped up in other peoples' lives. It gets lonely.' She lifted her skirt a couple of inches, but it was subtle and he could have been mistaken about her motive. With a smile she put her other hand on his and gave it a squeeze. There was no misunderstanding her intentions and Bill didn't like it. He pulled his hand away and got up.

'Things are hard and I feel for you. Life's certainly a challenge. It's not easy bringing up a handicapped child is it? I hope things get better for you. I'll be back in touch with the estimate, but I'd better crack on,' he said, not wanting to be drawn into a deeper conversation.

'If you ever want to come round for a drink one evening, you're very welcome. I can rustle up a bit of dinner too.' It was a nice offer, but Bill felt uncomfortable.

'That's very kind of you but as soon as I've completed my current projects we're moving south.'

'Oh?' Bill clocked the disappointment on her face.

'We need a fresh start after everything that's happened. I've been offered work at a residential home for handicapped children in Surrey and they can take Toby as a pupil. It was a stroke of luck really. Apparently the school have lots of positions they need filling.'

'What's it called?'

'You won't have heard of it,' Bill said dismissively, turning to go.

'Go on, try me.'

'St. Bede's in Haslemere.'

'No, you're right, I haven't heard of it, but look, I wish you and Toby well. I expect I'll see you again as I'll be over at mum's next week. It's been nice chatting to you,' she said casually.

As she closed the door on him, Bill wasted no time making his escape, it was too hot in there and he'd felt suffocated.

32

1973

Sandy

Preoccupied with the baby issue they'd never discussed being dog owners, but Sandy was certain that Jasper would love her surprise. She'd made the decision the day she lobbed the orchid, its foliage yellow and gnarled. She'd looked at its stick-like skeleton in the pot by the window and thought, I can't even keep a damn houseplant alive, what chance do I stand with a baby? All she needed to do was water the plant and position it towards the light. She'd never really nurtured anything in her life and hadn't been interested in her dad's tomato plants. Plants, babies, they were all so helpless and fragile. And then a smile broke across Sandy's face. *Maybe a dog is what we need.*

Throwing back the sheets she realised how wonderful it was to escape to a hotel for the night, enjoying a sumptuous bed and basking in the morning light as it filtered through the thin curtains. She had to stay in a hotel because the kennels that had been recommended to her were too far to drive to in one day. It was halfway across the country and set in a secluded corner of Exmoor close to Buckfast Abbey which they'd visited a few times on their travels.

She couldn't wait to see the selection of puppies. It was like choosing sweeties as a child on a Sunday with her father.

Jasper was uncertain about leaving her to go off on his tour. 'Are you sure you don't mind?' and, 'Are you sure you're going to be okay?' he'd repeated on loop, but this was his career and the biggest scoop of the century awaited him. It wasn't fair to try and hold him back. He was so excited by the prospect, after getting his boss to agree to using the story; it was an enormous project for him. Biting her lip and fighting back tears she'd waved him off, but as soon as she'd closed the door the silence hit. It was a silence that pierced her subconscious. The house was crying out for a dog and she was yearning for a four-legged companion. She imagined a small fluffy dog curled on her lap at night as she watched 'Corrie.' Stroking a dog would be therapeutic. Jasper wouldn't mind a dog. It needn't interfere with their lives, too much. She conjured images in her head of walks through woods - a dog would be something they could both focus on. The perfect child substitute without all the whingeing of a baby.

Being an only child she'd longed for a dog for company, but her mother had steadfastly and stubbornly put her foot down. Sandy wondered why she'd had a child and how on earth her father had put up with her all those years. The final straw came when Sandy found herself pregnant at nineteen with Jasper's baby and living at home. When Sandy refused to contact Jasper, her mother's plans for them to marry were dashed, and she'd herded Sandy off to a mother-and-baby home until after the birth and insisted she have it adopted.

Sandy remembered arguments with her parents about getting a dog. 'I'll take it for walks Mum.' And 'I'll train it to poop outside,' she'd promised.

'We are not getting a dog. I don't need another tie to stop

me enjoying my freedom. You can't expect us to be shackled to a dog as well as to you.'

Sandy presented them with a list of ten reasons to get a dog in an attempt to convince them, but her mother retaliated with her own list with reasons against it that Sandy found hard to disagree with.

God, Sandy reflected, why hadn't she bared her soul to Jasper and told him more about her childhood? It was all coming back and she realised that on marrying Jasper she had slammed the door on the past, to focus on the moments of gold that the future would bring, but it was returning to haunt her. The fact was, it was too painful to talk about half of the things that had happened within those walls. It was only as she drove that the memories were flooding back. They hit her like bullets. With tears pricking her eyes and obscuring her vision, she plundered on, dodging ruts in the road and braking when the hedgerow grew thick by the roadside, getting closer to the farm nestled at the bottom of a hill.

Approaching the farm, she slowed to let a gaggle of geese waddle across the road. Further along a farmer tipped his cap and smiled as she passed. In her excitement she had come unprepared, stepping out of the orange Cortina in dainty kitten-heeled shoes muttering, 'Shit, my favourite shoes,' as mud painted them brown and splattered up her tights.

She wanted to get a dog as a surprise for Jasper coming home, but she was worried that she should have discussed it with him first. Dogs were intelligent, sentient creatures, man's best friend, just waiting to be loved and ready to take that risk.

Sandy cast her eyes over the misfits and scrawny mongrels, with their ribs showing, shivering and unsteady on their legs; each of them came with a report about their mistreatment in a former life. None of them were for her. She avoided their doe eyes, threatening to break her resolve and melt her heart with their whimpering. She allowed the owner to talk her through each dog and how the farm worked to bring the dog's weight up to what it should be. Afterwards, she asked to see the puppies in the next barn.

'This one was adopted,' the owner said, before leaving the mongrel shed, pointing to a scraggy Labrador, 'but she came back to us because humans can be stupid. They didn't give her the stomach medicine she needed, then got upset when she was sick. Having a dog isn't cheap. It's a responsibility and you can't cut corners and think you can avoid vet bills.'

All the way to the farm, Sandy had visualised a small fluffy white dog, small enough to fit in a beach bag and adorable enough to shower with kisses, but as she walked across the mucky yard and entered the puppy barn another vision crowded her mind, startling her as it came out of the blue. The dog she wanted had big floppy brown-and-black ears, coarse hair and large paws. Not only would it be her companion it would be her guard dog and was big enough to ward off intruders, his presence settling her mind at night while Jasper was away. An inner voice spoke to her. 'You want something big, something reckless, something intense and something thick-skinned, the complete opposite to you.' When the owner asked her if she had any ideas regarding breeds, she answered, 'An Alsatian would be nice.'

'You do surprise me, the way you were talking I thought you were more interested in the smaller breeds.'

'Perhaps...' Sandy said, uncertainty creeping in. 'Show me what you've got, I'll know the one when I see it.'

'Matching dogs to owners is like matching a man and a woman. Opposites attract if you know what I mean,' he said, scanning her up and down, 'but not for long.'

Sandy felt muddled. This was like the day she chose her wedding dress. It was supposed to be one of the most exciting and glamorous purchases of her life. But it was an exhausting day sending her head into a spin with a migraine that had taken two days to shake off. She walked into the shop, saw the dress she liked but the assistant had put her off, encouraging her to try everything on. Standing in front of the mirror, with flattering comments from her best friend and the assistant, she'd loved them all. In the end she returned to the original dress that had caught her eye.

'How do I know which dog to choose?'

'I don't want to influence you, take a chair.' The owner offered her a plastic chair but noticing dried mud on the seat Sandy remained standing. 'Sit here for a while, take your time, watch how they play. Do you choose the smaller one who's a bit quicker around the food bowl, do you want one with energy or one who is going to sit on your lap and be clingy? Do you want a male or female? A lot of potential owners make their choice by looking at the dog's head.'

Sandy was relieved when he left her alone to make her decision amidst the howl and whimpers of fifty puppies. She wandered from pen to pen peering through the bars at the parade of applicants. The experience reminded her of how she'd felt as a model every time an agent licked his eye across her body deciding what contract to offer her based on individual parts of her body. Was he assessing her fingers for a glove advert or how toned and shapely her legs were for modelling hot pants?

Overwhelmed by the surroundings and the enormity of the decision, the smell and the warmth hit her. She realised she couldn't possibly make a decision on a whim and without Jasper's input. Reaching for the latch she paused with an intense sense that something or somebody was looking at her. Above the din, the cry of one puppy was distinct. Its whimpers pulled her towards the pen. How could she ignore its cry? Swinging round, she saw a Tibetan spaniel and their eyes met from across the barn. Sandy knew that he was the one. She stepped towards the puppy, crouching at the bars. There was something in his deep brown eyes and lion face, not a pleading, because pleading she could overlook. There was a dignity, as if he didn't need her to be nice. He turned away but in that gaze Sandy saw something she recognised in this creature. Maybe she saw her own independent streak or the eyes of a fighter down on his luck. He came across as a large dog within a small body and it appealed to Sandy.

33

1973

Jasper and Sandy

Taking her eyes from the road, Sandy looked at Jasper sitting beside her in the passenger seat. They were driving home from the train station where Sandy had just picked him up, after his trip to Whitby.

'I've got a surprise for you.' Grinning from ear to ear her face wore the expression of an excited child let loose in a sweet stop.

'I love surprises, especially your surprises.' He gave her an air kiss and reached over to stroke her cheek.

Sandy knew how to break the monotony of relationships, to keep the spark alive and show him how much she cared. She knew the power that surprises brought. If she'd picked him up from the airport, she would have been standing at the front of the crowd holding a sign. And she often surprised him with a cooked breakfast in bed, on one occasion the fried eggs were heart shaped and there was a love note on the tray. Her best surprises were food related and she was an amazing cook, experimenting with exotic ingredients he'd never heard of, and using ideas she'd gathered from magazines and TV programmes. She would put a well-presented dish on the table dressed in candles, linen napkins and a pristine tablecloth. Sometimes she invited surprise guests, but she knew when he wanted peace and quiet and just the two of them would sit across the table holding hands. The house was always immaculate. He couldn't cope with chaos and liked everything to be in its place, and in that sense it was good that they didn't have kids. He didn't have to ask her to do anything. She was one step ahead of the game on everything from taking his suits to the dry cleaners to mending his socks if a hole appeared. His shirts were ironed and hung in the wardrobe and his toothbrush was replaced when the bristles were worn.

God, he loved this woman. She was radiant and smelt amazing, she was always happy to see him when he returned from one of his trips. It was times like this that he knew their love and desire for each other was still as fresh and alive as the day they stood at the altar. He'd spent the entire journey dreaming about the things they'd do together during his few days off until he returned north. He needed this break and longed to switch off. He couldn't wait to take her to bed and languish there until mid-morning, with no responsibilities or interruptions. All thoughts about her having an affair were swept away the moment he saw her. Sometimes her beauty was too much for him to handle, moving him to the point of tears and making him question why she'd want to be with a journalist who left her for weeks on end in his pursuit of a scoop. But now that he was beside her again, his faith was restored. Wherever she'd spent the night, she'd soon tell him when they were home and relaxed.

Beaming at him, she removed the key from the ignition.

'Not long now. I can't wait to see your face,' she teased.

Jasper sensed that the surprise was about more than a bit of dinner. Maybe she'd booked a few days away. Her effervescence was contagious. And then the penny dropped. She was pregnant. With heart banging across his chest did he dare to believe this was the surprise?

'Wait there, I'm going to blindfold and guide you into the house,' she giggled.

Jasper waited until she reappeared at his side gulping back laughter as she tied a tea towel around his forehead covering his eyes and led him up the path to the house, clutching his holdall.

Over the threshold he stepped onto newspaper, yes he was sure it was newspaper. Maybe she'd had the house redecorated in his absence, but he couldn't smell paint. The house smelled different though, there was no doubting it. It was a sweet cloying smell, that he found nauseous and he wished it would go away. As soon as the blindfold was off, he'd open the windows to let in fresh air.

Gripping his shoulders, she twirled him around.

'Welcome home darling,' she shrieked lifting the blindfold from his eyes. 'Meet Tibs.'

Jasper's mouth fell open. They were standing in the middle of the kitchen. Every inch of the floor was covered with layers of newspaper and in the corner, blocking the back door, a puppy was curled up asleep on a red velvet cushion. He stared at the ball of fluff.

'You've bought a puppy.'

'Isn't he cute? Do you want to hold him? His fur is so soft.'

'Why didn't you ask me first?'

'I wanted to surprise you. I went all the way down to Devon to pick him up.' Sandy's excitement was gone and her voice was flat.

'I wondered where you were when you didn't answer the phone. You should have told me you were going away. I was worried.'

'I'm sorry. You don't mind though?'

'Given the choice I wouldn't get a dog. I'm not an animal lover, Sandy.'

Something niggled inside him. It was times like this, when she behaved like an impulsive, headstrong child that made him question whether their marriage would stand the test of time.

'You like my cousin's dog.'

'I tolerate it.'

'You love it really. You're always throwing balls for him.'

'What do you expect me to do, moan and complain every time we go around there?'

'Well I won't take you there in future.'

'Life's about putting up with things you don't like.'

'Exactly, and I put up with you going away.' Hands on her hips, Sandy had morphed into a petulant child.

'You think I enjoy trekking round the country listening to heartbreaking stories?' He'd said too much, had never meant to tell her how hard it was listening to the heart-wrenching tales of these families and feeling powerless.

'I'm sorry, all right. I thought you'd be happy.'

'I'm sorry I snapped at you. I wish you'd asked me first.'

'You'll get used to him.'

Jasper grunted.

'I get lonely and scared when you're away.'

Caught between a rock and a hard place he didn't know what to do. He could feel his eyes pricking but he wasn't allergic as such. He wished he was allergic, a full-blown allergy that left him sneezing and wheezing for England. That was the only way she would take him seriously. But maybe this was about more than the dog, and was symptomatic of something deeper going on in their marriage. It was about lack of communication and was the same problem she'd had when she didn't contact him to tell him she was pregnant all those years ago.

'The dog can stay, I suppose,' Jasper conceded.

'Thank you,' she said excitedly, giving his arm a squeeze. 'You won't regret it. I know you won't.'

Jasper eyed the whimpering puppy suspiciously.

Kneeling to pick him up, Sandy brought him to Jasper, clearly hoping his arms would welcome the little fella.

Jasper waved the puppy away. 'I might start sneezing.' He watched her put the puppy back in the basket, the newspaper rustling under her feet. The heading of an article in *The Daily Telegraph* caught his eye – Doctor Simon Gerard wins Top Doctor of The Year Award. Jasper picked up the crumpled sheet from the floor and began to read.

'There are awards for all sorts of things these days. Look at this. Awards for doctors, whatever next? They're only doing their job for God's sake.'

Sandy sat down next to him and peered at Simon Gerard's face. 'That's the doctor who delivered my baby,' she gasped.

'Really?' Jasper huffed. 'I'm surprised he's won an award. He was very blunt and uncaring from what you told me?'

'Winning an award? That does surprise me.' Sandy frowned at the beaming smile of Simon Gerard holding a gold-coloured trophy cup. 'His bedside manner was appalling.'

The phone ringing in the hallway finished the conversation, as Jasper rushed to grab it. His boss at the other end welcomed him back and told him that he was doing a splendid job.

'Sorry mate, I know you were hoping for a few days break.'

'What is it?'

Jasper was used to having breaks cut short and expected it, but it was tough on Sandy. Journalism was a fast-paced field and information developed rapidly. He went where the action was. It was expected of him. It was a challenging job involving long hours and tough competition and the pay wasn't great. They hardly lived in luxury. But it was exciting when a big news story broke and with that came the chance to meet interesting people.

'A thalidomide boy in Blackpool has suffered severe bullying and was hospitalised. It was reported in a Blackpool newspaper but it's going to go national. I've contacted the family. He lives with his dad. Mum recently passed away. They've lost their home due to a fire, although I don't know if this is linked to the bullying. I want you to get up there today. This could be just the story we need for our campaign.'

'Great, I'll get the story and write it up chief.' Jasper could hear the clatter of typewriters singing in the background. He wasn't missing the office.

'Make sure it pops.'

'Yes, chief.'

Coming off the phone, the issues of the dog paled into insignificance compared to the annoyance of having to go away again. This was all he needed.

'Who was that?'

'The boss.'

'What did he want?' Sandy asked with a knowing frown as she laid the table for lunch and put one of her delicious homecoming mushroom quiches, warm from the oven, onto a plate.

'It's bad news, I'm afraid.'

With a salad bowl poised in mid-air, Sandy shook her head and sighed. 'You've only just got back. Why do you let him do this to us?'

'I'm sorry.'

'You could say, no. Work always comes first. I haven't seen you for two weeks. Doesn't he have any respect for family time?'

'We don't have a family.'

'We do now,' she said nodding towards the dog.

'It's a big story, Sandy and relevant to what I'm already working on. The boss has organised everything. But I want to get this one first, before the other nationals get it––it could be the scoop of my career. I'm sorry, I know it's hard on you.'

Sandy thumped the bowl onto the table. 'For God's sake. I never get you to myself these days.'

Jasper glanced at the puppy. He was annoyed she'd bought it without asking him. Maybe they could find a compromise if she accepted some boundaries for the dog. His nose was getting used to the doggy whiff in the air. Once it was house trained, it might not be too much trouble and if it kept Sandy off his back it would be worth it. It was company for her and let him off the hook in terms of his frequent trips away. It irritated him that it was always him finding a way through their differences.

'I don't need this stress right now Sandy.' His head stabbed with the start of a headache. She was pushing all the right buttons.

'I'm sorry,' she said, standing behind him. 'I've missed you. It's feels as if you've been away for months.' She wrapped her arms around his neck. 'I'm sorry to have a go. I wish I was going with you. But I've got the dog to look after and work.'

'I've missed you too,' he said rubbing her hand. 'You're doing important work here for the campaign with your fundraising and support at the school. I'm really proud of you.'

'How's it going at the school? Are you still enjoying it?' Jasper asked Sandy after lunch.

Sandy poured coffee and sitting in the lounge she opened up and told him everything that had been going on at the school. It was only as the stories flowed, tumbling from her in animated bursts that she realised how much she was enjoying her work. The experience had opened her eyes to a different world of the less fortunate and made her appreciate all that she had, realising that actually her life had been sheltered and privileged even though it had never seemed that way. It was a far cry from the glamorous work she was used to as a model, but that didn't matter. She was giving something back to society and that excited her. No two days were the same and all kinds of things happened. It was fun getting to know the children and all of them were dear to her. For each child to trust her and let her be a part of their lives was an amazing feeling, and that sense of achievement never went away.

'Some of the staff have their favourites and they take that child home with them, for a day out. It's so unfair on the others. I've tried not to be like that. Little Eisha is beautiful with blonde ringlets tied into a red ribbon and she's so cute that you can't help loving her, but the trouble is she gets more attention than some of the others. Harry has piercing black eyes and a squint and it's hard to warm to him. His eyes make him look ugly. He can't help it but I've noticed the staff don't spend as much time with him. I'd like some of these negative attitudes to change but I'm only a volunteer, so I don't want to encroach on their work. They are trained teachers and carers and who am I to wade in with my opinions?'

Glancing at the clock Jasper realised that time was creeping on. 'It sounds like you're doing a marvellous job darling, but I'd better get packed. I won't be long.'

With Jasper upstairs, Sandy picked up the puppy and curling her legs on the settee, cuddled him on her lap. Her mind drifted to life at Haslemere; it had become a big part of her life. She liked the can-do attitude of the staff. It wasn't well-resourced but they did what they could with the resources they had. She arrived in the morning, after the children were washed and dressed. Each had their own wheelchair and for those who needed them, prosthetic arms and legs were strapped on every day. Sandy thought it was dreadful that the children were forced to wear these to make them look normal. They were ghastly things and hurt the children. She found it distressing to watch the children in pain. She thought it was strange how the handicapped children only ever saw able bodied adults. It gave a false sense of how society should be. She discovered through her conversations with the older children that they held all sorts of false beliefs about what would happen to them when they grew older. They believed that children were in wheelchairs but as you grew older you wouldn't need a wheelchair and would no longer be disabled. It was heartbreaking to tell them this was wrong, and Sandy felt very cruel telling them they would never be able-bodied. The unit was great, and she didn't see any abuse, but she felt that some of the practices were an abusive by-product of an institutional regime.

She recalled one lesson that she hadn't liked. One of the female members of staff brought in wedding magazines for the teenage girls to cut up and make wedding albums. After the lesson she had a word with the teacher, Mrs Simkins.

'I know I'm only a volunteer at this school, but I wasn't sure about that lesson. Surely, the magazines will encourage those girls to dream about their own weddings and indulge in fantasies. How likely are they to get married?' Sandy would never forget watching their faces as they dreamed of long white dresses because it was so poignant and so cruel.

Mrs Simkins looked at Sandy with a shocked expression. 'They like looking at wedding pictures.'

'But surely the chances of some of these girls getting married are slim? They already have the misunderstanding that they are going to grow legs when they were older, and I just think it's feeding into false notions about what their lives will be like.'

'How do you mean?' Mrs Simkins had replied.

'I hope I'm wrong and they defy all expectations and go on to marry. But the reality, for many of these girls is that they will be cared for all of their lives and many have bladder and bowel difficulties which will make intimate relationships difficult.'

'You're thinking too deeply. It was just a fun activity. I've been doing it with classes for years.'

'Maybe it's time to question what we do in class and the implications of the activities we choose to do with the children.'

JASPER DUMPED his bags at the foot of the sofa and kissing the top of Sandy's head he was mildly tempted to stroke the puppy but resisted, his hand hovering in mid-air.

'Don't worry about Tibs. I'll take him to the school. He'll be great with the kids. He'll spend so much time up there that you'll hardly know we have a dog.'

'I'm sorry I was harsh with you. It was a shock. It's not as if we've ever talked about getting a dog. They're not my favourite animals. When you were so excited in the car, I thought you were going to announce that you were pregnant.'

'We've been through that.'

'We can change our minds.'

Not wanting to get drawn into another conversation about starting a family, Sandy ignored the comment and tried to make light of the situation.

'I'm sorry I was impulsive. So, when I decide to get a big fat, hairy tarantula, I'll give you plenty of warning.'

'You'd better not.'

'Give you no warning? Okay, I'll just go ahead and buy one then, or a snake if I feel like it.'

'Stop teasing and come up to bed. I've got a snake you can stroke.'

Laughing, he took her hand and guided her upstairs. 'We've got ten minutes for a bit of nooky.'

'You really are the last of the romantics!'

34
1973

Jasper

Jasper had never been to Blackpool, but his grandparents had holidayed in the northern mecca, religiously each year. Occasionally, they broke the pattern by going to Skegness. A montage of posed photographs pinned to their cellar door captured their happy holiday faces. The photos typified what Blackpool meant to Jasper; cheap and brash with a hint of clean fun. When he'd been a child they had brought back a stick of pink rock for him; no wonder he had so many fillings.

After a short ride to Blackpool's bustling promenade the taxi dropped Jasper's case onto the pavement outside The Grenadier Hotel. In the front window a sign said 'Vacancies,' and below it was a potted aspidistra and a statue of an Alsatian. The paintwork of the hotel's facade was peeling, and it had clearly seen better days, but it was cheap, and Jasper wouldn't be spending much time in his room.

The Grenadier Hotel consisted of two houses knocked together, spanning three floors. According to a billboard on the street, it welcomed families, it had hot and cold water in every room and a resident's bar.

Opening the guest register the middle-aged receptionist with teeth like dirty pebbles and hair scraped into a bun, eyed him suspiciously.

'Room twelve, third floor,' she said, slamming a key on the counter.

'Thank you.' Jasper smiled picking up the key.

Putting his battered suitcase on the bed, he glanced around the room, the musty smell filling his nostrils. The room was devoid of luxury other than a dusty blue rug under the washstand in the corner. When he sat on the bed, he could feel the springs dig into him. He wasn't going to get a great night's sleep.

THE SUN WAS SINKING, spreading into a magnificent apricot hue. Jasper smiled as a tram passed, with a couple laughing on the back seat. He felt a tweak of envy. He would like to be here with Sandy. They would have bought ice creams and sat on the pier, nuzzling each other's necks like other couples relaxing in the beating warmth.

Finding a phone box along the busy thoroughfare he dialled home, welcoming Sandy's resume on her day at the school.

'Those poor thalidomide families, they've been through so much.'

'Yes, I know, and to think, we could have been one of them.'

'The children have been robbed of the magic of childhood.'

'They've been photographed by medical teams, they've had operations, they've been poked and prodded more times than a flaming pin cushion. And now they're entering adolescence without arms, without legs and in some cases without organs.'

'Adolescence is a time for exploring, having fun, learning

and discovering yourself and the opposite sex— but what kind of adolescence will they have?' Jasper sighed.

'Do you remember what you were like as a teenager?' Sandy asked.

'I remember the embarrassment of acne and greasy hair.'

'I remember looking in the mirror and wishing I was Marilyn Monroe.' Sandy giggled.

'It all seems so trivial compared to what these children are up against. The young girl with no legs watching from the sidelines as her able-bodied friends dance at the local disco, or the kid with one eye and no ears trying to be accepted. They're dealing with enormous issues.'

'And the powerful Distillers Company, worth millions have no compunction in fighting these children and offering paltry sums in compensation.'

'I hope the interview goes well,' Sandy said.

'Me too. I'm nervous about meeting this family. The boy has no arms, like our son— but he survived. It feels unfair. Why didn't our son live?'

'I wish I knew why, Jasper.' She sighed. 'We'll never know.'

'I'm in two minds about whether to tell the father about our experience. What do you think?'

'I'm not sure. I think it's better not to. Stay professional, don't bring your personal life into the interview.'

'It might help. To show them I have something in common with them.'

'You could do, but not on the first meeting.'

After the phone call Jasper sauntered along the seafront taking in the smell of candy mixed with fried onions as he gazed out to the vast stretch of glimmering sand and glassy sea, the tide a long way out.

. . .

THE FOLLOWING day started out well. It was sunny and warm and filled with hope. The delicious aroma of sizzling bacon and sausages floated up the stairwell as Jasper descended, enticing him into the day. He took a window seat in the breakfast room and looked out at the hazy mist dancing across the sea. The scenery was familiar to him through the memories his grandparents had shared, but he was seeing it through new eyes.

On the street the salty wind that whipped off the Irish Sea caught Jasper's breath and lifted his thin cotton shirt. The beach was already dotted with deckchairs and children armed with buckets and spades. Crossing the road, Jasper gazed up at Blackpool Tower, majestic and so out of place, as if it had walked from Paris and plonked itself there.

'Hey, want to buy some rock? Lovely Blackpool Rock,' a voice called.

Heading for the phone box, Jasper wheeled round to see an old man on a stall selling sticks of pink and striped rock, which, no matter how long you sucked it, magically had the name of Blackpool showing through its centre.

Jasper laughed. 'Do I look as though I'd eat rock?'

'You might have a kiddie at home.'

'Wish I did mate, but you know what, I am visiting a child today so it will make a nice present.'

Jasper took out some coins from his pocket to buy Toby a stick of rock. Toby was the boy he would soon be meeting.

35
1973

Bill and Jasper

At first, Bill wasn't keen to be interviewed. This was a big deal, a journalist from a national newspaper visiting all the way from London. He'd spent the past week worrying and going over all the possible questions that might be asked, with mixed thoughts about the publicity. There was no avoiding the story entering the local press. *Horrific bullying of local handicapped boy,* the *Blackpool Gazette* read. But this newspaper was in a different league. Bill was a simple man, all he'd ever wanted was a quiet straightforward life, but the day that Rona snatched Toby from the hospital changed all that. Considering calling the newspaper to cancel the interview, Rona's voice filtered into his head during the previous night as he tossed and turned. She would have wanted the interview to go ahead and would have welcomed it, as a chance to show to the world what a wonderful and strong child Toby was. All life's adversities, she used to tell him, all the troubles and obstacles make us stronger, but the world will try to break us. We mustn't let it. We must soldier on. Bill's stomach churned and his head pounded. He was doing this for Rona— and in her memory he'd find the strength.

'We're having fish and chips for our lunch; would you like some?' Bill asked Jasper soon after he had arrived.

'That's very kind of you,' Jasper replied, shifting uncomfortably on the settee. 'But I can eat later.'

'I'd like you to eat with us,' Bill said firmly, his grubby fingers wrapped around a chipped mug. 'I want you to see what our life is like. I've got rid of the mother-in-law for a bit. She's gone down the shops,' he added with a cheeky chuckle, smoothing away any awkwardness. 'It's been good of her to put us up, but I'm looking forward to moving on, I must admit.' With nerves taking over, Bill quelled the rising tide of Les Dawson mother-in-law jokes entering his head without warning.

'Yummy,' Toby enthused, getting up from the floor where he'd been sitting cross-legged. 'I'll lay the table.'

'That reminds me,' Jasper said, reaching into his bag for the stick of rock and giving it to Toby. 'I hope this won't ruin your appetite.'

'Thank you. Dad never buys me rock. I love it and candy floss. Can I eat it now Dad?'

'Thank you,' Bill said to Jasper. And to Toby he said, 'Not till after dinner and you'll have to clean your teeth after, you know how bad sugar is for the teeth.'

Toby tutted. 'Yeah I know. I won't eat it all at once.'

THE BOY WAS GOING to lay the table. How? thought Jasper.

'He's a great kid, he learns fast and can do a lot for himself,' Bill said, as if reading Jasper's thoughts. 'It's not lunch time yet, son, you can clean your shoes first.'

Grumbling that his belly was rumbling, Toby got up from the settee and plonked himself by the back door. Using his feet, he rifled through a box of old newspapers, clamping the paper between the balls of his feet and spreading it across the floor. Shuffling to the sink he pulled a box of tins and cloths from a cupboard.

'Open this,' he demanded.

'Only when you say please.' Bill raised his eyebrows to Jasper.

Jasper watched in awe as Toby settled to polish his shoes using his feet.

Bill rubbed the stubble on his chin and out of earshot of Toby said, 'When he was born, we faced a choice. We could either feel sorry for the lad and for ourselves, or we could cope and help him to cope. When he was little, we did feel sorry for him, but as he grew older, we thought why should we feel sorry for him? He's happy, he's thriving. We felt that rather than be at his beck and call we should treat him as normal as possible, protecting him from the obvious dangers no more than was necessary. He's growing up in a harsh world where people say cruel things and we wanted him to be able to cope, to compete with others and be as independent as he can be. That's why my late wife Rona chose the local secondary school. She wanted him to mix with able-bodied children rather than cocoon him in a special unit where he wasn't going to have to face the world and have to explain himself.'

'Has what's happened made you question things?'

'Definitely.' Bill raised his arm to scratch his balding head and as he did so, the belly fat protruding over the top of his trousers jiggled. He reminded Jasper of a toad, with its pouch full of air, ready to call into the night. Apart from his colouring and eyes, Jasper struggled to see Bill in Toby. They weren't cut from the same cloth and were as dissimilar as Laurel and Hardy. Toby was waif-like, a brittle leopard with long legs and strawberry tones to his curly hair. Bill's hair—— what was left of it—— was as dark and coarse as a black pig. With a bottom the size of a boulder, Bill looked as if he'd been raised on prime beef and Channel Island gold topped milk. It was hard to imagine Toby growing into a pint-sized Bill. 'I wish we'd never sent him to that bloody school. I thought it would be good for him to mix with the local kids, but in hindsight I think he needs to be with his own kind.'

'I'm going to a new school soon,' Toby said, looking up.

'Really?' Jasper instantly saw a storyline. *Handicapped boy driven from school of horrors.*

As Bill and Toby talked about their move south, Jasper witnessed something of himself in Toby's manner. He couldn't put his finger on what it was. He liked this lad. There was something about him that Jasper warmed to. As he listened to their story, he felt ashamed of himself that he was here in a work capacity. It felt wrong.

'What's your new school called?'

'St Bede's, in Haslemere.'

'No way, I live in Haslemere and my wife works at the school.'

'What a coincidence,' Bill said, poking his finger into his ear and waggling it around.

'What do you enjoy doing Toby?'

'Football, painting.'

Bill removed his finger from his ear and inspected it.

'They're two very different hobbies,' Jasper said, watching Bill from the corner of his eye.

'I taught him how to play football when he was tiny. He's going to miss his team.'

'I run a team in Haslemere,' Jasper said in a cheery voice. 'I'm a coach. We're looking for more coaches, so if you're interested, Bill, you can join us and there's a team for Toby's age group.'

Jasper's enthusiasm was running away with him. He could see them having fun on the pitch and he knew Sandy would love Bill and Toby. He'd only been in their company for a couple of hours but there was something about them, they were special people. He wasn't sure why he felt that way, especially given Bill's manners. Maybe it was the fact that they'd been through so much. They were strong people and he admired that. He'd invite them round for dinner, get to know them, salvaging his guilt at taking advantage of their ordeal in order to sell their story.

'So, Toby,' Jasper asked as he watched Toby eat. 'Have you always used your feet to eat with?'

'I wore arms for a while. They were heavy and I hated them.'

BILL SAW the pain on Toby's face at the mention of the arms. Feeling the familiar wave of guilt every time Toby reminded him of how much pain he'd been in, Bill's heart slammed in his chest.

'I wanted him to look normal,' he said, justifying himself. 'But my wife thought Toby should have the freedom to discover how he wanted to do things. I wasn't giving him credit for his abilities. He's a bright boy and will find a way. He's had to try harder than the average person.' Bill glanced at Jasper's polished brown brogues. They looked handcrafted and had tiny punched holes. Expensive shoes, Bill sniffed. How could anything ever go wrong in *his* life, with footwear like that? Bill stared at his own feet, with toes popping out of his worn socks and remembered Rona's darning skills. He felt embarrassed and should have been wearing shoes for their visitor.

JASPER WATCHED Toby wash the dishes after they finished eating. He used his feet, in a bowl on the floor. He found it incredible how the boy was able to squirt washing up liquid into the bowl, cleaning the dishes with a cloth between his feet and it was great that Bill encouraged him to do jobs around the house.

'Using his feet is a way of life for him.'

'You made me wear my artificial arms, Dad,' he accused.

Looking sheepish, Bill rubbed his forehead, which glistened with grease under the ceiling light.

Bill tapped the table with his big sausage fingers, biting his lip. Jasper's heart went out to him. The poor man, he'd taken on the world.

'I just wanted you to look normal, I thought it would be better for you. I didn't want people staring at you. But your mother was right to get rid of them.'

'You were embarrassed by me.'

'No, never. I'm proud of you. You know that.'

Bill ruffled Toby's hair, but the expression on his face and the grey under his baggy eyes showed that he felt he was losing a battle.

'Okay, I'll admit, I hate it when people stare. Old people are the worst. You'd think they'd know better.'

'That must be hard,' Jasper said.

'Some of the comments are awful. Rona was determined to take him out and not to let it get to her. But there are some nasty comments.'

'Like what?' Jasper asked, incredulous.

'People would come up to her and say, you ought to be ashamed of yourself, taking that pill.'

Feeling comfortable in their home, Jasper poured himself a fresh cup of tea from the teapot that dominated the table. 'How did the arms work?' he asked, stirring milk into his tea.

'They were made in Germany and powered by compressed gas kept in cylinders on the child's back and were controlled by switches under the chin. We had various hospital visits when he was small. Thalidomide problems were so new and complex, doctors were unprepared. The shoulders of most thalidomide survivors weren't strong enough to use the type of arms that were already around, which were used predominantly by war veterans and others. They needed arms that powered themselves. Scientists worked frantically to come up with a prosthetic.'

'Did the arm work like a normal arm?'

Bill laughed and shook his head.

'If only. They were limiting. By then he'd already learned to write and eat, using his feet.'

'That's a shame, but I can see that you can do most things for yourself Toby.'

'Yes, I use my mouth or my feet.'

'Research is moving ahead all the time. We went to a demonstration of a bio-electronic limb. The components are made in Russia. It had a rechargeable battery that lasted three days and you could charge it overnight, but it only had one function, it could grip but it wasn't really that suitable for the thalidomide children,' Bill said.

'So, did you give up on the powered arms?'

'More or less. He refused to wear them.'

'They hurt me and gave me sores and bruises.'

'The doctors were more interested in showing off their wonderful invention and didn't see how the children struggled to use them. Idiots.'

Jasper pulled a face and scribbled notes.

'We took you to exercises,' Bill said, looking at Toby. 'They helped to strengthen your arms and we bought gadgets to help with everyday tasks. I used to enjoy making the odd thing in my shed too. But I don't have a shed anymore.' Bill's eyes misted over, and he stared off towards the wall.

Toby scurried off to gather a few of the gadgets, bringing them to show Jasper who was impressed by how good they were. Bill had made a wooden stick that attached to a plastic beaker and a stick to help Toby dress. Bill continued to stare at the wall, blinking when Toby jumped in front of him.

'We lost you there.' Jasper smiled.

'Sorry, I was thinking about our home. And what we lost in the fire.' A look of defeat haunted Bill's face. 'I also fitted a new lock on the front door so that it was lower down and altered the door so that the lock was set on a wooden plinth making it easier for Toby to open, using his mouth.'

'Until Mum died, I prayed every night for my arms to grow. But what's the point? God can't stop people dying - even mums. I don't believe in miracles anymore. Or Santa. Last year we didn't put out a mince pie.'

'Who told you to pray for new arms?' Astonished, Bill's mouth fell open.

'I don't know. It might have been the vicar.'

. 'Which vicar?'

'Probably the same man who dressed up as Santa.'

'I don't remember him, but I rarely go to church. Bloody hypocrites. That makes my blood boil.'

'He did say it Dad, God's honest truth.'

'I believe you.'

'I guess you could complain.' Jasper suggested.

'Oh, what's the point, they're a law unto themselves, the bloody Church. I've enough battles to fight without adding to the list.'

'That must have been a horrible ordeal you both went through?' Jasper was referring to the recent bullying at school.

'Toby sees the world, not quite through rose tinted glasses, but he thinks that people are mostly kind, which they are, but there are the occasional nasty bullies that ruin things for other children, particularly vulnerable children like Toby.

'He's always spoken to everybody and people are generally very sympathetic and understanding towards him, and so it was a terrible shock. But he'd been bullied for a long time and I didn't know what was going on. He tried to be brave and handle it himself, but it only got worse. I wish I'd known what was going on, I could have done something. I feel so helpless.'

'I did tell you I didn't want to go to that school anymore.'

'You kept getting tummy ache and I thought it was nerves. I had no idea.'

'I wanted to move school, but you wouldn't let me.'

'We chose the school because we thought you'd be happy there. We had long discussions with the headmaster. I wanted you to be with local kids.'

'Well it didn't do much good'

'At primary school the children accepted the way you were, but at secondary school it was down to a few children who wouldn't accept you. That's their problem. They're just ignorant people.'

Jasper raised his eyebrows in agreement but stayed silent.

'Even if I had listened to you, I'm not sure what good it would have done moving school. I always think if you've got problems, you're just shunting them to a new place.' Bill sniffed and wiped his hand across his nose. 'Problems need to be tackled head on.'

Jasper listened without interrupting as father and son argued it out, and when they fell silent, they looked to him for inspiration.

Feelings were running high and Jasper changed the subject. 'Okay, tell me how things were when you were younger. What's your first memory Toby?'

Toby's eyes lit up. 'Knocking a conker from a tree in the park. Do you remember Dad?'

'No.'

Toby looked disappointed as if it mattered greatly to him that Bill could remember. 'It wasn't fair that other boys could knock them down and I couldn't. I was desperate to have a conker fight. But one day I took Mum's rolling pin from the kitchen and flung at the tree. It got lodged in the branches but loads of conkers fell.'

'Conkers are great fun.' Jasper smiled. 'And what's your favourite football team?'

'Man United.'

'No way, mine too.' And the conversation flowed from there.

By the end of the day Jasper felt compelled to tell Bill about the child he'd lost. It was right to tell him. He thought that it would bolster Bill's confidence, to know that he'd been fortunate, despite the loss of his wife, to have such a lovely kid— a strong and healthy kid. But when he told Bill his story, beyond asking a few questions, Bill didn't comment and seemed keen to change the subject. Embarrassed by his reaction, Jasper wished he'd kept it to himself. He felt like an idiot.

BILL SAID GOODBYE TO JASPER. He waited on the doorstep, watching as Jasper opened the gate, turning to wave, as he headed in the direction of the station, his briefcase swaying by his side. Bill kept his eyes on him until he disappeared from view, a cold chill creeping up his spine. Something didn't feel right, but he couldn't put his finger what it was. He shrugged, went back into the house but it wasn't until he was in the bathroom cleaning his teeth much later on that his thoughts became clearer. Was he mistaken or was there a resemblance between Toby and Jasper? He wouldn't have given it a moment's thought if Jasper hadn't mentioned losing his own child. He scrubbed his teeth longer than normal trying to work out why he'd seen a resemblance but as he spat the frothing paste into the sink, he chastised himself for being stupid. His mind was playing tricks. He was just tired and under a lot of stress.

36

1973

Sandy

When Sandy joined St Bede's as a volunteer, she was given a guided tour of the school and the background to the school was explained to her. St. Bede's was founded in the early twentieth century by a woman's inspiration to improve the lives of cripples who would have been discarded by society. It provided education, care and support to children with complex physical handicaps. Historically it charted and catered for a succession of conditions from rickets, polio and spina bifida to cerebral palsy and thalidomide. It was a former Victorian school but by 1973 had spread to five buildings, with further plans to expand. It had a residential block, classrooms and a church.

Set behind an imposing iron gate and surrounded by beautiful views over wild and open heathland— nestled in the Surrey Hills— it was remote and out on a limb with only two buses a day passing its gates. It was difficult to get staff because it was so remote and vacancies could take months to fill. A few of the teachers cycled in and one of the nurses took a train and a bus. Whatever their means of transport, the cost of getting there had to be factored in and tended to put some candidates off. But the world came to St Bede's through many routes, not least through its army of committed volunteers and Sandy was one of them. Some staff transferred from renowned institutions like Great Ormond Street Hospital for Children and they experienced two vastly contrasting places of work, but everybody who worked there loved St Bede's because it was quirky, an enclave set apart from the rest of society. It was an odd place that attracted odd characters and was a special home in the minds and the hearts of all who worked there. St Bede's did remarkable things for the children suffering from the consequences of many physical problems.

Even when Sandy was an outsider living in Haslemere, she was conscious of the importance of St Bede's. Not only were there reminders through the many people in the surrounding villages who worked there, but there were also collecting tins on the counters of local shops, jumble sales and other events raising money for their cause, as well as the coverage in the local press and there were occasional royal visits. Word got around the village that Sandy was a model and she was asked to take part in a charity event and from that first event, having given birth to a thalidomide baby in the early sixties herself, she was curious and keen to become involved with St Bede's.

Noticing a small wooden ladder on the desk of each child, Sandy smiled to herself as she entered the classroom. She was helping out for the morning and there were six children in the class, each with different physical needs but all mentally capable. From the beginning of St Bede's each child was encouraged to be responsible for their own future. Each child built a toy ladder and no matter how badly handicapped they were or how crude the result, they always had that ladder and kept it in front of them in class and it was a symbol of the ladder of life. Every rung represented an obstacle which had to be overcome in order to reach the final goal. Today's lesson was about aspirations and building self-confidence. Sandy slipped into a chair next to a thalidomide boy who had no limbs.

Sandy thought that some of the teachers were tough in their approach to attempting to build resilience in the children and the teacher standing in front of the class was one of those.

'You are what you are, and you have to make the best of it. The human being who does not use his or her skills is less than human, but the one who makes the very best of his or her incomplete self, excels.'

The teacher went around the classroom asking each child what their greatest skill was, something they were most proud of. One child without arms or legs said that she could paint with her mouth, another child with no arms said he wanted to be an athlete, and another sang in the school choir. Every child in the room had something to be proud of. One child hesitated for a few moments and breaking into a smile said, 'My smile, because friends always say it makes them feel happy.'

The teacher wrote on the board the words *I can*.

'There's no such word as can't. You can all do something,' she said. 'And, do that well.'

After the lesson, Sandy wandered through the school. In the early 1960s, she had been told, St Bede's gained a reputation for being an experimental centre where the most modern artificial limbs were made for thalidomide victims. Thalidomide came with a new set of treatment problems and medicine and science had to find ways to help the children adjust to their limb deficiencies. The armless children were good at using their feet and would eat and write with their toes. There were a few children without hearing or ears. St Bede's was experimenting with hearing aids and false ears, in order to give them a 'normal' appearance. They were stuck on with double-sided tape but often came off.

Sandy peered through the glass door into the sewing room where teachers and children were busy at work experimenting with different types of clothing to make it easier for the children to dress themselves. As a former model she was interested in fashion and gave her thoughts on fabrics and designs. Many of the girls found it difficult to put the uniforms on, which were difficult to wear and they weren't very flattering because of the nature of their disabilities. The sewing room was making pinafore dresses with front zips and they were using a great modern invention, Velcro, to fasten bras, shirts and shoes.

'Sandy, there you are.' Mrs Jones, the headteacher called as she entered the corridor, the swing doors flapping behind her. In many ways she was the archetypal, quintessential headmistress you might find in a children's novel. She was tall and dull, respectable and plain. Strict and stern, Mrs Jones could quell the unruliest classroom with her frown. Her mild rebukes, 'You can do better, dear,' were delivered with a patient sigh. Despite her dreariness and regimented ways, she transformed into a different person on stage, delivering stirring speeches to an assembly hall of voracious children. 'One day you will leave school,' her speeches began, 'and go out into the world as young people. Take your thirsty minds, kind hearts and a will to be the best you can be, given your unfortunate circumstances. Let your disability open your eyes to see your true abilities and use those skills and abilities wisely.'

'Lovely weather today.' Sandy smiled.

Mrs Jones grabbed Sandy's arm, making her feel as if she was about to be reprimanded for a misdemeanour.

'Come, follow me,' she said brusquely.

When they were out of the corridor she stopped. 'I've got somebody coming in an hour for an interview. It's for the post of school nurse that we've been advertising. It's so tricky filling vacancies because of the transport issue.'

'How can I help?'

'I want you to be on the panel of interviewers.'

Mrs Jones, recognising Sandy's personable manner often

asked her to be involved in interviewing candidates. It was good practice, she told Sandy to have a representative of the local community on the panel.

As they walked through the gardens, Mrs Jones filled her in with the details. 'She has a good career record. She doesn't drive. My only doubt is that she will get fed up with trekking over here.'

MARION INTRODUCED HERSELF; first to Mrs Jones and then to Mr Lee the deputy head and Sandy.

After the interview, Marion was told to wait outside the office while the panel of interviewers made their decision. When they were ready they called her back in.

'We think you'll be perfect for the job,' Mrs Jones told her. 'We would like you to start next week.'

37

1973

Marion

Marion had found out about the job at St Bede's through her Blackpool friend, Linda. The panel were impressed that Marion had worked for Doctor Simon Gerard at the mother-and-baby home in London. They had seen the recent article in *The Sunday Telegraph* about him winning The Doctor of The Year Award in obstetrics. Little did they know that she'd had an affair with him. Marion smiled to herself thinking of all the occasions they had got away with making love in the broom cupboard.

It would be interesting to work at St Bede's, in close proximity to Bill and Toby. She had felt her campaign of revenge slipping away when Rona died, but it had been fun to remind Bill of what he and Rona had done, kidnapping a baby.

Marion despised the dark side of herself - but the hatred inside herself was overpowering. Sneaking around inside Bill's garden after dark was one thing but tampering with Bill's oven was something that even she realised was going one step too far. She could make it end right now. It had been going on so long. This was her chance to make it - just stop. The monsters inside her mind made her do wicked things. She could have killed them both. She was like a rat trapped in a drain. For years she had been stuck. The drain ended in darkness. But now there was light at the end of that drain. If she took a job at the school, she could watch children playing - handicapped children, hidden from society and the troubles they faced. She had something in common with them. She too wanted to run from her demons.

MARION REMEMBERED how she'd met Linda for the first time - in a cafe along Blackpool's Golden Mile, several years ago. If it hadn't been for Linda's recent nugget of information about Bill moving to Surrey, Marion's summers in Blackpool would have carried on indefinitely. She would miss its brashness, the absurdness of Blackpool Tower dominating the landscape and the seafront awash in a myriad of colours all glitzy and brash. She'd felt compelled to return, year in year out, when she could have got on with her life, putting everything behind her and taken a package tour to Spain.

There was no need to go back to the brash capital of the north now. Soon everything she needed would be right there in front of her - apart from the man she loved. She'd never have Simon, but there was a glimmer of hope that one day they would be together. She truly loved him, always had and that meant never letting go, despite the situation being as tough as it was. She couldn't forget him, she'd tried and failed so many times. Even though it had been over twelve years.

Wedged into a narrow space next to the window, on the train from Haslemere back to London, the job offer was in her handbag, she cast her mind back to how she'd met Linda, in Joe's cafe, on Blackpool seafront. Wherever Marion travelled to, more than museums, monuments, temples or churches, she sought out cafes. Joe's cafe gave her a good vantage point to people watch, but there were only two people she had ever wanted to watch. Rona and Toby. Marion had followed Bill and Toby into the cafe several times wearing a scarf around her head, sitting at a nearby table, listening to their conversation above the din of crockery and the tinkle of cutlery.

The cafe wasn't anything special, but it was her favourite postcard scribbling spot and space to relax and contemplate her next move and gather thoughts. The floor was a yellow and white checked boarded lino and the tables were Formica. The rod holding a net curtain covering the lower part of one of the windows had broken and nobody had bothered to fix it. The gooey, old-fashioned cakes reminded her of her nan's kitchen, and the smell of bacon, the sizzle of sausages and a builder's mug of tea drew her back time and again. The window ledge displayed a row of dusty plastic knickerbocker glories, the colours of the fruit and ice cream long faded and doing nothing to entice customers.

'May I borrow your ketchup?' Marion had asked the woman at the next table.

'I don't think there's much left, but yes, of course.'

'Staff are too busy.' Marion glanced over at the counter where the owner and his wife were bickering about an order.

'Service isn't what it used to be.'

'Are you on holiday or do you live here?'

The conversation with Linda had flowed from there. And then one day during the summer, she discovered she had a connection with Linda.

'Sometimes I wish my mother would just give up and move into a care home,' Linda confided. 'She's ninety-five but refuses to give up her independence. She's bloody hard work at times. She called a builder in to make some changes to the house, three years ago. But if you ask me,' she said, glancing round conspiratorially, 'he took advantage of her because she's old. He did a shoddy job.'

There had to be hundreds of builders in the Blackpool area, but Marion's interest was piqued. 'What's his name?' she asked casually.

'Bill Murphy.'

Taking a nerve-steadying sip of tea, Marion tried not to sound too interested.

'Tell me more.'

'I don't feel as if I can complain, but I'd like to.'

'If he's done a shoddy job then you must complain. Get him to come back. Mind you, three years is a long time ago.'

So, he wasn't the perfect builder that Rona had made him out to be, all those years ago when she'd worked with Marion at the mother-and-baby home. This information could be useful, Marion thought, as she stirred more sugar into her tea.

'I can't. The poor man's been through so much. I kept going to confront him, but somehow I couldn't pluck up the courage to approach him. He probably thought I was a stalker and thinks I'm a nutcase looking up at his house, too afraid to approach.'

'His personal life isn't your concern.'

'I know. But I'm too soft. His wife recently died of cancer, leaving him to bring up their disabled son.'

There was no doubting this was the same Bill Murphy. 'It's negligence. Your mother could have had an accident. Sorry, it's none of my business. I'm probably overreacting. Shoddy work you say?' Marion frowned.

'And he had a house fire. The poor chap's had a lot on his plate.'

'It's still not your problem,' Marion said dismissively, feeling a surge of annoyance that made her want to take revenge on Linda's behalf.

'The dreadful thing was, I watched his house burn. I'd just been visiting a friend who lives around the corner from him.'

'Don't you go feeling sorry for him.'

'That's a bit heartless.'

The comment hung in the air like a piece of rope and then, after years of holding it all in, something popped inside Marion. 'The man's a criminal.' She stopped and clamped her mouth shut, stopping more words from escaping.

Linda leaned in, her lips twisting.

'Hang on, lady, those are strong words. You've never met him.'

A moment ago, it had seemed she was going to open up, but the shutters were down and all Marion could do was stare into her egg and chips.

'I think you need to explain,' Linda whispered.

'I've said too much.'

Marion prepared to leave the cafe but as she stood, Linda stood too, their eyes locked as if preparing for a showdown.

'Stay for a while.' Linda said.

Trancelike Marion sat, pushing the plate to one side and covering her face with her hands. After a moment of silence, she uncovered them and with a wariness in her voice she whispered, 'Okay.'

'Go on.'

'You've got to swear to me not to tell a soul.'

'You have my word.'

Marion was very still, looking beyond Linda towards the sea, hesitating. 'How can I trust you?'

'If you don't feel comfortable telling me then don't, but if you don't, I'll continue to sympathise with Bill's plight.'

Words were rearranging themselves in Marion's head. 'I worked with his wife, Rona, years ago at a mother-and-baby home in North London.'

'Really?'

'It was during the late fifties, early sixties. We delivered two or three babies with missing limbs. They weren't expected to live. The doctor I worked with, Doctor Simon Gerard, considered it kinder to let nature take its course.'

'How do you mean?'

'He ordered Rona to put a baby in the cold room, on the windowsill, effectively to die.'

'That's shocking.'

'You have to remember what it was like back then. They didn't expect thalidomides to live. The truth came out much later. Sometimes babies were so deformed that they didn't survive. Of those who lived, half died before they were one.'

'And did the baby die?'

'No, he's very much alive. His name's Toby and he lives with Bill.'

'Bill's son?'

'Only in name. Rona refused to let him die. She made Dr Gerard falsify birth papers and write a death certificate for the authorities. She planned it all. She escaped with the baby that night. Until this day it's been our secret.'

'Why would a doctor go along with that? If he'd been found out he would have lost his job. My God, he risked everything.'

The light left Marion's eyes and she looked away, the dull ache in her heart returned. 'Because of me.' Taking a deep intake of breath, she prepared for the next stage of her speech. 'I was having an affair with the doctor. Rona saw us together. In fact, she caught us in the broom cupboard.'

Linda burst out laughing and finding the funny side to her story, Marion joined in.

'You come across as so prim and proper, who would believe it?' Linda spluttered.

'I was committed to him; he just wasn't committed to me. He was the love of my life. Sadly, he was married.'

'Oh, one of them.'

Thinking of Simon made Marion's eyes water, but she sniffed her tears away.

'Men, they think through their dicks.'

'That bloody woman Rona, she held him over a barrel, threatening to expose our affair if he didn't falsify the papers and let her take the baby.'

'It sounds as if she was desperate for a baby, poor woman.'

'Yeah well, we've all been desperate, it doesn't mean we steal to get what we want. Whatever her reasons, I can't condone what she did.'

'Look at it this way. She was rescuing the baby.'

'He was the boss. She should have followed his orders. When you work in a hospital you learn to park your emotions at the front door. You can't get involved.'

'But we're all human. She acted from the heart.'

'Whose side are you on?'

'It's not about taking sides.'

AND HERE SHE WAS NOW, a couple of months on from the conversation with Linda in Joe's. As Marion stared out of the train window, she wished she hadn't opened up to Linda, but a burden had been lifted from her and one good thing had come out of the conversation. Bill had returned to make the repairs to Linda's mother's house. It had felt good to spill the secret to someone. And if Bill hadn't told Linda about St Bede's she would never have known that Bill and Toby were moving to St Bede's.

As Marion stepped off the train back in London – having enjoyed her interview and tour of St Bede's and very much looking forward to her new job - she thought about Simon. When she'd read the article in *The Sunday Telegraph* she had been absolutely livid. How on earth did somebody like him win an award? He had a brusque manner with his patients, but more to the point he had ordered a nurse to put a handicapped baby in a cold room to die and then allowed the midwife to kidnap the baby. She had to confront him. He couldn't get away with what he'd done and he'd torched her insides for too long. The need for revenge was like a rat gnawing at her soul, it was relentless. Revenge was sweet, but spiteful. Old scores needed to be settled. Unless she did, the monsters in her mind would never be hushed.

38

1973

Sandy

It was a wet Friday afternoon, a relentless downpour pelting the ground so loudly it almost drowned out the teacher's voice as she addressed the class. The children, used to spending lots of time outside at St Bede's, were stir-crazy, for it had rained all week. The teachers were trying to keep them engaged and the focus for the week was on preparation for the annual festival, to be held at the end of the term. There was going to be a music concert, a flower show in the chapel, an art exhibition, a disco, a barbecue and a display of old photographs.

In the afternoon the weather brightened up. The rain stopped and the sun came out and the children were excited as the build-up began when their parents would come to pick them up to take them home for the weekend. This happened at four o' clock, but Sandy had come to dread Friday afternoons because a straggle of children stayed, waiting on the sidelines as the others left, their parents never turned up for them and the look on their faces was heartbreaking. Some parents didn't come for weeks and there was no phone call to say when they would visit. It was disruptive and unsettling for the children.

'Some families can't face having children with limb deficiencies at home, so they're left here at weekends,' Elizabeth, one of the teachers, told Sandy.

Walking in the gardens at the end of the school day the two women had grown close to each other and enjoyed their strolls, sharing thoughts and bouncing ideas around. Occasionally they met for coffee outside of St Bede's at the weekends and Sandy enjoyed Elizabeth's company, particularly when Jasper was away.

'I find it very upsetting when I see Edward or Sally not picked up for the third or fourth Friday in a row. It's not fair. An institution can't replace a family,' Sandy mused. She felt that she could trust Elizabeth and opened up to her about what she thought of the school without fear of it getting around.

'Weekly boarding is better, I agree.'

'I guess it's too far for some families to come every week to pick their child up.'

'There is a strong move in the country to get handicapped people to be looked after locally but, as things stand, the services are inadequate, so we plough on doing our best.'

'I'm not saying you don't do great work here. You're an amazing place, offering a great service for children with severe physical handicaps-- but there's something missing. This place can't replace home and family.'

'I agree, they are deprived of a normal family life. Some of them never know when their parents will visit. They're left waiting and wondering every Friday afternoon.'

'It's almost as if you are a refuge for these children, as if they would be homeless otherwise.'

'And it doesn't help that we are isolated.'

'I'd like to take them out and show them the town or go

down to the seaside. It would be great to take them home with me.'

Elizabeth laughed. 'You're ambitious I'll give you that. I love your spirit, it's what we need here, but I don't think that would be practical.'

'I don't see why not. I could take one or two out at a time. I've seen the limbless ones transferring on a banana board into cars.'

'Some of the children have medical issues, requiring medication or treatment every few hours. Some have had operations. A few thalidomides have had rods put in their backs to straighten them and stop them toppling over and others have had spinal cord corrections. We have to be careful. It would be a big responsibility.'

'I can cope with whatever is thrown at me. There's no reason why some of the children couldn't go out for an afternoon with me. Sally is cooped up here for weeks at a time. Her parents rarely visit. And I can't remember when I last saw John's parents.'

'You've got a point. I'll discuss things with the Head, but I can't promise.'

'Thank you. I just want to help.'

'I know you do,' she said smiling. 'I was the same when I first came here. I used to take children out on my days off because I felt sorry for them, like you do. But they were much younger then and it was easier. I took more children than I should have done, piling them along the back seat of my car. I loved it. I'd take them to my house and play with them in the back garden. I had to take them straight into the house so that the neighbours didn't stare. I couldn't give a damn, but with being cushioned here, they aren't used to being stared at. My house was a change of scene and somewhere to escape to. I wanted my home to be somewhere they could relax and have some fun, away from this place, which after all is just an institution. What I was doing felt useless, but it was the only thing I could think of to do. It wasn't easy. One child fell onto her face and broke a few teeth. She was using crutches. We had to return to the school immediately.'

'What did you do with the children in your house?'

'We baked biscuits and watched TV. On sunny days they played in the garden or played hide and seek in the house, shuffling around the furniture on their bottoms. It was amusing to see.'

'Why did you stop taking them home?'

Elizabeth came to a halt under an apple tree as if in deep thought and with a grave face looked at Sandy. 'One of the children thought that I was going to adopt her. There were several times when she came alone. I don't know where she got the idea from, but it made me very wary. These children are vulnerable, we must never forget that. I thought I was doing good but actually in some ways I was encouraging their dependence on me. I was filling a void their parents couldn't fill. We become like second parents, but we mustn't see ourselves as parents, we're paid staff, we have to be detached. We're here to gently encourage their independence.'

'Yes, it's all very sad.'

'That little girl, Sally, has a hard time of it. We often chat. She doesn't like going home, her mother's harsh with her. She expects her to be presentable by wearing her prosthetics when the poor girl hates wearing them. She's told quite categorically by her mother, '"When you come home you've go to wear your arms and legs."' She tells her mother, 'But I don't want to wear them today.' Sadly, she has to do what her mother wants, otherwise she doesn't get collected on a Friday afternoon.'

Head-to-head in conversation as they crunched their way around the rain drenched path, the women arrived at a bench on the south side of the gardens.

'It's a bit wet to sit down.'

'No problem,' Sandy said, pulling a cotton scarf from her bag to wipe the seat.

'So how did the interview go the other day?' Elizabeth asked, avoiding the area of the bench that Sandy hadn't wiped. 'Did they fill the position?'

'Yes, a nice lady with a background in nursing who also trained as a medical secretary. She's called Marion and she's perfect.'

'Where did she work before?'

'Well bizarrely our paths may have crossed, although I don't remember her. She worked in the mother-and-baby home where I gave birth twelve years ago to a thalidomide baby with no arms.' Sandy explained.

'Really? That's a strange coincidence.'

'It's unnerved me, to be honest, it's all I've thought about since meeting her, I can't wait until she starts.'

'It can't have been easy losing a baby.'

An image of the baby, tiny and lifeless in her hands, snapped before Sandy's eyes, then it was gone. Over time that image changed, faded and blurred. It had the same effect on her now as it did all those years ago, emptying her of everything, hollowing her from the inside.

'I never got to see him. That was the hardest part. It's the not knowing. I took the doctor's words at face value but a part of me doesn't believe he died. I have this sense that he's alive and out there somewhere. We put all our faith in doctors, too much sometimes. It wasn't as if the doctor offered any comforting words. He was blunt, his manner was brusque and that just added to the pain that I felt. I know it sounds stupid, but I would have liked the chance to hold him to believe that he was dead. I feel cheated. I know that I was going to have him adopted anyway, but that's not the point. I carried him for nine months, I had a bond with him. I had feelings––I still do–– and they'll never go away. I just want a sense of closure and meeting that woman might bring me closure to my baby. I've pinned all my hopes on chatting to her. I don't know what she can tell me. Nothing I expect. I mean, how many babies were born in that place during that year?'

Sandy could remember the day he was born so clearly, the 1st of February 1961. The weather was unusually mild for the time of year. JF Kennedy was President of America. The memory of JFK and his tragic death two years later was linked in her mind with the tragic death of her son, except that her baby's death didn't matter to the world at large, but JFK's death was still plastered across newspapers and magazines and still talked about years later.

Elvis Presley's gravelly voice singing 'Are You Lonesome Tonight?' played on the radio in the ward, the words seeping into her troubled mind because they echoed how she felt in the hours and days to follow. 'Is your heart filled with pain?'

'Yes, but how many had deformities and how many had no arms, like your son?'

'Whether she'd remember though.'

'You'd be surprised what people remember.'

'I know I'm being daft, pinning all my hopes on her. I'm living in a fantasy world.'

'Have you talked to anybody about how you feel? A professional? It can't be doing you any good bottling it up inside. What does your husband think?'

Sandy sighed. Jasper. She didn't want to consider how it had affected their marriage and how she'd pushed aside his desire for a family. She knew she was being selfish but as the years went by it was harder to imagine their lives with a child in it.

'It affected me so badly that I aborted our next baby. I couldn't face going through all that again.'

'Your next baby will be healthy.'

'There won't be a next time. I was one of the first women to have an abortion, it was soon after the law changed.'

'Is that why you bought a dog?'

'Yes, is it that obvious?'

'And I'm guessing Jasper isn't best pleased with a canine replacement for a child?'

'You have a habit of hitting everything right on the nail. I don't know what to do Liz. I had no idea when I bought him, that Jasper wasn't keen animals.'

'What's there to hate about puppies? I'm looking forward to meeting him. Who's looking after him while you're here?'

'My neighbour. She's very helpful. I think it's driven a wedge between Jasper and I. I need the dog. I need something small to love.'

'Are you absolutely sure you won't want another baby at some point? You can't reverse the body clock once it starts to tick. Think how things will be in old age. So many people decide they don't want kids but regret it years later when there's nobody to visit them in the care home and loneliness kicks in.'

'The dog's all I need right now, I'm certain of that, but I feel cruel making the decision for both of us, knowing that Jasper wants a child more are than anything in the world.'

'Take your time,' Liz said, patting Sandy's leg. 'Don't be too hasty, that's my penny's worth.'

39

1973

Marion

Marion sat in the garden at the end of her shift, taking in her new surroundings and relaxing in the late sun before heading home. She liked working at St. Bede's. Staring at the blue sky scribbled with gauzy clouds, her eyes were drawn to two squirrels engaged in a territorial dispute in a nearby tree, chasing and nipping each other across the branches in a spiraling pattern, their bushy tails sweeping the bark like dusters on furniture. Fascinated by them, she watched their small bodies, marveling at their speed and agility, so perfectly adapted to their environment. Nature was a wonderful thing. If only humans could be like that she mused, moving through the tree of life in such graceful fashion, pushing past obstacles in such an effortless way, climbing to the pinnacle, achieving all of the things they wanted to achieve. If only her life had followed a predictable pattern, instead of everything that wasn't supposed to happen happening, and all of the things she'd wanted were snatched from her. Things should have been very different. All she'd wanted was security, stability, a home filled with happy children and a loving husband. These simple things were so hard to achieve.

She saw a small olive-brown warbler flitting through trees and shrubs, with a distinctive tail-wagging movement and light chirrup carried on the breeze. Being among the flora and fauna at the end of the day helped her to think and gave her a brief respite from the tortuous thoughts. She basked in the warmth of the low sun that kissed her face. A series of smoke trails criss-crossed the sky. She thought how wonderful it would be to be one of the plane's passengers––to be transported into another existence, away from the demons that troubled her. Closing her eyes, she emptied her mind and let the warmth of the sun take away the pain. She shut out dreams of happiness and contentment; it was too late for those. She was old and weary. She forced herself to focus on the present - she'd make do with what she had. This was where she would spend her days. And she was happy here.

Her eyes abruptly snapped open and she let out a small gasp. *I will not allow them to win.* Simon will pay for what he did. She'd allowed him to trap her and make her feel desperate all of these years, her mind brittle and damaged. She'd lived her life his prisoner, his captive, interred against her will and if she continued to be his prisoner, she'd go mad.

From behind her, she heard the crunch of leaves, somebody was making their way through the clearing. She turned to see who it was.

'Sandy, how nice, want to join me? I was just enjoying the peace at the end of my shift.'

'I saw you come down here and hadn't had the chance to get to know you yet, after being on the interview panel. It's a busy place, the weeks fly by.'

In a cloud of floral perfume, Sandy joined her on the rickety bench.

'How are you getting on?' She smiled at Marion.

'Good thank you. I like it here. It's very different to other places I've worked.'

They'd only spoken briefly in the staffroom between lessons, snippets of conversation that lasted minutes. It would be nice to get to know this beautiful woman. She always wore flowing dresses and her make-up was perfectly applied. But Marion was guarded, wary of people judging her and not wanting to reveal too much about her life so soon. It was easier that way and it seemed to her that this woman had it all. Beyond her smiles and her warmth there was something about her that Marion was intimidated by.

'I noticed on your CV that you worked in a mother-and-baby home in North London,' Sandy said.

'Yes, for many years.'

Sandy twisted her hands in her lap. Marion sensed that she had something that she wanted to share.

'Were you there in February 1961?'

Marion froze. 'I'm not sure.' She tried to keep the wariness out of her voice.

'I gave birth to a baby there. He was a thalidomide baby, he had no arms. Sadly, he died.'

'I'm sorry, that must have been a very painful time.'

Marion leaned down and carefully bent the stalk of a nearby flower towards her face, its velvet red petals yielding to her touch and the light scent wafting up. She opened her fingers and released the thin stem before sitting back and wondering where the conversation was leading.

'Yes, it was, but there are so many unanswered questions that I have in my head. Sometimes I think I'm going mad.'

She barely knew this woman and yet she was revealing her inner fears. Thinking it was better to listen than comment, Marion stayed silent, fixing her eyes on a distant tree, as a range of emotions coursed through her veins as the lie reared its ugly head again. Her stomach knotting, she reminded herself there were several handicapped babies born around that time. But only one on the 1st February.

Scared to ask and with her innards twisting, she forced herself. 'What date in February?'

'The first.'

It was a date that Marion would never forget, as if it was carved across her palm. Along with the day that Kennedy was shot, and Neil Armstrong stepped on the moon, this was a day committed to memory. It was the day when everything in her life changed. 'I might have been away, I don't remember. I'm sorry.'

'It doesn't matter, it was a long shot.'

In the minutes that followed, they filled the silence with a spray of words about the view that served no purpose other than to cover the awkward atmosphere that had settled between them.

'If you ever want to talk, I'm a good listener,' Marion offered.

'The doctor told me he'd died. His named was Doctor Simon Gerard. I only know his name because I recently saw an article about him. He's won an award. I didn't get to see my baby. Without the physical evidence how do I know he really died? I smell his scent, even though I never smelled him. I wanted to hold him and kiss him and say goodbye. I hope his very short life was for a purpose. People tell me I should forget it happened, that he was handicapped so it was a blessing, but it doesn't feel like a blessing. I imagine him and what he would be like if he'd lived.'

Marion just listened as she watched the light fade from the woman's eyes, her body slumping forward as she spoke, years spent festering over what might have been had drained all her energy and strength. Marion wanted to say something to make her feel better, but the damage was done. Marion's lips twisted but no words came, for there was nothing she could say that would take the pain away. But the campaign she'd embarked on, instilling fear in Rona for all those years, went some way to bring justice.

'I'm sorry,' was all she could manage. But sorry fixed nothing, it didn't cut it.

'No, I'm sorry, for unburdening myself. I'm quite a private person. It's just that when I read that you'd worked there, I thought you might remember something.'

40

1973

Marion

It was several days after her chat with Sandy in the garden at St Bede's and after making her mind up – particularly after hearing about his award - Marion prepared to confront Simon. She had seen his picture recently, in a medical journal. He had been promoted. It wasn't right. How did a doctor like him get to be promoted?

A few days after coming to her decision, she headed to London on her day off. Over the years she'd come to enjoy surprising people. Surprises took careful planning and she had plenty of experience in that department. It was her forte, a skill she'd honed over the years. Flowers left on Rona's doorstep, with no message attached. A letter on her table. A card. Cryptic messages. She called it the sweet medicine of revenge. Anything to warm her soul and give meaning to her existence. She was the last person that Simon would be expecting. They hadn't spoken in years.

Stepping off the train at Waterloo, Marion joined the throng of people flowing towards the exit. Marveling at the gigantic Victorian edifice and the frenetic hustle and bustle, she realised how much she missed working in London. This was in complete contrast to the slow pace of life in sleepy Haslemere where dandelions on the station verges and the whiff of cow poo greeted her. Passing so many different faces, colour and activity, everywhere she looked something was going on. It was a hive of activity, there was no time or head space for loneliness. There were stalls selling flowers and newspapers, commuters checking watches and glancing up at the station clock, ladies in pretty pastel coloured coats and pigeons swooping.

It was twelve years, since she'd stepped inside the mother-and-baby home. She knew that he still worked between the home and the adjacent hospital and probably from the same office, on the ground floor of the home to the right of the entrance.

On the bus, Marion sat on the top deck craning her neck as they passed solicitors, accountants and architects' premises. When the road dipped, they turned a corner and St Agnes came into view, the bus coming to a halt on a tree-lined avenue.

Standing on the pavement outside St Agnes, Marion gazed at the familiar wrought iron gates and the building beyond. It was a former lunatic asylum. The building overlooked a park where she and Simon had taken snatched lunchtime walks together, kissing between the trees where they were thickest and away from the prying eyes of onlookers. Marion noticed new flower beds in a swirly pattern close to the pavement and a couple of new benches under the ancient oak tree that stood in the middle of the lawn.

The familiar creak of the gate sent memories scudding through her mind. She had never failed to be amazed by the strength of mothers pushing with all their might to bring babies into the world and it had been a privilege to witness each miracle, a tiny bundle in its mother's arms waiting to make its mark. She remembered the joy of birth and being enthralled to see new life starting out, but it was always tinged with flecks of sadness that she was denied the miracle for herself.

A set of steps led to wooden doors and Marion went in, managing to avoid the woman on the reception, behind a glass panel. She had her back to Marion and was jabbering away to somebody as she waved a file around. Sneaking past the reception in big strides she headed towards Simon's office. An aluminium door plaque affirmed that Dr Simon Gerard still occupied the office which was halfway down the corridor and opposite the broom cupboard where they'd been caught scantily clad by Rona on one occasion. With nobody in the corridor her luck was in, she'd chosen a good time to visit and––taking the plunge, with her heart hammering in her chest, she knocked on the door.

'Come in.'

Fighting her anxiety, she was lost for words.

'You.'

The room was the same as she remembered. It was a light office with a large window and a black-and-white lino floor. Its white walls gave it a surgical appearance. Books, mainly medical manuals lined the left wall and information posters adorned the right wall, some were old and curled at the edges. Simon sat at his desk.

The shock registering in his voice drained all volume from it and his face turned a shade of grey. Digestive biscuit crumbs were gathering in his moustache. How many times had she asked him to get rid of his moustache? Still, why did it matter, they were over a long time ago.

'Long time no see, thought I'd pay you a visit, Doctor Gerard,' she said, giving emphasis to his title in a sarcastic tone. A proper doctor wouldn't behave as he had.

'I've got an appointment in five minutes, this had better be quick.'

His eyes anchored themselves on her and his hands were

clasped on the desk in front of him. His face had a sour expression as he looked at her in disbelief.

'Thought you'd never see me again, didn't you?'

'I hoped I never would,' he sneered. 'I see the years haven't been kind to you.'

'You can't hurt me with your cruel words any longer. And you don't get away with what you did to me that easily.'

'What do you want?'

'My money for a start. I see you've been promoted. You can pay me back. That money was supposed to be for us. I want to move, and I need it for my retirement.' She should have asked him for her money years ago, but stupidly a part of her had harboured the thought that one day he would come back to her.

'Why have you waited till now?'

'I want it back.'

'Well, I don't have it.'

'Fine, I'll go to the police then.'

'And what do you think they'll do?'

'Take you in for questioning.'

He laughed. 'It was a gift. I didn't want to take it. It was your bloody money, you insisted I take it.'

'You took advantage. That money was supposed to make things easier so that we could get together.'

'If you were that naïve, Marion, that's your problem,' he snarled. 'You knew I was married with a family. But you saw an opportunity to upgrade yourself, like all you cheap tart nurses and receptionists do. You gave it away so easily. I didn't even have to try that hard. You were more than happy to spread your legs. You're the typical nurse, going after a doctor, a gold digger. What did you think I'd do? Just give it all up and run off with a two-bit dolly bird? And the only reason you're here now is because you've heard about my promotion. You're a bloodsucking bitch only interested in money.'

'If you don't agree to give me my money back, I'll walk out of this office and tell everybody exactly what you did with the baby. They would soon take that award away from you.' She laughed.

'Nobody would believe you. If you don't go, I'll call security. Now if you don't mind, I've got work to do.'

With both hands on his desk she leaned towards him, inches from his face. 'I want my money.'

'You've had your money.'

'No, I haven't.'

'When you resigned, I gave you a fat cheque. Spent it already? You always were flush with cash.'

'You evil bastard.' She reached out grabbing his cheeks with one hand, surprising herself with her strength.

'Take your grubby hand off me. Bitch.'

He pushed her hand away and she buckled, knocking her elbow on the desk with a painful thud. Ignoring the pain, she ploughed on. 'That money was hush money. You sacked me. You got rid of me and paid me to quietly walk away.'

'You gave me a letter of resignation.'

'Under duress.'

He sniffed and opened a file on his desk clearly showing her that he had better things to be doing with his time than arguing with her.

A flush crept up her neck and anger grew like a fire raging in her belly. How dare he twist the facts? Her fury threatened to erupt but she kept it contained, worried he'd call security and have her removed. She had to turn things around and gain the upper hand.

'I know where the boy is. I know where they live and soon I'll be spending a lot of time with them.'

She wasn't going to tell him everything; how she'd spied on the family for years, sending letters and making Rona's life difficult. And she wasn't going to tell him that Rona had passed away. Let him find that out for himself.

'What are talking about?' he asked behind shifty eyes as he picked up a pen and twiddled with it. She could see that he was nervous and for the first time since entering his office felt a surge of power.

'I'm working at a school in the countryside where some of the thalidomides board. He's called Toby, nice name, don't you think? A modern-sounding name. I rather like it. Toby's joining the school very soon.'

'Enough. Meet me in the park at one.'

He got up and, moving towards her, ushered her out with a sweep of his arm before she had the chance to protest.

'All right, I'm going, but you'd better start thinking about how you're going to pay––and how much.'

He held the door open, his face giving nothing away.

Marion walked over the road, glad that she didn't see anybody she knew and waited for him by the pond. Taking a sandwich from her pocket she took out her frustration on the bread, pulling chunks off it to feed the ducks quacking near the reeds.

With the sandwich gone, she was hungry and wished she'd kept some for herself. Her stomach growled and her mind was on food as she heard familiar footsteps on the path.

'So, what's all this with the boy?' Simon asked, digging his hands in his pockets.

'He's joining the special school I'm working at,' Marion told him, wiping leaves from the bench before sitting down.

'And what's that got to do with me?' He lit a cigarette.

'I thought you'd be interested.'

'Why would I be interested?'

'I just thought you'd like to know that I'm in contact with the family. I have been for some time,' she lied.

'Stay away from them.'

'Scared I might say something?'

'They're nothing to you.'

'Rona's dead.' She hadn't planned to tell him, but it just came out.

'Oh.'

She saw the creases on his face relax with relief.

'You think that's all right then? That it lets you off the hook? I can see it in your face, you think it makes things easier for you - you fool.'

'How did she die?'

'Cancer. Bill's found it hard to cope and the boy's been bullied at his secondary school in Blackpool. I guess they thought it was best to make a fresh start. Integrating handicapped children into the mainstream isn't always the best approach.'

'You seem to know a lot about them.'

'I've made it my business to.'

'Sounds as if you've been following them. There are laws preventing that.'

'And I suppose you're above the law?'

'Just let them lead their life in peace. They got what they wanted.'

'Oh, I see.' Marion sprung from the bench and faced him, red mist swirling before her eyes. '*They* got what they wanted.' She pointed at him, inches from his eyes, her voice raised. '*You* got what you wanted. Me gone. And your family got what they wanted. What did I get in all of this? Wasted years, that's what. Believing you when you said you'd leave her.'

'You've turned into a bitter woman.'

Marion turned her back and walked towards the pond, flustered, fuming, her heart pounding. 'I hated Rona. Thinking she could just steal a baby because she couldn't have her own, manipulating you and threatening to expose our affair. She got her own way and destroyed us.' Marion was out of control, her face contorted. She was beside herself. People walking in the park and children playing, stopped to stare.

'There was no us.'

'I'm glad you thought so little of our relationship.'

'Where's this conversation leading?'

'You either pay me a considerable sum of money to stay quiet or you do the decent thing and tell your wife we had an affair.'

Simon threw his head back and laughed. 'You're deluded.' He put a finger to his head and twisted it.

'Or I tell her myself and I tell the police what really happened that evening. They'll do you for medical negligence - you left a baby in a freezing room to die and then let a midwife kidnap the baby. You couldn't make it up.'

'And you'd be in trouble too, but you're too stupid to see that. You've withheld information for all of these years. You knew what happened, but you've kept it to yourself. That makes you an accessory.'

Marion hadn't considered that. But she had nothing to lose. Her old cat with arthritis would die soon and then she'd have nothing. Prison couldn't be any worse. For years she'd been alone with her feelings, and there was nowhere to run from them. Staring from her single bed in her dreary flat that overlooked the gasworks she'd watched her world fall apart. Her parents were gone. She had no siblings, no children, no partner and no friends. She'd never really liked dances and pubs and crowded places, or mingling with stupid people, but the terrible itch of loneliness never went away. The annual trips to Blackpool were her way of scratching that itch. Stalking Rona was a banquet of revenge and an entertaining game, knowing that Rona would never phone the police. She felt safe in her hatred. She loved the unexpected games, like a slashed tyre, a scratch on their paintwork, a series of untraceable phone calls. And watching her tears of frustration from afar. But returning from Blackpool to her grubby flat, holiday memories turned to ashes. It was an obsession that needed feeding.

'Gone quiet then? Hadn't considered that, had you?'

Miles away, Marion snapped round to face him. 'The police would be more interested in you.'

Damn it. She stood tall, pressed her shoulders back. This wasn't going to destroy her. The new job in Haslemere was a fresh start and she was enjoying it. There was hope, she had skills to offer and had become a part of the St Bede's 'family.' For so long she'd felt unloved, as if nobody cared but these children cared. She could see it in their eyes and the way they asked questions and engaged with her. She'd formed bonds with several children already. Despite all this, she was shackled to the chains of revenge which was why she was here now.

He sat down, exhaustion manifesting itself in the way his shoulders slouched as he looked at the pond. She saw the pink-eyed look. His face, cadaver-like and sagging, lacked the liveliness she remembered of years ago. She saw it then, the lack of fight in him, as if he'd readily admit the truth if the police came knocking. It was all working in her favour. Maybe she could expect a phone call from him, soon, with the promise of money.

'I've heard enough Marion, I'm not playing your games.' His words were sharp but reading between the lines she knew he was acting. He had no strength left in him to fight her. 'You need to get a life and I'm getting back to work. Don't come back. I don't want to hear from you or see you again.'

'Don't think this is the last you'll be hearing from me,' she spat after him, then turned in the opposite direction and hurried off.

41

1973

Bill

Bill loaded the last of Celia's boxes onto her removal lorry. She was finally moving to Yorkshire. And Bill and Toby were heading south in their van, to Surrey to begin their new life.

'I thought we'd never get to the end of that lot.' He stuck out his bottom lip and blew air onto his face, as he thought about the journey ahead.

Toby looked at their van which had taken all of five minutes to pack.

'Don't pull that sad face.' Bill ruffled the lad's hair. 'I know we've lost everything but it's going to be okay. Who needs belongings when we've got each other?' His words felt weak but he couldn't think of anything else to say to take the pain away. Losing his mother, his home and everything that was familiar was a lot for a twelve-year old to go through and there were times when Bill felt inadequate.

'All my games have gone and my picture of Mum.'

Bill pulled him into a hug and slapped his back.

'Look at it as an adventure. New school, new home.'

'When will we get to see Grandma?'

Bill had no idea. Yorkshire was a long drive from Surrey and maintaining contact with his mother-in-law was the last thing on his mind. It wasn't going to be possible to cut ties, but he was looking forward to seeing less of her.

Celia came out of the house and stood on the path. She had that 'poor me' expression on her face that Bill had come to know so well and the slumped posture, as if the weight of the world was on her shoulders. As their eyes connected, she pouted her lips.

'I don't know how I'm going to cope at the other end.'

Bill gave a half laugh and wiped his brow of sweat. 'Come on, Celia, you'll have your daughters to help.'

'Amy and Rachel lead busy lives.'

'Yes, well we all do, but Rachel's coming to stay for a few days to help you sort things and settle in.'

Sometimes Bill despaired. It was her decision to move to Yorkshire, she knew what she was in for. She always seemed to find something to complain about.

'You'd better be making tracks,' she said evasively

He wasn't going to swallow the bitter pill of guilt she was offering. 'Yes, it's a long way,' he replied, checking his watch.

'When will you be able to visit? I will be very lonely up there.'

Bill had the impression that she was only moving so that she could have a further reason to complain about her life.

'I've got no idea. We need to settle in first.'

'Well don't leave it too long,' she ordered.

Bill's heart sank. There was no escaping from her.

'I don't even know your new phone number,' she said, ramping up the sad expression on her face.

'I have your new phone number. I'll give you three rings to let you know we've arrived. Thank you for everything and for putting us up these past few months.'

Celia stood back, looking affronted. 'It was the least I could do for my family.'

As much as he found her difficult to get along with, she had just called them family, but he still wanted to step away from Rona's family and make a fresh start. Moving south was, after all partly about that. He hadn't forgotten the way her family had treated Rona: she was the black sheep of the family for no apparent reason other than the fact that she'd married a man who used his hands for a living.

Celia bent down to kiss Toby's forehead, in a rare act of affection. 'How long will it take you?'

'Several hours, but we've been invited to that journalist's house, Jasper and his wife for a welcome dinner.

'I'd be careful what you tell that journalist. Remember there's a court case going on.' 'That doesn't affect us.'

'It should do. You need compensation, too.'

'Rona wasn't sure if she'd taken the tablet. I've told you this, many times.'

'Doesn't matter. It's obvious he's been damaged by thalidomide.'

Bill smiled to himself. Rona hadn't taken the tablet. Because Rona had never been pregnant. She couldn't have children, but Celia didn't know that. Before Toby came along, Rona's sisters, Amy and Rachel were the golden girls because they had children and Rona didn't. Bill had felt inferior to Amy and Rachel's husbands. He was the outcast, just their sister-in-law's grubby builder husband. Toby hadn't changed how things were between Rona and her family. The animosity was still there. Bill could see why Rona had been driven to fabricate a pregnancy and snatch Toby. Their endless, unrelenting questions: 'When are you two going to have a baby?' had really got to her and tipped her over the edge. But pretending to be pregnant, was a foolish idea. 'What are you going to do when they discover you've made it up?' Bill had asked Rona. At the time they'd lived at opposite ends of the country and hadn't seen her family for months. 'I'll think of something,' she'd replied. And then she brought Toby home, at around the time that her phantom pregnancy reached full-term.

'I don't know about that journalist.'

'I liked him, so did Toby.'

'I thought he was creepy.'

'How do you mean?'

'I don't know. There was something about the way he was looking at Toby.' Her face melted into a smile and then she raised a hand towards the van. 'Come on,' she goaded, her tone friendly and less hostile than it had been earlier. 'You better make tracks.'

As Bill drove out of Blackpool, with his old life and Rona committed to memory, he felt exhilarated to be starting a new life and wondered what the future held for both of them. But there was also a dark side to his thoughts. Meeting Jasper had troubled him. Bill had been thinking about Jasper and Sandy's loss. He didn't know what was troubling him exactly, it was more just a feeling he couldn't shake off. He wished that Jasper hadn't mentioned about losing his own baby son. It got him thinking and wondering. He didn't want to acknowledge his own thoughts. It was easier to push them aside and focus on all the good things that were going to happen now that they were finally moving away.

42

1973

Simon 'Are you visiting Mum later? Could you take these new bed socks? I bought them the other day. You know how cold her feet get.'

Carol rubbed the fluffy pink socks against her cheek and passed them to her husband, Simon.

'They shouldn't be cold. It's boiling in that place,' Simon said, dropping the socks on the table.

'Well are you going or not?' she snapped.

Christ he was doing her a favour and this was her attitude. He was tired of popping in to see his mother-in-law, but the care home was near to the hospital and the mother-and-baby home where he worked and not on Carol's route to work. They'd thought about moving her, but she was settled and the staff were good. He didn't mind the old bat, in fact he quite enjoyed her muddled conversations but - and he hated admitting this to himself - it was time she popped her clogs. This had gone on long enough. She'd eaten into a fair chunk of their inheritance, after living in the care home for four years and really, what was the point to her life? A hamster had a better quality of life. At least hamsters had wheels to run on. She sat in a chair all day, never left her room and most of the time forgot who'd visited and sometimes she barely recognised him. When she didn't recognise him she was rude and obnoxious. It was times like this when he longed for the end. He'd been through a similar situation with his own mother and had longed for that old bitch to die too. But it had been different with his own mother. He'd loathed her. She'd deserved to die a painful death after what she'd put him through. The memories of his awful childhood, his mother regularly beating him, making him stand in wet pants in the corner of the kitchen, still haunted him.

'Yes. All right. I'll pop in to see your mother, then I'll come home and mow the lawn, cook the dinner and hoover the lounge. Satisfied?' he snapped.

'Don't be like that. You know I would go if I could. It's not much to ask,' she said, as if talking to a disobedient child.

'That's a matter of opinion,' he muttered, grabbing the socks and heading for the front door. He left the house without saying goodbye.

After work he diligently dropped into the care home. Dinner had long been served but a boiled cabbage-and-gravy aroma filled the corridors. As he neared Mavis's room the pleasant voice of Andy Williams singing 'Moon River' filled the air.

'Two drifters...'

That was exactly how he felt about his marriage. They'd drifted on, the love and romance had gone, and the fireworks had fizzled to dying embers. Having spent years longing to leave her and waiting for the children to grow up, the urge to go was no longer there. He had meant to leave Carol to be with Marion all those years ago but leaving Carol, in the end, had seemed too big a thing to do. Selling the house and splitting the equity was too much effort and meant they would both be worse off, so what was the point? It was easier to sleep in separate rooms and pretend that it was okay.

'We're after that same rainbow's end...' sang Andy Williams. Maybe they were but couldn't see it. What did he want at the end of his rainbow? Probably the same as for her. Happy children, grandchildren, a fat pension and a retirement in the sun. Just not with Carol.

Mavis's door was open so that passing staff could glance in. She was slumped in an easy chair fast asleep; a pleasant evening sun was streaming through the window and across her face, casting a warm glow across the orange-and-amber spangled carpet.

Simon's nose wrinkled at the pungent odour of urine and, glancing down he noticed a heavy used pad in the corner of the room and a bundle of dirty sheets. What was going on? Were they short staffed? Perching on the edge of the bed, he hoped the creak would wake her, but she was out for the count. He'd wait till she woke and any delay in getting home was always a good thing.

What a sorry state she was in. Her hair was matted and didn't look as if it had been brushed. Her neck looked like bark on a tree, she had egg stains on her beige cardigan and a bulge in the sleeve where she kept tissues. Her pop socks strained like thick bands over bloated purple legs.

Bells rang, doors slammed, there was shouting. Simon peered into the corridor to see what the commotion was about. The medicine trolley was in the corridor. The lid was open, the trolley unattended–– creating the ideal opportunity for drug theft. He stood by the door, expecting a nurse to appear but nobody came. An idea struck him as he stared at the trolley. He could steal some medicine and kill Marion. He stepped towards the trolley, his heart racing. No, it was a stupid idea on so many levels. Whatever was he thinking? But he was fiercely proud of his award and had to stop Marion. His children and Carol were too. They'd celebrated with a meal out and he had seen pride in their eyes. The award was not going to be taken from him. He'd do whatever it took to keep it, even if it meant scaring Marion and putting her in her place.

He turned and went back into Mavis's room to wait. Several minutes passed. He heard footsteps and turned to see the nurse at the door.

'Hello, Doctor Gerard, come to see Mum?'

'She's asleep.'

'She needs her tablets, I'll come back when she's awake.'

'I can give her them when she wakes, if you like.'

'Would you mind?'

She returned with the tablets and gave them to Simon. Such slack security Simon thought and how easy it would be to steal the tablets. They'd never win an award, he thought smugly.

'As soon as she wakes up if you don't mind. I'll sign that she's had them.'

'There's dirty laundry on the floor by the way and a pad that hasn't been collected.'

The nurse turned and stared at the mess, looking shocked.

'Oh goodness. We've got a couple of new staff started this week. Things have been a bit chaotic and we've new residents too.' Scooping everything up and tutting to herself she bustled out of the room.

Mavis woke and looked alarmed as if she'd seen a ghost.

'Sorry, did I shock you? You were fast asleep,' Simon said.

'Take me home,' she ordered.

'Not this again, Mum this is your home.'

'I want to see my mum and dad.' Her mouth was dribbling.

'I've bought you some new bed socks.'

'Put them in the drawer, I don't want the place cluttered up, I'm going home.'

Simon sighed. 'It's time for your tablets, Mum.'

'Do I know you?'

'Yes, it's Simon. Your son-in-law.'

She stared through him with vacant eyes. 'Oh.'

'You need to take these.'

'There won't be enough for the other people.'

'They've got their own medicine.'

'The other people need it.'

'What other people?' he asked.

'The people who have left their homes,' Mavis said.

'Why have they left their homes?'

'Their houses have been bombed, stupid, don't you read the news?' Her mind had gone back to the war.

'I've taken care of them. Now if you just open your mouth.'

She opened it slightly, her eyes wide, then snapped them shut. 'No.'

'I'd better go now. I'll see you tomorrow.' He stood to go. He wanted to get out of the room, and get away from her so that he could think about what to do about Marion.

'Okay dear, give my love to the baby.'

'What baby?'

'I saw you pushing his pram the other day. He looked just like you.' She was away with the fairies.

Simon leaned down and kissed her on the head. 'Goodbye dear.'

Out in the corridor, the nurse was locking the medicine trolley.

'Did she take them okay?'

'Yes, Nurse, she did. All good, see you again.'

'And Doctor,' she called after him, 'well done for winning an award. Your family must be very proud of you.'

'Thank you, Nurse. Yes, they are.'

Wherever he went he received compliments and people were impressed. He liked that. It made him feel good and on top of the world and he glowed with pride. He was somebody that people looked up to and respected.

43

1973

Simon

Simon hadn't been to Marion's flat since the day he'd sacked her. Emotions slammed into him as he parked his car, tucking it away in a quiet road under a tall tree off the main thoroughfare. He strode along the pavement clutching the bottle of token Martini, breath chugging from his mouth, his wedding band winked in the evening sun. He reflected on how he used to prise the band from his finger before their clandestine meetings.

The gate leading to the front door squeaked mournfully as he opened it, as if it sensed trouble ahead. It was amazing how plans and ideals went out of the window so easily. He remembered the hundreds of times he had promised to leave Carol for Marion.

He'd never forget the first time he saw Marion. Rounding a corner along the hospital corridor they'd bumped into each other, the stack of files she was holding crashed to the floor, scattering across the tiles. She had changed out of her uniform and was about to go home. Bending to gather the papers, their eyes had met and there was a huddled handshake. The dance of courtship began. She had safe eyes that told the world she was a good listener and a keeper of secrets. It was the type of scenario only seen in films. A bubble formed around the space where they crouched and breathed, the corridor blurring. She was beautiful but not in a stunning way, she was quite ordinary. Her dark eyes and dark hair fell in waves and reminded him of a princess he'd seen on TV depicting Richard III's era. Her skin was milky and soft. Laughing at their clumsiness he saw the most astonishing woman he'd ever met. As they got to know each other he found her easy to get on with and enchanting. But now, all those feeling were gone. He hated her.

'Martini?' he'd casually suggested when she'd rang him out of the blue that morning, two days after their confrontation in the park. Martini reminded him of their weekend in Dorset, a wonderful escape with no expense spared. They'd stayed in a fifteenth-century manor house, with a four-poster bed. His heart jolted when he remembered watching her sleep in the early hours of the morning, her locks splayed across the pillow. But that was then. It was a heady mix of Martini and making love. Tonight, it would be Martini and murder.

She'd hesitated, not expecting this friendly response to her avalanche of hostility. 'Why would I want to spend the evening with you? I loathe you. I want you to face up to what you did.'

'I'm just suggesting a civilised drink like two adults. We need to talk about what happened. We need to put it to bed.'

After a cold greeting on her doorstep, he followed her into the kitchen and put the bottle on the worktop.

'I'm surprised you'd want to come here,' she said in an icy tone.

'It's been a long time.'

'How's Carol?'

'The same, pretty much.'

She shrugged but said nothing.

'Why ask?'

'Just making conversation. I bet she's proud of her husband winning an award and getting promoted.'

Simon saw the sarcasm in her face and in the tone of her voice but ignored it. She was a threat, there was no doubting that.

Taking two glasses from the cupboard, she poured the Martini over ice and added a splash of lemonade, her back to him. Now that he was here, the air filled with her delicious scent, he found himself wavering. He was an idiot. What was he thinking? How was he going to scare her?

Marion took a gulp, throwing her head back like a cowboy drinking whisky. She seemed on edge, but he was too. He was glad that nerves were getting the better of her. He smiled inwardly but warned her to slow down. They'd not even left the kitchen but in a matter of moments the glass was empty, and she slammed it down on the counter.

'Steady on Marion.'

'You can't tell me what to do,' she hissed, taking a step towards him with a pointed finger. 'Remember all those times you promised me you'd leave her.'

'Get over it. It was years ago.'

'No, I won't just get over it,' she screeched.

She reached for the bottle and unscrewed the top.

'It's strong stuff.'

'Why do you care?'

'You need help. Your behaviour isn't normal. You need to see a psychiatrist. We dealt with this years ago.'

He wanted to get sloshed too, but now was not the time. He enjoyed a few drinks. Drink turned down the volume of his thoughts, allowing him to dwell on happy memories, blotting out the stain on his career, the ugly secret weighing down on him, like an appendage to his body. Drink steadied him, gave him the resolve to carry on, but there was no way he was about to join her in the land of oblivion.

'You ruined my life. I want you to pay for what you did. I want to see you rot in a prison cell. It's what you deserve.'

'You never used to be a big drinker,' he commented as she took a swig from a fresh glass. 'Since when did that happen?'

'Being in your company is making me nervous, but now it's making me sleepy.' She yawned. 'I think you should go. I will go to the police.'

'Not so fast. I don't like the frosty you.' He stepped towards her. 'What happened to the friendly you, the one that couldn't get enough of me?'

'Being with you is making me feel…' She yawned and clapped a hand to her mouth. 'You can stand here all evening if you like, but you know where the door is.'

As the light caught her face, he could see now how she'd aged. There were crow's feet around her eyes and her neck sagged. His eyes fell to her belly. She'd put on weight. It was probably cream teas. She liked her cream teas. Occasionally they'd met on a Sunday afternoon when he'd been able to sneak away, pretending to the wife that he was going to watch cricket.

He followed her into the lounge, where she slumped inelegantly onto the sofa. Her skirt rose to her knee, revealing still-slender, unblemished legs as she curled them under her bottom. Something was triggered inside him; he longed to kiss those legs again. Correcting his thoughts he perched on the edge of the sofa.

She stifled another yawn. 'What are you waiting for? A deep and meaningful conversation?'

'Why not?'

'If that's what you want.' She sat up and suddenly her tired features were gone. With alert eyes and folded arms, she stared at him as if expecting him to inspire her.

'What do you want to talk about? We need to talk about the evening that Rona took the baby.'

'Your callousness that evening shocked me. I bet there weren't many doctors that would have put him on a cold windowsill to die.'

'My only thought when I looked at those tiny twisted digits - was that he could not possibly survive. I thought that his internal organs would be deformed too. We didn't expect him to last the night. But Rona didn't agree with me.'

'Toby is a strong boy with a fighting spirit. There's a saying I read somewhere. Who are we to translate what is written on the body as a judgement of the spirit?'

'I was wrong. I made a mistake.'

'Why did you become a doctor?'

'You know why. Or have you forgotten the hours we spent together?'

Simon remembered the series of events that culminated in his decision to become a doctor. He was twenty-two and training in architecture. He was standing outside a London pub when a bus ploughed into a group of his friends, killing two of them. A few months later his father died and then an ex-girlfriend passed away during surgery. Amid the grief he dropped out of the course and stayed at home to support his mother for a few months, but he'd loathed her and couldn't wait till she'd popped her clogs. Seeking a complete life change, he decided to travel to the Himalayas to train as a Buddhist monk.

'Something to do with seeing death all around you.'

'Something like that.'

Up in the hills under a scorching sun he contemplated where his life was heading and decided the best way to find himself was to lose himself in the service of others. When he became a doctor, he was the public face of a complex new service. The idea of a 'womb to tomb' service without charge excited him and he felt privileged to be joining the NHS in its infancy.

'Would you be a doctor, if you had your time again?'

'It's a stressful job at times.'

'Especially when faced with life-and-death decisions. You shouldn't have done what you did.' She waggled her finger, her eyes rolling, the booze talking.

Simon was thinking about how the workload had increased. Thanks to a booming birth rate and fewer women dying in childbirth and people living longer. These factors added to the stress he was under. He was overworked and underpaid. A loyalty to the health of mothers in childbirth had shackled him to the job for years, but cracks were appearing.

Marion gave a spectacular yawn and rubbed her eyes. Her head resting on the arm of the sofa she was close to drifting off.

His body prickled with heat and his palms were sweaty. He needed to go away and come up with a plan.

'Just nipping to the loo,' he whispered, hoping to slip out as she drifted off. A germ of a plan was forming in his mind. Her eyes were closed, and she was snoring lightly. He inched towards the door, half expecting her to spring to life, but she was under and he was able to open the door quietly and leave.

44

1973

Toby Bill and Toby drove down the M6 and M1 at a steady speed. Toby stared out of the window at the bland concrete, fields and the occasional herd of cows breaking the monotony. Sports cars raced up the outer lane, older drivers hogged the middle lane and lorries thundered down the slow lane. To pass the time he counted the lorries and then the bridges, but there weren't many bridges.

'Let's play I Spy,' Bill suggested, sensing Toby's boredom.

'Me first,' Toby shrieked. The guessing game, I Spy was his favourite car game but realising that it was less fun without his mum, a pang of sadness washed over him. Bored of playing the game having exhausted the objects on view, from 's' for sky to 'c' for car, she'd livened it up with made-up objects like lion, giraffe, boat. 'There's no giraffe here,' he'd shout. 'I can't see an aardvark on the motorway.' He wished she was still here. Sometimes that wish filled him with such rage and bitterness that he thought he would explode. It was hard to accept that she was gone.

'I know,' Bill said thumping Toby's leg, 'I've got a new game for you.'

'I don't want to learn the times table. They do that at school.'

Bill laughed. 'It's one we haven't played before. One person begins with a sentence that describes a situation. For example, one day I woke up in the jungle. Taking it in turns each person makes up one sentence to the story but the beginning of the sentence must alternate between unfortunately or fortunately. So, the second person would add to the story, for example unfortunately I came face to face with a lion which chased me. Then the other person adds–– but fortunately I had a superpower and could fly away. Do you get the idea?'

'Me first,' Toby said excitedly.

They played the game from Leicestershire through Hertfordshire, before Bill had to break off to navigate their way through London. When suburbia trickled into open countryside and winding lanes, they made up stories about the lives of the people in the houses they passed.

After a period of silence, Bill spoke. 'I know you miss her, and I'm sorry I don't talk about her. It's hard to accept that she's gone.'

A lump rose in Toby's throat and he thought he was going to cry.

'When we think about her, we don't always need to be sad. She was a fun person and we need to hold those fun memories inside us like a flame, and enjoy that flame and never let it extinguish,' Bill said.

'Do you remember when she used to play I Spy?'

'Yeah I do,' Bill smiled. 'I know it's tough, but we'll get through. We've got each other and that's never going to change.'

'I don't want you to die too.'

Bill glanced at Toby, horrified.

'Of course I won't die, Toby. Why on earth do you think that?'

'I don't want to be an orphan.'

Bill took his foot off the accelerator and glanced at Toby. 'Now you listen to me. That's not going to happen. I'm not ill. I intend to live for many more years.'

'But Grandma says you drink too much and that too much alcohol isn't good for the liver.'

Bill sighed. 'That's true alcohol isn't good for the liver or a person's health in general, especially blood pressure. And yes, you are right, I have been drinking too much lately, because I've been under a lot of stress, but that's all going to change. This is a fresh start for us.'

Toby wasn't so sure now that it was happening. He missed Melanie and Fred. Fred wasn't always the good friend that he should have been, but he was the nearest thing to one that he had, apart from Melanie. Toby had caught Fred looking embarrassed to be seen hanging out together on the school field.

Toby's mind drifted. The only time that he felt normal was on the football pitch. The best times were when he'd scored a goal and everybody cheered and congratulated him and thumped him on the back. He felt on top of the world and felt as if he belonged. But the feeling never lasted because their praise and good comments were always short-lived. When the match finished and the referee blew the whistle and everybody had sung his praises in the changing room, it was as if the Toby they saw kicking the ball into the goal was a different Toby to the boy who needed assistance to eat and go to the toilet. Toby hoped things were going to be different at the new school.

'Do we have to go to that man's house for dinner? I can't wait to see our new house and my new bedroom.'

'I thought you liked Jasper?'

'He's okay.'

'They've got a dog.'

'I love dogs. Big or small?'

'I'm not sure.'

They pulled up outside Jasper and Sandy's. It was a modern house in a leafy cul-de-sac, with a grass island in the middle. It was a quiet road and Toby didn't see any cars cluttering the driveways. He guessed they were in the garages to stop them getting rusty. He sniffed. 'I bet this road is full of snooty people.'

Each house was different. One or two had thatched roofs and a few had criss-crossed window-panes. They were all detached with neat front lawns and an array of bedding plants and birdhouses on poles. The houses were set back from the road, some were hidden behind tall hedges and one of them had an evergreen tree–– the type he'd seen in churchyards. Some of the branches were touching the windows and Toby imagined living there and climbing down the tree at night, but without arms climbing a tree could only ever be a dream.

'It's stockbroker belt.'

'What's that?'

'Areas near to London, like this, where rich people live and go to work in the City. Bankers and financial people, those sorts.'

'Toffs you mean?'

'Maybe.'

'We're not going to stay long, are we?' Toby felt the start of a nervous tummy ache.

'It would be rude to rush off as soon as we've eaten, but I promise we won't stay too long.'

They rang the doorbell and Jasper, more casually dressed this time, in a blue shirt and denims welcomed them in. The house was even bigger inside. Toby had never seen such a large hallway. It was square with a wide staircase to the right and several doors leading to rooms on the ground floor.

Jasper asked about their journey as he guided them through the hall, in a cloud of heavy aftershave that made Toby feel queasy, as they went to the kitchen at the back of the house. French doors led onto a patio and a garden at least three times the length of the house they'd left behind in Blackpool.

In the steamy kitchen, which smelled of roast meat and vegetables, Sandy was crouching to remove a sizzling chicken from the oven. Although her face was flushed and her apron was splattered with fat, Toby instantly thought she was the most beautiful woman he'd ever seen, not counting the ones on TV. She glanced up at Toby with a hassled expression on her face. The only warmth radiating from her was the warmth escaping from the oven.

Putting the chicken on the hob, Sandy smoothed her hair and untied her apron. She extended a hand to shake Bill's and turning to Toby touched his shoulder, with warmth now in her eyes.

'I expect you're very hungry after such a long journey. Help yourself to the bowl of crisps outside while you're waiting. Dinner's taking longer to cook than I expected.'

'How's the chicken darling?' Jasper asked, opening a cutlery drawer and pulling out a carving knife and fork.

'It's stopped clucking.' She winked at Jasper, then playfully flicking a tea towel at him she said, 'You get the drinks, take our guests outside. I'll be out as soon as I've got the dinner under control.'

Toby, feeling like a spare part, followed Jasper and Bill out onto the patio and sat politely while they discussed motorways, roadworks and bad driving, until something brushed against his leg. He looked down to see a small fluffy caramel-coloured dog with a pink bow on its head and a yellow knitted wrap around its belly.

'Do you like dogs, Toby?' Jasper asked, sweeping his fingers through his blond layered hair in a way that Toby had only seen women do. He was a stylish man and reminded Toby of the singer, Elton John. But he had a plummy voice that made

Toby feel inferior. He wondered if his dad felt the same. Toby was glad that his dad looked rough and had a steak-and-kidney pie belly, because that meant that ladies wouldn't be interested in him. The last thing he wanted was a stepmother.

'We've never had a dog. Dad won't let us get a pet.' Toby bent down to stroke Tibs. 'It's so soft.'

Addressing the dog Jasper said, 'We don't want you anymore, do we?'

'You're not giving my baby away,' Sandy simpered, stepping onto the patio and putting the plates on the table.

'She bought him without telling me. It was a shock but I'm getting used to having a dog around the house.'

Sandy picked Tibs up and planted kisses on his head and in a childish high-pitched voice, said 'You're Mummy's baby aren't you? Yes Mummy's little baby.'

'She molly coddles that thing, as if it's a child,' Jasper said, smoothing his hair.

'Mummy's got some nice chicken for you later on, if you're a good boy.'

'You spoil him.'

Sandy planted more kisses on the dog's head, like tiny arrows. 'And we'll save some gravy for you my little munchkin.'

Jasper tutted and raised his eyebrows in Bill and Toby's direction.

Toby was both horrified and intrigued by this woman's behaviour towards the dog.

'We don't have children,' Sandy said, 'but having a dog is like having a child.'

Your dog, Toby wanted to say, is nothing like a child. Sandy was making Toby cringe. You can knit sweaters for it and put bows in its hair and talk to it in a baby voice––but it's still a bloody dog.

The dog ran off to the bottom of the garden, cocked his leg against a bush and ran back to Sandy.

'Good boy,' she said in a baby voice, patting the dog's head. 'Have you done a little wee-wee?'

With plates brimming with chicken and vegetables, Bill picked up a fork and started to feed Toby.

'I can feed myself,' he protested.

Bill pushed the fork towards Toby's mouth, but Toby pursed his lips and hoisted his foot onto the table. He hated it when his dad insisted on feeding him when they were with other people. His mother would never have been like this. She encouraged him to make his own decisions and do what made him feel comfortable. Sadness washed over him as he thought about how different his dad was. He felt like a small child and could see his independence slipping away, his life being controlled by others.

'Come on,' Bill whispered. 'Open wide.' Toby couldn't believe that his dad would make a big deal of this in front of people they barely knew. In any case, Jasper had seen him eat with his feet the first time they'd met. It's because he fancies the woman, Toby thought. That's what it was. He was embarrassed.

'Give me the fork.'

'Where are your manners?'

Toby went as red as a beetroot, radiating heat like a hot pan. Feeling all eyes on him, he wanted to 'Do a Daphne' and drop through a Scooby-Doo style trap door in the patio.

'I want to eat with my feet.'

'You *can* do, later. Not now.'

'We don't mind,' Jasper encouraged.

'Go ahead, don't mind us,' Sandy added. 'Lots of children at St Bede's do.'

'I try not to encourage it when we're out,' Bill said firmly.

'It's fine, really,' Sandy said, picking up her glass. But when she smiled at Bill, Toby noticed pity in her eyes.

'It might be okay now, but as he gets older his body won't be so flexible. I worry that he'll develop problems. We aren't designed to eat with our feet.'

'I wouldn't worry about hip replacements yet,' Jasper laughed. 'All that football will keep you fit Toby.'

Toby picked up the fork between two toes and skilfully stabbed a carrot.

'Well I'm very impressed, I couldn't eat with my feet.' Sandy laughed.

'Don't be daft, of course you couldn't. The lad's used to it. It's all he's known,' Jasper said.

Picking up his glass of beer, Bill changed the subject. 'Did you always want to be a journalist?'

'From a young age I loved writing, but my parents were factory workers and could barely read and write themselves, so they didn't encourage me to do well at school. I got a scholarship to the local grammar school. It was a struggle for my parents to pay for the uniform. After school I went straight out to work and trained as a draughtsman. Then I did National Service and after National Service I went back to being a draughtsman at the same engineering firm but I hated it. I was hopeless at drawing and it was boring work. They were similar drawings each day, of transformer pipes. I knew I had to get out when the chief draughtsman told us individually what our increase would be for the next year. Mine was the lowest in the department.'

'You seem to have done well for yourself though.'

Toby saw jealousy in his dad's face as he glanced around the garden and up to the house. As the evening sun caught his cheeks, he thought his dad looked older somehow. The lines around his eyes were deeper and his skin was leathery. For the first time Toby was seeing him, not as his dad, but as a beaten, broken man. His heart jolted. He felt suddenly fiercely protective of him. He was doing his best. He'd been through so much and he worried about Toby's future. His dad didn't have the money this couple had, their comfortable lifestyle was a world apart and their only worry was a spoilt yappy dog and keeping their sports car polished. His dad had bigger things to worry about. Pride washed over him. They didn't always agree on things, but his dad was always there for him.

'Every morning at work I went to the loo with the paper and started looking for jobs. I spotted a job and rang them from a public telephone.'

Toby was itching to ask about Jasper's background. 'How come you talk so posh if your parents were poor?'

Bill glared at him.

'Good question, Toby,' Sandy chuckled.

'I was the black sheep of the family. My mum didn't always like it that I had, as she put it, ideas above my station. My mum and dad struggled. I can remember the bitter winter of forty-seven and trudging for miles with an old pram through thick snow to nick coal from the coalyard,' Jasper sniggered. 'When I was your age I used to walk past the big houses in the village and think to myself, one day, Jasper, you're going to be rich and live in a house like that.' Looking at Toby, Jasper added, 'It's important to hold onto your dreams, you can be whoever you want to be. All it takes in life is a bit of hard work. Don't let your handicap get in the way.'

There was hard work, and there was hard work, in Toby's opinion. Jasper didn't look overworked, at least not in the same way his dad did. Jasper was a calm man, relaxed and unstressed. His hands were smooth, and his hair was slicked back. Maybe his job wasn't easy, but it was well paid. He looked unfazed by life, as if life just happened around him. His dad was a hard grafter. He could smell it on his sweaty skin and on his dirty clothes, and in the way he slumped in front of the TV each evening, snoring himself to sleep, always with a medicinal whisky.

'Enough of this heavy talk,' Jasper breezed. 'Are you looking forward to starting at St. Bede's?'

'Yes, but I'm nervous.'

'Don't be,' Sandy reassured him. 'Everybody's lovely. You'll be fine.'

'What's it like?' Bill asked.

'It's geared up for handicapped people with all the subjects you find at other schools, like drama, sport, geography and history...We're fortunate to have a workshop and they make perfectly adapted spoons and all sorts of utensils. Each child is different, with different needs and the workshop makes things for them to help with cleaning their teeth, dressing, toileting and schoolwork. There are pencil and paintbrush holders for the mouth and something quite new called Velcro which is fitted to clothing to make doing things up easier. I think you'll find school easier to cope with and as a result, life in general. A physiotherapist will meet you to talk about what you need and you'll be measured up.'

'You'll love it.' Jasper smiled at Toby.

'And there are occupational therapists whose job it is to help the children learn how to do everyday activities. A lot of the time the children learn by making mistakes. Last week we had a shopping trip for a few children in wheelchairs. They went to the greengrocers and were faced with a new set of difficulties to overcome. How do you get into a shop when you are in a wheelchair and there is a two-inch step? And having got in, there is no rhubarb for your crumble? How do you get the things off a high shelf when your artificial arms haven't any power in them? How do you use a trolley when you use crutches? The triumph the children, and the teachers, feel when these problems are solved is enormous.'

'Dessert anyone? Sandy's made a lemon meringue pie. It's one of her specialities, you've got to try it.'

'I will,' Bill said, patting his belly. Toby noticed his eyes light up at the mention of pudding and hoped his dad would be given a big portion to save the embarrassment of watching him ask for seconds. His dad ate like a gannet, shovelling food down as if it was his last meal on earth.

Silence fell around the table as they tucked into the sweet, sharp lemon filling and billowing meringue top.

'What is your favourite subject Toby?' Sandy asked, putting her spoon down and delicately patting her mouth with a napkin. He wondered if she was going to finish it, because there was still half of it left.

'Why do adults always ask boring questions?'

Bill glared at him. 'Toby, don't be rude.'

'Well what am I supposed to say?'

'What questions would you like me to ask you?' Sandy asked.

Toby shrugged. 'Dunno.'

Sandy crossed her legs and folded her arms. She looked as though she was waiting for him to answer, but he didn't want to talk about school and was bored with the conversation. She'd given him a rambling description of St Bede's. Toby knew he was being obnoxious but there were too many bad memories and he didn't want to be pulled into a conversation about his old school. This was a fresh start. He wanted to forget the past.

'You like maths,' Bill prompted.

'No, I don't.'

'He's top of the class in maths,' Bill enthused.

Toby scowled at Bill, wishing he'd shut up, and they could leave. They'd been here long enough.

'No, I'm not,' Toby scoffed, pinning his dad with a cold stare. Why were parents so stupid?

'Yes, you are.'

'I'm top of the bottom class. It's not the same thing. Being in the bottom set is not something to brag about.'

'You always get top marks.'

Toby huffed. His mouth was almost too dry to speak.

'It sounds as if you're being modest.' Jasper smiled, showing his perfect white teeth. 'I'm more interested in how you kick a ball. You both coming to my Wednesday evening football team?'

Toby watched his dad's face brighten at the mention of football. 'You bet we are,' Bill said.

As they said their goodbyes, Toby wondered if Jasper and Sandy were going to be a big part of their new life. If they were, he wasn't sure how he felt about that. They weren't the type of people his parents socialised with. They were refined sort of people. His dad didn't fit in with them, but *they* seemed to like him. He could tell his dad felt uneasy in their company, because of the way he'd tapped his heel under the table. This was his nervous tick.

45
1973

Toby and Bill

Bill pulled onto a sandy track flanked by gorse, bracken and scattered pine leading into St Bede's car park. Toby gasped as he saw his new surroundings. It was beautiful and wild, but there was a peaceful feel to the place, as well as a sense of adventure. He wanted to get out and explore and play hide-and-seek among the bushes and trees. Beyond the sprawling buildings, in the far distance were blue tinged hills. For a moment his fear was gone, but with adrenaline pumping through his body his excitement quickly turned to fear, gripping him, vice-like. His eyes fell to the floor as Bill swung the car into a parking bay, a sense of foreboding crept into his chest. His dad was busy chatting about how lovely it looked, and it was only when Bill removed the keys from the ignition that he noticed the tears trickling down his son's face.

'Hey, wipe those tears away, you'll be fine.' Bill pulled Toby's ear affectionately and winked.

'But what if I'm not?'

'I have every faith in you, you mustn't doubt yourself. I'm proud of you, son.'

Bill pulled him into a reassuring hug. Not wanting to pull away from the warmth and smell of Old Spice, Toby clung to his dad until Bill pushed him away.

'What if I don't fit in?'

'All you can do is be yourself, think before you speak and be considerate. There are kids here with far worse problems than you. Remember that.'

'It's going to be strange. Will they be offended if I ask them about their problems?' Toby sniffed.

'You'll know what to do. There are children with all sorts of handicaps. Some have something called cerebral palsy, others have spina bifida and there are thalidomides like you.'

'Will I though? And what is spina what did you call it?'

'We'll be sitting here all day if I explain.'

'It sounds complicated.'

'Forget about labelling them with whatever condition they have, just get to know them as people.'

'Okay.'

'It'll take a while, like any new experience, but it will be so much better than the last school. I'm only sorry I listened to your mum. She wanted you to go there, I wasn't so sure, but she had your best interests in mind when she made the decision. She just wanted you to fit in.'

'I wish she was here now.'

'We've got through these past months, I don't know how, but we have. I know it's hard, but life goes on. Things can't get any worse. We've got each other. We can't see Mum, but I think she's always at our side watching over us.'

Bill and Toby were met by the caretaker who walked them over to their accommodation - a small cottage in the school grounds. As they approached the cottage Toby could see the uneven slate roof through the bracken and gorse. As he got closer, the occasional flash of colour – some blues, others green or brown – emerged from the mottled stones that looked like eyes trying to steal a glimpse of the world. The cottage looked alive and welcoming, like a creature crouching on the heathland. Toby was excited and ran towards his new home.

Toby loved his new room even though it was plainly decorated. It had a small bed which was neatly made with crisp white linen sheets and two wooden chairs. The evening sun was streaming in and the little room was like an oven for heat. It was going to be strange to be here, Toby thought, but wonderful at the same time.

IT WAS two in the morning and Bill couldn't sleep. Something had been troubling him all afternoon and it wouldn't go away. Was he imagining it, or was Toby uncannily like Jasper? Over lunch he'd studied Jasper's face at every opportunity. He couldn't put his finger on what it was exactly but there was no doubt in his mind – Jasper and Toby were very similar. Their noses were alike and their cheekbones. They each had a facial mole to the left of their mouths and a kink in their fringes. But there was something Bill detected in both of their eyes that haunted him. If Toby really was their son; it had to be a terrible coincidence.

Bill wished he could roll over and doze off, but when he finally drifted to sleep, he slept for only a couple of fitful hours. It was around four, the room was still dark and he heard the sweet melody of the dawn chorus.

BILL AND TOBY got up at seven and after breakfast they headed to the school entrance. The secretary told Bill to wait in the reception area for the headteacher while she took Toby to his classroom and knocked on the door. His dad's words of reassurance had carried him into the building, but his heart was now beating a rapid rhythm of fear and uncertainty. The door squealed open to a peel of noise and laughter, and he found himself staring into the eyes of his new teacher, Mr Hendon. He was a Billy Bunter look-a-like, a red-faced barrel of a man in a beige suit and round rimmed glasses. Mr Hendon beamed down at him. Toby stared up at his long, hooked nose and took a step backwards nearly stepping into the path of a boy, propelling himself along in a walker and wearing a funny pair of shoes that looked like duck's feet. Toby felt a familiar choking panic start somewhere in his stomach and his cheeks flamed. He had to pull himself together.

'Toby,' Mr Hendon said, in a booming voice, causing Toby to take another step backwards. Toby imagined him practising the Boom and Beam in front of the mirror. He wasn't like any of Toby's previous teachers. He couldn't possibly be a teacher. *He's a bank manager. He counts money all day.*

Toby tried to smile back at Billy Bunter Banker and started to say, good morning, Sir, but the words died in his mouth halfway through 'morning' when he realised there was a boy standing next to him.

Mr Hendon was still beaming. 'Toby, this is Steve.' He gestured to the lanky boy with wild hair at his side who was smiling at Toby. Steve had shortened arms and no ears. Mr Hendon clapped a hand on Steve. 'I thought it would be a good idea to choose somebody from the class to show you around and be with you for your first days here.'

'Thank you.'

'You need to look at Steve when you speak, he has impaired hearing.'

'Okay,' Toby replied looking straight at Steve.

'Steve's just going to a physiotherapy session, but you come into the lesson with me. It's not unusual for the children to leave sessions for different reasons, like physio or x-rays. We can do everything in this one place, rather than children having to visit the local hospital. Don't be alarmed,' he said pointing to a metal bed in the corner of the classroom. 'Annie's just had an operation. Beds are often wheeled into the classroom so that learning can carry on.'

Toby stared at the sea of faces and, despite feeling overwhelmed by the shock of the range of different problems the children had, when they smiled at him, he instantly knew he was going to be safe. He also had a strong sense that this was going to be a fun place to be. He'd already seen the possibilities for adventure outside. Inside the classroom was chaos, paintings hung on the wall, and there was a music corner with a large drum and guitar and along one side of the room were parallel bars and a large mirror along the wall. A girl with leg straps was walking by clinging to the bars and a nurse stood behind watching and waiting to catch her if she fell. Toby could see that her muscles were too weak to walk unaided.

He took a seat, glancing out of the room onto a large playground where a girl was playing in an oversized tricycle with straps around her feet; a teacher was close by helping. On the other side of the playground a small group of children, older than Toby, were playing wheelchair basketball. They were whizzing round and it looked such fun. He wouldn't be able to play this game, but he was okay, he loved football, but wanted to watch them enjoy themselves.

After lunch the children had half an hour in the playground and Toby and Steve sat on a bench watching the others play. Toby made sure he looked at Steve before he began to speak.

'Can I ask you...?'

'About my ears?'

'I didn't mean to be rude.'

'It's okay. My outer ears didn't develop and I can't see out of my right eye, but that's not something you would notice.'

'Is there anything they can do?'

'My mum took the drug thalidomide when she was pregnant and it caused the problems I have.'

'Mine too.'

'I did wonder. I couldn't hear at all when I was born. They were experimenting with hearing aids. I began with something called a bone conductor, which was strapped to me with a bright red headband, but I was too young for it. I switched to headphones, which improved my hearing by twenty five percent.'

'I guess I'm lucky, it's just my arms that were affected.'

'We're both lucky, things could be a lot worse. Look at Jenny over there, she's got no limbs.'

'What is the outer ear for anyway? Do you need ears?'

Steve laughed. 'They collect sound waves and direct them into the ear. They also stop insects getting in.'

'No way.' Toby pulled a face. 'I hate creepy crawlies.'

'I've got false ears to make me look normal and they're stuck on with double-sided tape. They're quite realistic until the sun tans the rest of my face making them too pale. I've lost one of them, that's why I'm not wearing them.'

'That's annoying. I'll help you look for it if you like.'

'Thanks mate. I can't wear just one ear.'

'No, that would look really stupid.'

'I play football. But you should see their faces when one ear gets knocked off by the ball.'

'I can imagine,' Toby chuckled. 'At least you can see the funny side of it. Excuse the pun.'

'You gotta laugh, what else can you do?' Steve kicked at the grass in front of his feet. 'Did your parents get a payout for damages?'

'No. The kids at my old school thought I had. They thought we were rich because of it.'

'That's a shame.'

'I think it's because my mum didn't have proof that she took the pill. I think she borrowed a few pills from a friend. My dad doesn't talk about it. They don't like begging for money.'

'It's not begging.'

'They didn't get anything, all right?' Toby felt tetchy. The conversation was irritating him. He wished his parents had fought for what they were entitled to.

'Sometimes I want to blame my mum. If she hadn't taken that stupid pill, I'd be normal.'

'She wasn't to know.'

'A toffy-nosed judge came down here to assess some of the children to see how much we would be awarded. We were known by a number - I was number ten - and we had to take our clothes off and walk naked down the corridor and into a room full of doctors. It was horrible. When I went into the room they said, "Here's number ten." They pulled us about and prodded us.

'Well money or no money, having no arms isn't going to stop me having a good life. I can ride a bike, play football and I paint, using my mouth.'

'Me neither. I'm going to drive a car when I'm older. A flashy sports car. They can make adjustments to them so that I can drive, it won't be impossible.'

Toby had a positive feel about his new school. It was about living with his handicap and overcoming limitations and it was about strengthening and correcting his body. At last he felt that he fitted in; he wasn't the odd ball and knew that he could succeed and even do well.

46

1973

Simon

Simon parked his car in a lay-by halfway between the bus stop and the train station. Although the station was bathed in orange light, it didn't spill into the unlit lane, which was shrouded in a cloak of darkness. It had been a gothic sort of day, grey and brooding and with the clocks going back it was the perfect timing for abduction. Simon rubbed his hands in anticipation. He wasn't going to let the bitch get away with it; demanding her money back after all this time was lunacy. Did Marion seriously expect him to write a cheque for such a large amount and for Carol not to notice? How dare she come slamming back into his life, digging up old bones and taking the high moral ground over the thalidomide baby and threatening him with the police? If the police found out, there was no telling what his fate would be. He'd lose his job, his family. It could cost him everything he'd worked hard for and destroy his good name. He'd gone over that night, in his mind and genuinely believed the baby was too weak to live–– and under pressure from Rona, who believed otherwise, he'd given in to her, let her take the baby. The child's mother wasn't a consideration. She wanted him adopted. She was just a dirty slag, in the family way and caught out of wedlock.

Simon knew Marion's new routine. One morning he'd followed her to work, keeping his distance and hidden under a hat and long coat. Luckily, she hadn't seen him but he had been very careful. She took the train to Haslemere each day, hopped on the number thirty-seven bus, which took her to the gates of St Bede's, and she returned to the station for the five-thirty train.

As the bus came to a halt a short distance in front of him, it suddenly started to rain heavily. Coming down in handfuls, he couldn't see clearly, but turning on the window wipers he saw her getting off the bus and battling against the strong wind with her umbrella. Putting up the hood of his jacket, he got out of the car. Without looking at her, he opened the boot, remaining there as if looking for something. Despite the rain, he could hear the tip-tap of her heels getting closer and the bus pulling away. He poked around in the boot until she was walking past him. Picking up a spanner, he spun round and hit her hard on the back of her head.

She fell to the ground, dropping her bag and umbrella in a puddle. He quickly hoisted her up, shocked at how easy it was to bundle her into the boot, and he threw the umbrella and bag on top of her. Two natures were at war inside him, the good and the savage, both fighting for control as his conscience played havoc. He'd never done anything like this before, was surprised how cool and at ease he felt. Staring down at her crumpled body, he wavered, tiny prickles of the love he still felt for her invaded his head. But it was only for a moment, before his head snapped back to the task in hand; he valued his freedom too much to let sentimentality get in the way. He slammed the boot and returned to the driver's seat.

47
1973

Jasper and Bill

'How's the campaign going?' Bill asked Jasper. They were standing on a muddy field rubbing their hands and stamping their feet to keep warm, as they watched Toby play football. This was a weekly occurrence. Jasper sometimes coached the boys, but Bill always went. He liked to support Toby.

'It's a hard slog, Sandy thinks I work too hard.'

'You wrote a great article,' Bill said, referring to Jasper's three-page spread about the three hundred-and-seventy victims of thalidomide.

'Glad you liked it.'

'What effect do you think it will have?'

'We're seeing a shareholder revolt. Distillers share price has plunged. They'll have to take notice now.'

'And up their offer to the families?'

'Indeed. I'm hoping the campaign will force them to do that.'

'So when this is over...'

'It will never be over. The children need a lifetime of care. And care doesn't come cheap.'

'You know what I mean. Any other stories in the pipeline?'

'Not really. I'm writing a piece about the new Capital Radio station. And there's a pay dispute in Glasgow. We need something exciting to happen like another train robbery.'

'Yes!' Bill screamed at full pelt. His son had just scored a second goal. In the short space of time that he'd been playing football with Haslemere Under Sixteens, his skills had improved no end. His reflexes were quick and he could read his opponents well.

'Nice one Toby,' Jasper said.

'Don't you ever let rip, just for once and yell across the pitch?' Bill laughed. The two men were very different, but over the weeks they'd learned to laugh at each other's different mannerisms. 'You sound as if you're watching polo or cricket, not football.' Bill nudged Jasper.

'My dad would turn in his grave if he saw me behaving in anything but a dignified way. He worked in a factory, but he had standards.'

'I can see you was brought up proper,' Bill said, pulling a packet of Rothmans from his pocket and lighting one. He inhaled with a pensive expression on his face. 'Mate, I want to talk to you about something important.'

'What, now? When your son could be about to score another goal?'

'His luck's bound to run out.' Bill sniffed.

'What is it?' Jasper asked, turning from the pitch to look at Bill.

'I don't know how to say this... but I think Toby is your son.'

A smile of amusement flickered across Jasper's face. 'My son's dead.' He spread his fingers into a fan and clamped his chest.

'What date did you say he was born?'

'1st February '61.'

'Toby's birthday.'

Toby was running around the pitch trailing the ball, his head flicking in both directions like a meerkat. Silence fell between them as they stared at the pitch.

Bill's eyes were dark and brooding as Jasper cast him a calm but doubtful look.

'You've lost me. What are you talking about? He died soon after birth...Now if you don't mind, let's concentrate on watching *your* son play football,' he snapped.

Bill's frown deepened as he persisted through the awkward atmosphere. 'I'm certain... he's yours.'

'STOP THIS.' Jasper was beginning to think his voice was coming from somewhere else. It felt as if the air was being sucked from his stomach and he couldn't quite pull himself back to reality.

'The doctor...'

'What about the doctor?' Came Jasper's sharp reply.

THIS WAS the hardest thing Bill had ever had to do. He'd kept the secret for so long, that it had become a part of him. He'd agonised for weeks about telling Jasper and playing out all of the consequences in his head. There was a sense of relief and one of foreboding. From this point on, everything was unknown. He was terrified––but knew that it was the right thing to do.

'My wife delivered Toby. The doctor insisted on putting him in a cold room, thinking he would die. He'd already delivered a baby affected by thalidomide, which died soon after birth. I know that what he did was wrong, and it was gross negligence, but if you look at it from his point of view maybe he was frightened of watching another baby die. Doctors are human after all.'

Jasper listened; his face white. He looked as if he was going to throw up.

'Sit down.'

'I don't want to sit down.'

'You don't look well.'

In a raised voice Jasper said, 'I don't think you'd look well if you'd been told...'

Heads turned. The two men in heated debate were more interesting than the football match.

'Let's walk over there,' Bill suggested, pointing to the other side of the field, so that they could talk privately. 'Wait till it's half-time. You need a few minutes to digest this and then I'll answer all of your questions and we can decide where we go from here.'

'It will take longer than a few minutes to take in what you've just told me.'

They stood in silence, their eyes on the game until half-time. Jasper kept tutting and huffing, shifting between his feet. Bill found the silence stifling. He wanted to make everything all right, but it was far from all right.

Bill broke the silence. 'Rona and I had been trying for years for a baby.'

'So, you took someone else's baby? You know I should call the police?' Jasper said, his finger pointing at Bill.

'And you've every right to. But please, I'm begging you not to. Toby knows nothing. As far as he's concerned, I'm his father.' Bill looked over at the boys having their drink and biscuits. Toby was standing away from the other boys, watching them. This was all he needed. How was he going to explain the fact that they were arguing? Toby mustn't find out. I'd rather die in a ditch, Bill thought, than tell him the truth and watch his world come crashing down. What the hell have I done? Maybe it would have been better to stay quiet, but the truth was festering inside him.

'Rona pleaded with the doctor not to let him die. She saved him. She took him home so that he could live.'

'And you went along with it? Your wife was a kidnapper. And you're just as guilty. You could go to jail for this. It's aiding and abetting.'

Bile rose in Bill's throat and he thought he was going to throw up. His words felt flaky, ugly and grimy.

'Did nobody stop to consider what my wife wanted?'

'She wasn't your wife at the time.'

'That's not the bloody point. She was Toby's mother.'

'And she planned to have him adopted. We didn't get her permission, but we did in effect adopt him.'

'Unbelievable.'

Neither of them saw Toby until he was halfway across the field. 'What's the matter? Why are you both arguing?' Toby shouted.

'It's okay, your dad and I are friends,' Jasper smiled through pursed lips, the smile failing to reach his eyes. Jasper slapped Bill on the back. 'Just a friendly disagreement over the rules of football.'

'It looked a bit more than that. Like you were really angry with each other.'

'You know what men are like when they get discussing football,' Jasper added.

At the end of the game Bill said, 'Go and get changed, I'll wait by the truck.' He waved Toby away, watching him disappear into the clubhouse before turning to Jasper. 'Thanks mate.'

'Thanks? I didn't do it for you. He's just an innocent kid.'

'And I love him and want what's best.'

'How can you be certain he's our child?'

'There was only one thalidomide boy born without arms at that nursing home, and certainly only one in February 1961.'

'What are you going to do?'

Jasper bent towards him, his temple throbbing. 'I haven't decided yet.' Startling Bill, he jabbed his finger into Bill's chest and through gritted teeth whispered, 'I'll make you pay for what you did, you're not getting away with this.'

JASPER FELT as if he had been kicked in the stomach. He couldn't get his head around it. If this was true it was one hell of a revelation. Why hadn't Bill discussed his thoughts before now? No wonder he went quiet in Blackpool, Jasper thought, when he had told Bill about their loss.

48

1973

Marion

Marion had no idea what had happened to her when she woke in a dimly lit, windowless room. When she had first woken she'd realised she was in a car boot, because she could hear the engine and car tyres screeching round bends at speed. The back of her head hurt and when she touched it she found a lump, which was bleeding. It was only then that it dawned on her that she'd been knocked out by someone - no not just someone - it was Simon, she was sure. Where was he now she wondered, and why had he brought her to this dilapidated place? All she'd wanted was her money, but maybe she'd gone too far in threatening to call the police. What did she hope to achieve after all these years? She'd been motivated purely by a desire to wipe the smugness from his face, he wasn't going to get the better of her. Anger burned inside for retribution after the way he'd sacked her, in order to save himself. Bitterness had imprisoned her all these years, weaving around her heart and changing the person she was. She couldn't forgive. She hated his power and the way he always came up smelling of roses. She'd long pushed aside her love for Simon, condemning it to a dustbin and replacing love for bitterness.

God damn it, why had she let him drag her down to his level? She was better than this. What would retribution solve? It would break a family. Toby and Bill looked so happy together. She had seen Toby's adoration for his dad and the way he looked up to him. She couldn't destroy that love. It was too precious a bond. Strong, unyielding, everlasting. And Toby was happy at Haslemere, she could see that, in the way he interacted with the other children, laughing and smiling. She didn't want his world to be shattered and for him to lose his dad. Bill was an amazing dad and throughout the ordeal, she had to give it to him, he'd stuck by Rona.

Marion had no shoes on, and her coat was draped over her like a blanket. Her legs ached from being scrunched up in the boot. She remembered screaming when he'd hauled her from the boot, but he'd slapped her hard across the face.

The first lump of dread settled in her stomach as she thought how prison-like the room was. It was damp with brick walls and flooring and one dim naked bulb overhead and she guessed this was a cellar or basement room. There was no furniture other than the bed she was lying on, a chair, a toilet and washbasin behind a plastic curtain.

She got up from the bed that smelled heavily of mould, her feet connecting with the damp bricks. She shuddered, pulled her coat from the bed and wrapped it around her shoulders as she went to the door. It was locked. Fear rippled through her. Icy nerves had destroyed the bravado she'd built when they'd met in the park.

She screamed and pounded on the door, until her voice was hoarse. It dawned on her that he'd gone. Wherever it was he'd brought her to, no one was going to hear her screams. She realised she had to calm down and try to work out a plan. Getting angry wouldn't help her escape. Anger hadn't helped in the past and it wasn't going to help now. She had to be strong and rational.

There was no way out other than the locked door. She tried to remember what she'd seen outside, but it was too dark to take in her surroundings.

The school would sack her if she didn't turn up for work, or they'd worry if it dragged into days. How long would it be before anybody reported her disappearance? Apart from the school there were few people in her life that would miss her. There was nobody she saw regularly who'd notice her gone. And even if the school reported her missing, how would the police find her? He could kill and dispose of her body long before the alarm was raised - if it ever was.

Nausea clawed at her throat, and she tried to swallow down the bile, but it was too late. Her stomach contracted violently and forced everything up and out. She lurched forward and sunk to her knees on the damp bricks, the pungent stench of her vomit invaded her nostrils. She wished more than anything else in the world that she'd defied Simon and gone to the police all those years ago. But it was too late for the police; he planned to kill her. What else could he do with somebody who knew enough to send him down?

She wrapped herself in her stinking, vomit-strewn coat, it was so cold. Her head was throbbing and she still felt queasy, but the worst thing was the tendrils of fear gripping her. How would he kill her? Would he leave her to starve to death?

1973

Jasper

'Are we having Bill and Toby round for dinner this week?' Sandy asked Jasper as he ate his breakfast, while standing at the kitchen sink surveying the garden. Fallen leaves blanketed the lawn, reminding him that he needed to spend Saturday raking them up. Autumn had come early this year. Sandy was sitting at the table cradling the dog as if it were a cuddly toy. 'I was just wondering what to cook.'

'Bill said they were busy this week,' he replied, with his back to her. They had fallen into a routine, cooking for Toby and Bill every Wednesday evening. Jasper stared out of the window, finding it difficult to look at her while they talked about Bill and Toby.

'Oh?'

'I thought you'd be pleased. You don't like them.'

'That's a bit harsh. I've never said that. I find Bill amusing, but Toby's irritating, as kids go. I'm always glad when the evening's over.'

'You should have said.'

'They're no problem, really.'

'What is it about Toby that you find irritating?' Jasper dragged himself from the window and sat opposite her.

'I think he's spoilt. Bill doesn't tell him off for things he does.'

'He's not a bad kid, he's always polite and well behaved.' Jasper found himself feeling defensive towards Toby.

'I don't know, it's just small things. I don't like it when he pulls the dog's ears with his feet and the way he flops onto the settee, leaving no room for anyone else to sit down. It's so rude.'

'Have you ever stopped to consider, what if he was our child?' With nerves coursing his body Jasper got up and filled the kettle, to keep himself busy.

'You've got a coffee over there,' Sandy said pointing to his cup on the windowsill.

'Oh yeah.'

'I'd be a stricter parent than Bill, for sure.'

'Yes, but don't you ever wonder, what if he was ours?'

'Not really.'

'I do. Our child would have been like Toby.'

Sandy shrugged. 'Why would I? You forget that I work with handicapped children. I'm used to it.'

'I'm fond of Toby, partly because he *is* like the child we lost.'

'I don't know, Jasper,' she said stroking the dog's ears. 'I'm relieved things worked out as they did. I can see how hard life is for Toby and for Bill bringing him up and trying to make life easier for him. Does that make me a wicked person?'

'If he was yours, you'd love him?'

'It's hypothetical, Jasper. He's not ours. I don't have to love him. I love you, I love the dog and I guess since having the dog I see things differently.'

'How?'

'I'm happy with a dog, they're easier than children, less demanding and they stay small forever.'

'When I look at Toby I think of our child.'

'All this thalidomide reporting is getting to you. Your imagination is running wild. We need to put it behind us. It happened a long time ago.'

Jasper watched her stroke the dog. He'd got used to Tibs. Tibs had a strong bond with both of them and his expressive eyes and plumed tail were endearing. He was a smart dog and eager to please. And true to his Tibetan spaniel heritage, he made an excellent watchdog. But it wasn't the same. A dog wasn't a replacement for a child.

She cupped the dog's face in her hands and made cooing noises. 'The world would be a better place if everyone had the ability to love unconditionally like a dog. He snaps me out of any mood. It's amazing how much love he brings.'

'He can't speak though.'

'Dogs do speak. But only to those who know how to listen.'

Jasper got up. It was time to go to work, but sadness drained through him. He was lost.

50
1973

Jasper

It was Saturday morning and with his head feeling as if it was about to explode, Jasper slipped out of bed. He needed to go for a drive to process the turmoil playing havoc inside him. He made an excuse to Sandy that he was nipping out to get the paper and some bacon for a late breakfast.

'Can you nip into Boots and pick up my photos?' She asked as he left.

Jasper was having a hard time digesting Bill's confession and working out what to do. There was a living, breathing part of him in the world, somebody who shared his DNA. That was both wonderful and unsettling.

Once he had calmed down and got his head around the situation, hard though it was; Jasper had met Bill in a quiet pub to discuss the situation a couple of times since the football match, but neither man could come up with a way forward. The more they talked, the more shipwrecked they both felt. At first, he'd wondered if Bill was even telling the truth. He had no reason to lie, but every reason to keep it a secret. Now that the idea was rooted in Jasper's head, it needed to be investigated. The truth was terrifying and made him feel out of control. If Toby really was their son, what next? It was like staring down the barrel of a gun. This was enormous. And explosive. And hard for him to contemplate the ramifications.

At the bottom of their road, unsure which way to turn, Jasper forgot about the paper and the breakfast he was supposed to be buying. Lurching onto the main road, grinding the gears, he headed in the direction of Guildford. As the road rumbled under him, he thought about Toby. He didn't see traits of himself or Sandy in the boy, but that wasn't reason enough to doubt Bill. Jasper tried to conjure a paternal feeling, but he couldn't. He hardly knew the boy. As far as he was concerned, he was Bill's lad. He even had Bill's mannerisms; the way he cocked his head to one side sometimes and in the way he stood, with his feet about a foot apart.

As he neared the city centre, Jasper found himself driving towards the police station. He was in two minds about the whole Toby situation and couldn't think straight. He pulled over, cut the engine and stared up at the concrete monolith. It was never good news when a police officer came to your door, removing their hat and politely asking to come inside. But today he was visiting them and that felt surreal. He was struggling to feel human. Leaving the comforting smell of his car's interior, Jasper stepped onto the pavement.

As he walked towards the entrance, he tried to switch off the voice in his head telling him to stop, go home. About to push through the door, a thought popped into his head. There was too much at stake. And he hadn't told Sandy. He dreaded her reaction. He turned away, looking towards the sky for answers. A feeling of panic coiled around him as he imagined everybody in court, fighting a custody battle. Toby losing his dad. Tears, pain, separation. Bill was his dad. Maybe not biologically, but in every other way. And he was doing a great job.

There was no denying that. He liked a drink and he wasn't perfect, but he'd tried his best. Together, father and son had built dreams and goals. They'd been through so much together; they were best buddies and shared a history.

What should he do? If only Bill hadn't told him, he would never have known. Better that, than this anguish.

Returning to the car, having gone to the shops, Jasper was curious to see the photos that Sandy had taken. He pulled the packet from his coat pocket and opened it. Leafing through pictures of the dog and landscapes, there was nothing of interest, so he slung them onto the passenger seat. About to start the car, he saw a picture of Toby peeping out from the bottom of the pile. His heart jolted. He took a closer look, enjoying eye-to-eye contact with his son's smiling face posing for the camera in a wood. He remembered the walk - it was one Sunday, with the four of them. Their pathway through the wood was lit by new beginnings, new friendships and memories born. With his finger he traced around the outline of Toby's figure. 'Are you really mine?' Maybe he could see a hint of his grandfather in Toby's face, but the flicker of familiarity disappeared, replaced by a younger version of Bill. It was perplexing. He blinked and looked again, as if blinking would cause him to see something different in Toby's face.

Jasper tore around Toby's face and slipped the picture into his wallet. Sandy wouldn't notice the missing photo. Sadness spread through his body like ink. *This thumbprint size photo might be the closest I get to my son. It would do, for now.*

51

1973

Jasper
It was the following weekend. Glancing from the basket she was in the process of filling at the kitchen worktop, Sandy smiled at Jasper, standing in the kitchen doorway in his underpants.

'What you up to?'

'I'm just putting a basket of food together for the school trip to the New Forest.'

'That's not today?'

'Yes, it is. Did you forget?'

'Sorry, yes I did. That's fine, you go and enjoy yourself, it'll give me a chance to catch up on the news.'

She put the basket down and wrinkled her forehead. 'Jasper, we need a big favour. We don't have enough adults going. Marion was supposed to be going but she's not been into work for a couple of days and nobody can get hold of her. It's very odd and not like her at all. Anyway, I said you were free.'

'Oh, cheers for that. I only get the weekend to relax. Can't someone else go?'

'Nope, you'll enjoy it, you'll know Toby, he's going. There

are two other adults going. Rachel and Alex. They both work at the school. And a man called Jack is driving.'

'A bit more notice would have been nice, darling.'

'The dog's taken care of. The neighbour's looking after him.'

On the Variety Sunshine coach, that had been donated to the school, they headed south. With the chatter and laughter of children of varying ages, from twelve to sixteen, Jasper relaxed, glad he'd joined the trip. One of the boys had long arms and no legs. Pressing his muscley arms on the seat the boy bounced up and down like a monkey for the entire journey, making everybody laugh much to Jasper's amusement.

They followed the old road into the middle of the New Forest, the coach slowing to catch glimpses of deer. Jasper enjoyed the views over the wild terrain of brown heather and bracken and pointed things out to the children, but he avoided engaging with Toby. Every time he glanced at the boy his heart jolted and he found it hard to talk to him, stuttering and getting his words mixed up. He wondered if Toby noticed the difference in him.

Nearing Lyndhurst, the landscape changed. They passed groves of oak, open fields cropped by stocky little ponies and pretty thatched cottages with brick or white-washed walls. They stopped by a shallow river to eat lunch, the adults pushing the wheelchairs over the bumpy ground. A few children staggered across the field on crutches. The air was thick with the scent of peat mingled with the mustiness of fallen leaves. Is this what the future was going to be like? Watching his son enjoy himself from a distance?

As they ate, watching the ponies, Jasper was awkward around Toby and went for a wander. A short way off, behind a tree he smelled smoke and hidden behind the low branches was one of the older boys smoking.

'Sorry sir. I'll stub it out.'

'I won't tell, this time, but give me the packet. You shouldn't be smoking.'

The boy pulled his trouser leg up and removed a packet of fags from his tin leg.

'WE'VE GOT A TREAT FOR YOU,' the driver declared after they had eaten fish and chips for their supper, huddled on a deserted beach. They had driven a long way in one day, through the New Forest and to a town on the coast. 'There's a disco in town this evening. I'll drop you all off and pick you up at ten-thirty sharp.'

'Shall I stay with them?' Jasper asked.

'That would be great, if you don't mind,' Jack the driver said. They'll need a few adults with them to help out.' Jack asked Rachel and Alex to go with Jasper and the children. 'There's a cafe in the next road. I'll wait in there with Sandy. The kids love a spin on the dance floor in their wheelchairs, don't you kids?'

'I'm on crutches,' a girl of about fifteen piped up. 'But I can still dance. I've got my own special dance.'

'Does that involve waggling your hips by any chance?' Her friend laughed.

When they queued to get into the hall, a burly bouncer in a black suit and dickie bow tie stepped forward.

'Oi mate,' he said to Jasper, who was standing at the front of the queue. 'Can I have a word with you?' He gestured to the wall. 'Step aside.'

'Is there a problem?' Jasper gawped at the man.

'I can't let you all in.'

'Why not?'

'They look like freaks and they pose a fire risk. Perhaps you'd prefer a quieter venue, Sir.'

'We've driven for miles to get here.'

'Not my problem.' He sniffed, adjusting his tie.

'If you knew who I am, you wouldn't be turning us away.'

'I don't care who you are, you lot ain't coming into *my* disco.'

'You'll regret this, you mark my word.'

'Clear off, the lot of you.'

'But we've paid to go in,' Toby pleaded, standing at Jasper's side.

'Bog off,' he sneered. 'I don't want no freaks in my disco.'

'Who are you calling a freak? My...' Jasper nearly slipped up and said my son, swallowing the words before they could escape. 'These kids are not freaks. How dare you insult them?'

'Go,' he barked in a venomous tone.

'You're more interested in how your guests look.' A flush crept up Jasper's neck as anger took hold. 'I don't think we want to go into your bloody stupid disco, but this isn't the last you'll be hearing from me.'

'I don't care who you are, bloody toff, get off my premises,' he smirked. 'You could be Prince Phillip for all I care.' A smile flickered at the corners of his mouth. He was clearly enjoying the power he wielded.

'But we've paid,' one of the boys said. 'Are we getting our money back?'

'Clear off.' The bouncer swept his arm towards them.

'We're not allowed to go in,' one of the girls whispered to her friend.

They returned to the kiosk and Jasper asked for a refund.

'No refunds.'

'But we've been refused entry.'

'Not my problem,' the woman shrugged dismissively. 'I don't make the rules.'

. . .

ON THE WAY BACK, Jasper absorbed the enormity of what had happened at the disco - for the first time in his life he appreciated the challenges that faced handicapped people. With fire burning in his belly he was going to tell the editor what had happened. This would give extra weight to the reports they were writing about the thalidomide scandal.

52

1973

Marion

Marion must have slept. But with no watch, and no window to see if it was light, she couldn't work out whether she'd been asleep for one hour or five. More time passed. She had never experienced such boredom for so long. With nothing to do except focus on the terror mounting inside her, she wondered whether she'd been left here to starve to death.

As she lay there, her hunger pains unbearable, she heard a door being unlocked from somewhere in the house and footsteps drawing closer.

The door opened, and although Marion thought she could spring at him and knock him down, she couldn't move when she saw him.

'Hello Marion,' Simon said. 'I'm sorry I had to hit you over the head to get you into my car. But you shouldn't go threatening me with the police. If you go to the old bill, I'm likely to lose my job.'

'So, what are you going to do, kill me?'

His eyes narrowed and his mouth tightened. It was hard to believe that the cruel man standing in front of her had once been her lover. She quaked inwardly.

He laughed and passed a bag to her. The bag was hot and looking inside she realised it was pie and chips and a bottle of lemonade. She devoured the food, cramming it into her mouth, three chips at a time, like a hungry wolf. She polished it off with a long glug of lemonade, burping as the fizz hit her stomach.

'Elegance was never your strongest quality,' he sneered.

'How long are you going to keep me down here?' she asked, wiping the grease from her face with the back of her sleeve.

'All in the fullness of time, my dear.'

'What do you want from me?'

'You can calm that attitude of yours for a start. You'll stay down here for as long as it takes.'

'As long as what takes?'

'You need time to think around all of the consequences of going to the police, for everybody, and especially for yourself. We all stand to lose. Nobody gains from knowing the truth. I need to be certain you won't report me.'

'I won't, I promise, I've been down here long enough. How long have I been down here?'

'A day, but that could turn into a week.'

'Well I've had plenty of time to think and you're right, it wouldn't be good for any of us. Least of all Toby.'

'I can't trust you, not yet, I need to be absolutely certain.'

'I just want my money. If you give me my money, I won't go to the police.'

'I don't owe you a penny. I paid you off when I told you to leave the job.'

'You do owe me money and you know it.'

'And what proof do you have?'

. . .

AFTER SIMON LEFT, Marion thought about the terrifying prospect that he wouldn't come back, that he was just playing games with her and didn't intend to let her go. She'd never seen this dangerous side to him and wondered where it had come from. The man was a complete psycho. When they were seeing each other they'd shared stories about their childhood, and his hadn't been a good one. She remembered him telling her that his mother had made him stand in the corner for hours if he was naughty, even denying him the toilet. And when he wet or soiled himself, he was beaten. This went on for years. She wondered if the trauma of this early abuse had stayed with him, only now coming to the surface now that he felt powerless again.

But considering why Simon hurt her, wasn't going to get her out of this situation. She had no means of escape. She was at his mercy. She still had fight in her and a sense of dignity.

When Simon stomped off, she thought he would leave her for an hour or two to mull things over and punish her for her stubbornness. But she expected him to come back with food, eventually. But he hadn't come back and despite having no clock, she was certain that about ten hours had passed. All she could think about was the terrifying prospect that he'd never come back. If he left her here to die, he wouldn't have to worry about her going to the police. Did he have it in him to be that brutal?

Her stomach was empty, and it hurt. It was lucky there was water in the room otherwise her mouth would be as dry as baked earth. Food dominated her thoughts as the hours rolled by. To take her mind off food she thought about Toby and how happy he was at the school. Simon might think she was going to the police, but seeing how adjusted Toby was, how could she rock his world? Marion had always harboured vengeful thoughts about Rona. Rona had a child. She didn't. A child she'd snatched. Marion's spite and malice had driven her revenge: anonymous letters, cards and even dog dirt through her letterbox. This had gone on for years. But Rona was gone. None of it mattered anymore. Toby's happiness was paramount now. Marion had lost her mother at around Toby's age. The pain never went away. She knew how it must be for him. She didn't want to make things worse.

When Marion was giving up hope of Simon coming back, he returned. This time she didn't rush to get up from the bed. Feeling too weak, she remained in a foetal position, huddled under the smelly blankets.

'When are you going to let me go?' Her voice was shaky, the strength he must have seen in her the last time had ebbed away.

'You'll go straight to the police, the minute I let you go.'

'I know you don't really want to kill me,' she said, trying to sit up with every inch of her body aching. 'I've got an idea. If you dump me by the roadside, I'll walk to the nearest house and get them to ring the police. I'll say you kept me blindfolded and that you wore a mask. And that I have no idea who my attacker is.'

'You've got it all worked out then? You don't fool me. What would a stranger want with you? They'd be suspicious. They'd ask questions and get to the bottom of it. The police can be clever bastards, but when you need them, they're bloody useless.' The chill in his voice was alarming.

'Toby's happy. Why would I tell the police?'

'I'm keeping you here longer, just to make sure.'

'Without any food?'

'Oh, I'd almost forgotten.' He pulled a box of cakes from his pocket and threw it at her. It fell to the floor. Marion eyed it but had no strength to pick it up.

'Go on,' he gestured, 'before I feed them to the mice.'

'Just leave me alone,' she whispered, regretting her words when he turned on his heel and left. When the footsteps had retreated, Marion sat up to pick up the cake. Her whole body ached and she had never felt so alone and so scared. She tore open the box and sunk her teeth into the cake, but far from satisfying her hunger pains she felt nauseous and couldn't swallow even a tiny mouthful. With her hand over her mouth she staggered to the sink to be sick.

GROWING INCREASINGLY WEAK, Marion knew that she had to do something, before she fell into a deep sleep and never woke up. After vomiting she tried again to eat the cake and this time managed to keep it down, although it was a struggle. She needed a plan. *Think woman.* Staring at the floor, it came to her. One of the bricks wasn't fixed into place. If she could prise it out, she might find a way of hitting him over the head. But did she have the strength and how would she distract him? He was much stronger than her. Willing to try anything, she knelt and slipping her fingernails into the cracks rocked and wiggled the brick back and forth. It was taking ages and she didn't think it would ever work itself loose, but when it eventually did, she breathed a sigh of relief. After pulling the brick out, she realised that he'd notice it was missing. She stood up, regaining her strength with every moment that passed, the sugar in the cake giving her energy, and walked around the bed, pushing it with all her might until it covered the hole.

All she needed now was to wait behind the door, holding the brick until he came. But she had no idea when or even if he'd come.

Hearing the door open at the top of the house and his feet on the stairs she took up position behind the door, her hands cradling the brick and her heart banging in her chest. If she missed, he'd turn on her and kill her with his bare hands or grind the brick into her head. As he drew closer, she shuddered, nerves getting the better of her and for one awful minute she thought she was going to faint. She kept her nerve, gripping the damp brick, praying for her plan to work.

The door opened and lifting the brick above her head she whacked it right into his face, simultaneously kneeing him between the legs. He crashed against the wall with blood trickling down his face. Slamming the brick hard into his head again, it felt as if she was watching the scene from above. This wasn't her, it didn't feel like her acting in such a brutal, barbaric way, grinding a man to death, but she carried on, like a robot, with all emotion swept to one side as she pounded her way to safety.

She ran up the steps in the dark and tripped. Hearing him groan, she looked back. Was he stumbling to his feet? About to come after her. Terror gripped her, she had to carry on and not look back.

It was dark outside and drizzling, but there was a watery moon and she could see her way along the path. She had no idea whether it was early evening or the middle of the night. She saw that she'd been held captive in a small cottage in a wood. The smell of rain hung heavy in the air, wet earth and damp leaves. Following the path, she ran as fast as she could, dodging trees roots and trying not to stumble. Twigs and acorns cracked underfoot. The dark shadows of the tall trees sent shivers through her. Clutching her fists, she kept moving forward, her aches and pains dragging her down, until she reached the main road. There were no houses nearby and she had no idea where she was. She didn't recognise her surroundings. The moon flitted in and out of clouds scudding across the sky, momentarily leaving her in complete darkness. New dangers lurked. It could be hours until a car came by and would she get into a stranger's car? Worse things could happen to her, before the night was up. And even if she could get to a hospital, to get her head seen to, what on earth was she going to say had happened? She'd murdered a man. It wasn't even in self-defence. How was she going to justify her actions without the whole story unravelling?

53

1973

Jasper

Disappointed they couldn't go to the disco, the children, Jasper, Rachel and Alex returned to the Sunshine coach where Jack and Sandy were waiting and headed back to St Bede's. As they drove, thunder growled in the distance, like a beast prowling the forest. Lightning flickered, cutting zig-zags of white in the granite sky and the wipers moved at full pelt as sheets of rain hit the window screen, obscuring the road ahead. Jasper had volunteered to drive back because the driver had a headache, but concentrating hard because of the bad weather, Jasper felt drowsy and the children, chatting and laughing were a distraction.

The rain petered away, and Jasper flicked the wipers off. Turning a bend, he swerved to avoid a large pool of water. There was something ahead, in the road.

He took a sharp intake of breath. 'Somebody's in the road.' Leaning forward, he peered through the glass and could make out the figure of a woman, frantically waving both arms, panic in her wide eyes. He took his foot off the accelerator and applied the brakes, the tyres squealing on the wet road and his headlights illuminating the woman. He could see her distress; she was crying and looked hurt.

'My God, Jasper,' Sandy gasped, 'I think it's Marion.' Sandy bellowed orders. 'Stop. Get out. Quick.'

Jasper cut the engine and they rushed towards the woman. Her hair was unkempt, and blood was crusting on the side of her face.

'Marion. Is that you?'

'Sandy?' Marion lurched forward, her voice cracking as sobs ripped through her. 'What are you doing here? Have you come looking for me?'

'Not exactly, we're on our way back from a day trip. What on earth has happened? Why are you out here?'

Sandy put her arm round Marion, whose own arms were tightly folded as she stood shivering.

'I was attacked,' she blurted.

54
1973

Jasper

'I'll drop into the hospital on my way to work,' Jasper suggested to Sandy on Monday morning. 'I'll see how Marion is.'

Finding Marion in the middle of a dark country lane had been very upsetting for everyone, especially the children. Jasper had rushed over to a nearby cottage to call an ambulance and they waited for an hour for it to arrive. Jasper also phoned the school caretaker to let him know what had happened and the caretaker then phoned the Head. They got back to St Bede's very late.

'If you could, that would be great. Tell her I'll be in later.'

As Jasper entered the hospital corridor the stuffy air with an undertone of bleach, tickled his nostrils. He noticed how tired the place looked, the white walls were ready for a coat of paint and scraped from the hundreds of trolleys that had bumped into them.

Marion was the youngest on the ward. The other beds were occupied by women old beyond their natural lifespan, waifs with wispy grey hair and fragile skin, locked in bodies that refused to quit with dignity.

'I should be coming out today,' Marion said. 'I haven't got concussion. It's really nice of you to come.'

'We were worried. It sounds as though you've been through quite an ordeal.'

'The police are going to the cottage where I was held. They'll find him dead. What's going to happen to me? I'll be charged with murder.' Her face had drained of colour and her eyes flickered with fear.

'No, he abducted you. If you hadn't killed him, he probably would have killed you.'

'You can't say that, not for sure.'

'Yes, I can.' He touched her arm and gave her a reassuring smile. 'You should rest.'

'I loved him once.'

'I thought you said you didn't know him.'

'That's what I told you, when you found me, but I've had to tell the police the truth...some of the truth,' she added, lowering her voice to a whisper. 'They'd keep asking questions until they got to the bottom of things.'

'Some of the truth?'

'I had an affair with him years ago. He's a doctor. He owed me money. A few weeks ago, I went looking for him, at the hospital where we both worked.'

'Where was that?'

'We knew each other in the St Agnes Mother and Baby Home.'

'North London?'

'Yes,' she said, looking surprised. 'Do you know it?'

'My wife had our baby there.'

'Oh.'

'He died. He had thalidomide damage.'

'I'm sorry. Sandy told me you had lost a baby.'

'She didn't tell me you'd worked there.' Jasper was irritated. Why hadn't Sandy mentioned it?

'Simon delivered two or three thalidomide babies while I was there.'

'What was his surname?'

'Gerard.'

The mention of this doctor's name sent a chill down Jasper's spine, but he kept his composure. This was the doctor they had seen in *The Daily Telegraph*.

'He did something, years ago, that I didn't agree with,' Marion went on. 'I threatened him with the police if he didn't give my money back. That's why he kidnapped me. To keep me quiet.'

An unease passed between them as they lapsed into silence, her eyes taking on a guarded expression. He stared at the lino, unsure what to say. The missing pieces of the puzzle were slowly slotting together. Jasper wanted to ask questions and fill in the gaps, but a part of him wanted to walk away and leave it all behind him.

'And will you tell the police what he did, now that he's dead?'

'No good will come of it.' She reached out, touching Jasper's hand, her eyes pleading with him. 'I want you to forget that we had this conversation.'

He anchored his eyes on Marion and took a deep breath, relief washing over him. 'I won't breathe a word. He's dead, that's all that matters.' Jasper patted her arm, turned and left with tears pricking his eyes and a knot twisting in his gut.

There was nothing he could do. He needed to settle for that and accept that doing nothing was the best thing to do. He could show Toby that he cared, by the small things he did. They might be little things, but they could make a difference. He could help Bill when he needed help and be there as a support. But he had to make his peace with Bill in order to move forward. The more he thought about it he realised that Bill was doing his best under difficult circumstances and in a situation that had been created by his wife, Rona. It was best that Sandy didn't know the truth. It would only stir a hornet's nest if she knew the truth.

55

1973

Bill It was Christmas Eve and Jasper and Bill were in the *Swan Inn*, a nineteenth century pub on Haslemere's High Street, enjoying a quick pint before heading home to get ready for Christmas. It was their favourite pub in the area and the staff were always friendly. The room was warm and bright and there was a roaring fire. Bill didn't like leaving Toby for too long, especially as it was Christmas Eve but Celia had come to stay for a couple of days and was watching a film with Toby. Jasper had suggested coming back to the cottage afterwards dressed as Santa, although for how much longer Toby continued to believe, Bill didn't know. He was getting a bit too old.

'I've done very well these past few months. I've cut right back on the drinking and I feel so much better for it. I only drink a couple of pints of beer a week and I've given up whisky completely,' Bill proudly told Jasper.

'That's excellent,' Jasper said, clinking Bill's glass in celebration.

'I used to cover up my feelings with drink so that I didn't

have to deal with them, but I'm slowly pulling myself together. It's been a difficult year.'

'I can't imagine what you must have been through, losing your wife.'

'Are you still angry with me?' Bill asked.

'I'm not angry with you. I feel very sad. I think you've done a brilliant job with Toby. I'm angry with your wife for what she did. But she's dead. What can I do?'

'I'm sorry. I know I keep saying that, but I am. I begged Rona to take Toby back to the hospital, but she wouldn't. She said he would die if he went back.'

'Before the doctor held Marion in that basement I would have disagreed. But now I see that she was probably right. Doctor Gerard was a very cruel man. I'm surprised he lasted as long as he did in his job.'

'The man must have had a screw loose,' Bill said.

'Yes, I reckon he was a psycho to behave as he did. Poor Marion. She seems to have recovered from her ordeal though.'

'It must be hard for you, watching your son grow up with another man.'

'It is hard. Very hard. I can't deny that. But I've come to terms with what happened and the situation we are in.'

'Come on,' Bill said. 'We better get back to Toby. Are you going to put your Santa outfit on in the gents before we leave the pub?'

'Yes. Good idea,' Jasper said finishing his pint.

Bill was looking forward to getting back to the oversized tree he'd put up in their small sitting room, trussed with tinsel and baubles and an angel with a startled expression on the top.

Bill laughed when he saw Jasper emerge from the gents clad in red, the white puff ball on his Santa hat swinging back and forth like a pendulum.

As they left the pub the sky had turned white and it had

begun to snow. Bill and Jasper looked up at the feathery flakes and smiled.

'A white Christmas, how wonderful,' Jasper said. 'Sandy will love it. I won't be long at your place. I better get back to her. All this time I spend with you, she will begin to wonder if I'm abandoning her.'

Bill had always loved this time of year, especially the bright colourful lights, the carol singers and the general festive cheer. He remembered Christmas long ago, when he was a young boy and the mad snowball fights with the other kids in the street. How he'd battled to keep the snowballs coming to defend himself, hurling them too soon in his excitement so that they ended up as little more than puffs of snow rising up into the air. Snow always brought memories of good times. But Christmas didn't always bring good memories. Rona was in hospital during the previous festivities. It had been a worrying time and impossible to enjoy. This year was going to be hard too because she was gone. But as he dug his hands into his pockets; Bill was determined to turn his sadness around, for Toby. And then a thought hit him. Toby had no hands to make and throw snowballs. A wave of sadness washed over him.

'I was just thinking about snowball fights. Toby won't be able to make snowballs,' Bill said.

'No, but he can run in the snow and dodge them.'

REACHING THE COTTAGE, Bill parked the van a short way along the lane, hidden from view. They closed the doors quietly and Bill waited a short distance from the cottage, his head peeping out from behind a tree as he watched Jasper hammer on the front door and a few moments later took great delight in seeing Toby's excitement when he saw Santa.

56

1974

Toby

'Tell me one of your stories Jasper,' Toby raved.

It was the weekend after New Year and Bill, Toby and Jasper were walking through the park enjoying what they had come to call, 'boy' time. Toby was confined to a wheelchair, having torn the ligaments in his left ankle after a bad fall doing a hundred-and-eighty degree turn while playing football, and his leg was encased in plaster. If he had normal arms, he could have used crutches, but he had to be ferried around in a wheelchair. Toby looked forward to the holidays, because despite not being able to walk, he was enjoying the freedom from his artificial arms, which had been rammed into the wardrobe, until the new term started. All of the thalidomide children suffered from sores and bruises where they rubbed against their skin. Toby liked showing everybody how well he coped without them.

'Give Jasper a break, let him enjoy the scenery.'

'But I like his stories.' Toby was enjoying the effect that his breath had in the cold air, rising as vapour as he spoke. He lifted his head to the sun, closing his eyes to its warmth. 'Were your mum and dad rich?'

Bill parked the wheelchair by a bench, and they sat in a line overlooking the frozen pond. The wintry trees stood like ballet dancers, poised in elegance and ready to perform.

Jasper rubbed his gloved hands and turned up the collar of his sheepskin coat and Bill tucked a blanket around Toby's legs.

'Lord no. What gave you that idea?'

'Toby, Jasper's already told us he came from a poor background, don't you remember?'

'Yeah, I know. I was just checking in case I got it wrong. He's posh. It doesn't make sense.'

'My parents *were* poor. And I suppose I do sound posh. My parents had a regional accent but I dropped it.

I remember the day our headmaster announced in the school assembly that I'd won a place at the grammar school. When I rushed home to tell my parents, their only reaction was worrying about how they were going to pay for the new school uniform and the many extras. The school sent the list, recommending we buy it all from Colemans, just about the most expensive shop in town. My parents were horrified and to my embarrassment they bought it all from the local Co-op where they could get credit and a dividend for shopping there. Clothing was still on ration and as far as I can remember, most of the family's allowance went on me.'

'But were they proud of you?'

'I think so, in their own way, although parents don't always show it.' He winked at Toby. 'Or get the chance to show it… because life gets in the way. Sometimes it's a struggle to survive each day.'

'Dad relies on his whisky to get through the day.'

Bill sighed.

'Your dad's been through a lot and drink can be a crutch. But he does his best.' Jasper slapped Bill on the back. 'I can see how much he loves you and he's very proud of you.'

They were silent as they watched the ducks sliding on the frozen lake.

'There will always be struggles.' Jasper rubbed his hands. 'But when we look back on life, we see the sunny spots. You can be anything you want to be Toby; you just have to believe in yourself.'

'Yup, it's called counting ya blessings.' Bill smiled.

'Can I give up football and learn to dance instead?'

Bill and Jasper exchanged a horrified look. 'Give up football,' they said in unison.

'Dancing is for girls,' Bill said.

'But one day the lad might meet a nice girl on the dance floor.' Jasper winked at Bill.

'Can we go and visit Mum's grave soon?' The anniversary of Rona's passing was approaching.

'Yes, son.'

'Can children have two dads do you think?' Toby looked from Bill to Jasper. 'If they don't have a mum?'

'Maybe,' Bill replied.

'Well we could pretend that I've got two dads. Just for fun.' Toby giggled.

'What about Sandy?' Jasper asked.

Toby wrinkled his nose. 'Boys only, remember? She's a girl. She's not playing this game.'

57

A YEAR LATER

Sandy and Marion

Jasper was spending more and more time with Bill and Toby and although Sandy loved the company of her dog when Jasper wasn't around, she felt left out. He always seemed to put Bill and Toby first, arguing that they needed his support. It was very virtuous of him, but she needed him too. She was his wife.

'I'm not deliberately excluding you. They'd love you to come too and so would I,' Jasper said one Saturday in August as he packed a picnic. He was heading down to the coast for a couple of days with Bill and Toby to camp near Swanage.

'You know I don't do camping. Sleeping on the ground with a thin piece of fabric between me and the rain and squatting over a hole to take a pee is really not my cup of tea. And where would I dry my hair?'

'Well you know that you're always welcome to join us.'

Sandy knew that but still didn't feel welcome. Somewhere along the way Jasper, Bill and Toby had become a team and like all teams they had their in-jokes which she didn't understand.

And as far as she was concerned Toby was an irritating little brat and Bill was an oaf.

Sandy grumbled to her friend Elizabeth at St Bede's, during one of their walks round the garden after work.

'He'd rather spend time with them than me.'

Elizabeth said, 'If you don't like something change it. And if you can't change it, try another approach.'

Elizabeth's words jarred and made her think. The weeks passed by and after much soul-searching something shifted inside her; she found her answer. She would have another baby. She was ready for one.

Marion wasn't sure what she was going to tell the police when they interviewed her, but the words came to her and she managed to keep the secret surrounding Toby's birth safe. The last thing she wanted was for Toby and Bill to be separated. The police came to their own conclusions after she told them about her affair with Simon and the money she'd lent him. The case went to court and Marion was acquitted of murder but found guilty of voluntary manslaughter and given a suspended sentence. Marion enjoyed Carol's squirms in the courtroom. Carol's perfect husband wasn't such a perfect husband after all.

'Simon was prepared to do whatever it took,' the judge concluded, 'to protect his reputation and glowing career record. Women trusted him at one of the most vulnerable stages of their lives.'

Marion took time off work after her dreadful ordeal. When she shut her eyes to try to sleep the nightmare was always the same. A masked man in a cellar would come closer and with a knife in his hand he would make sweeping movements. Every night it was the same and she woke screaming. At home, hidden from the world consumed by her nightmares wasn't doing her any good.

After a break she returned to work and this was the best thing she could have done. It gave her a focus to the day and the company of some of the loveliest people she'd ever met and in particular one person, Pete the new caretaker. The children called him Disco Pete because he was the disc jockey at the school discos. One evening Pete invited Marion to the cinema and they started seeing each other. They felt comfortable and relaxed in each other's company and after several weeks together Marion knew that she was ready to love again. She had found romance for real, would treasure it always, the right way, as something special between the two of them.

THE END

Read the prequel to this story: ***Every Mother's Fear:*** My Book It is the story about what happened before ***Every Father's Fear.*** Set in the late 1950s and into the 1960s. The story follows Sandy, an aspiring model and Rona, a midwife, caught up in the thalidomide scandal.

THANK you for reading ***Every Father's Fear*** which I hope you enjoyed. Please would you kindly leave a review on Amazon even if it's only one line. Reviews are the lifeblood of authors and always appreciated.

NOW READ 'EVERY SON'S FEAR,' the 3rd book in the series!
My Book

. . .

YOU MIGHT ENJOY my entertaining blog which is about all sorts of issues that get my goat!

Here is the link: https://joannawarringtonauthor-allthings-d.co.uk

Joanna Warrington has also written the following books:

OUT NOW! DON'T BLAME ME' My Book

EVERY FAMILY HAS ONE My Book

THE CATHOLIC WOMAN'S Dying Wish
My Book

HOLIDAY
My Book

A TIME TO Reflect My Book

POSTSCRIPT

According to Thalidomide UK there were 458 people in the UK affected by the drug and for every thalidomide baby that lived there were 10 that died.

The UK distributors of thalidomide, Distillers (now Diageo, successor to Distillers) agreed to compensate victims in 1973 and the Thalidomide Trust was set up. Fifty years on and hundreds of victims have never received any compensation for their life-altering conditions. Grunenthal, the German manufacture of the drug has always maintained that it is not liable because it met contemporary industry standards for drug testing. It argues that back in the 1950s nobody tested the effect of drugs on fetuses.

In January 2010 the British government expressed its "Sincere regret and deep sympathy for the suffering caused," for its decision to give the drug the stamp of approval. Survivors in the UK received £80 million in compensation from the government to help with their on-going needs.

Grunenthal set up a fund of 50 million euros for victims mainly on the Continent and unveiled a memorial in 2012 when it expressed its "sincere regrets." It has never compensated British victims.

Printed in Great Britain
by Amazon